A SISTERHOOD OF
SECRET AMBITIONS

A
SISTERHOOD
OF SECRET
AMBITIONS

SHEENA BOEKWEG

FEIWEL AND FRIENDS
NEW YORK

A Feiwel and Friends Book
An imprint of Macmillan Publishing Group, LLC
120 Broadway, New York, NY 10271

Our books may be purchased in bulk for promotional, educational,
or business use. Please contact your local bookseller or the Macmillan
Corporate and Premium Sales Department at (800) 221-7945 ext. 5442 or
by email at MacmillanSpecialMarkets@macmillan.com.

Library of Congress Cataloging-in-Publication Data is available.
ISBN 978-1-250-77098-1 (hardcover) / ISBN 978-1-250-77097-4 (ebook)

Book design by Trisha Previte
Feiwel and Friends logo designed by Filomena Tuosto
Torn page © heathenphotog/Shutterstock
Paper texture © Lukasz Szwaj/Shutterstock
Watercolor illustrations by Sofia Bonati
Pen & ink illustrations by Trisha Previte

First edition, 2021

2 4 6 8 10 9 7 5 3 1

fiercereads.com

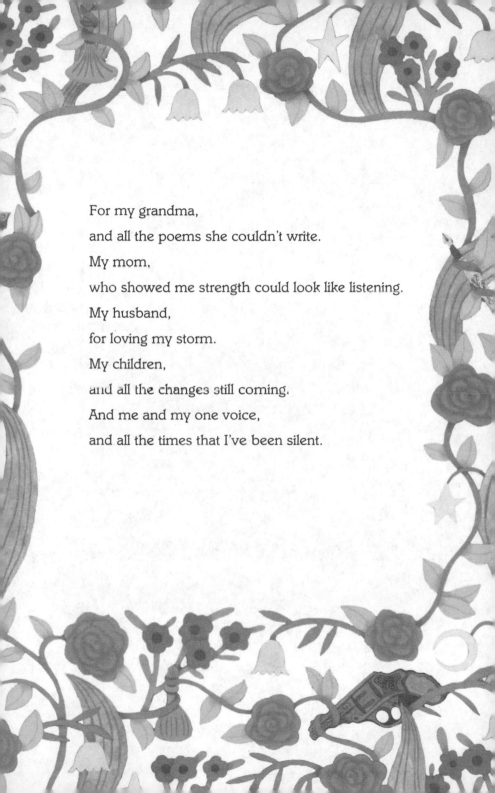

For my grandma,

and all the poems she couldn't write.

My mom,

who showed me strength could look like listening.

My husband,

for loving my storm.

My children,

and all the changes still coming.

And me and my one voice,

and all the times that I've been silent.

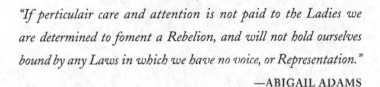

"*If perticulair care and attention is not paid to the Ladies we are determined to foment a Rebelion, and will not hold ourselves bound by any Laws in which we have no voice, or Representation.*"

—ABIGAIL ADAMS

"*As to your extraordinary code of laws, I cannot but laugh. Your letter was the first Intimation that . . . a . . . Tribe more numerous and powerfull than all the rest were grown discontented.*"

—JOHN ADAMS IN RESPONSE

"*Remember the Ladies, John. ~~Or we will remember you.~~*"

—ABIGAIL ADAMS

SPINSTERS!

Why listen to Gossips when there is work to do?

Don't spend your father's money on drinks with your Chatty friends, when you could be home cleaning with new Scouring Kitchen Powder. Even if you are 127, it's not too late to impress a charming Adam with your thrift and skill!

You'll be a Wife in no time!

CHAPTER ONE

A storm cloud rumbled above the rooftops, the salted wind tossing a newspaper across an empty street as we parked the Model A two block away from our target—the house at 127 Adams Street. In the seat next to mine, Mira clenched the steering wheel so tightly she creased her leather driving gloves. Well, mine actually. She'd borrowed those gloves from me. But I didn't say anything.

I couldn't.

There wasn't supposed to be a car in the driveway.

I folded the advert in fourths. The coded message clearly stated it was only supposed to be a Chat, an assessment of the safety of the family who lived at 127 Adams. We'd done those plenty of times before.

Behind me, Bea cleared her throat. "Perhaps we should notify the Matrons?"

Thunder rumbled above us.

The Matrons were the leaders of our society, but this was just one car, and one man. There were five of us, and we'd been trained.

"There's no call for that," I said. "The advert said the Spinsters and Gossips are watching our backs. One quick Chat and we'll be home before supper."

"Meadow Lark?" Iris suggested. She was the Spinster assigned for up-close protection for this assignment, and a dear friend whose usual smiling eyes were focused and deadly as she scanned the street.

I bit my lip. Meadow Lark was a reliable plan, but with children in the home . . . "That could get messy. We need eyes closer. It'll have to be Saint Sebastian."

"Do you think this is a test, Elsie?" Bea asked. With her wide brown eyes she looked younger than she was; her brown hair longer than was fashionable, tucked in two braids, freckles across her upturned nose. A stray shadow darkened her plump cheeks. "Ada told me—"

"Ada was just trying to get under your collar," Mira said. "I'm glad that milquetoast's married and minding her own beeswax."

"Watch your slang," Greta said in the back seat, squashed nearly against the window as though she thought poor was catching. With her blond curls combed out, she looked like a sunflower or a movie starlet; either way she followed the light and the light loved her back. She stared out the window like she was bored. "It's unladylike."

"Yes, Mother," Mira, Bea, and I muttered in unison. At twenty-two, Greta was the oldest of us Wives-to-be, and we never let her forget it.

I stared at the house beyond the car as if wishing this would go well would make it so.

Mira let go of the steering wheel. "I say we blow the house up and go find a soda fountain."

Bea pressed her palms together. "Or a bakery."

Mira grinned back. "Wouldn't pie be luxurious?"

"Oh pie," I squealed

"There are children in there," Greta said with genuine concern.

I fought a laugh. Greta didn't always understand our sense of humor. I reached over the seat and tapped her knee. "You're right. I guess explosions aren't the answer this time."

"One day they will be." Mira pulled off my gloves and adjusted her short hair in the rearview mirror. "And I'll be ready." Mira was the bravest of us, the first to adopt the garçonne fashions, the first to bob her hair. She wore trousers, a collared shirt and vest, while I stuck to dresses and stockings rolled at my knees. I kept my hair to my shoulders, curled up to be closer to fashionable, while Mira's dark, slicked-back hair was so short she had the barber take a razor to her neck. Short hair didn't tend to get stuck in the car engines she liked to tinker with. According to her stories, she'd hot-wired a car, a plane, and the box of explosives they'd used in our training.

But Mira's stories were fairy tales wilder than the ones I had on my shelves.

"We're starting to gain attention," Iris said.

"I'll act as cover," Greta said as she opened her door, her bright eyes sparked with worry as she glanced down at her delicate heels. "Those trees will do."

"I've got my work boots in the basket," Bea offered.

"No offense, Bea," Greta said with a look, "but I'd rather die than wear boots you wore in a pasture full of cows."

Mira turned around in her seat. "You can't just say no offense before you say something really offensive."

"Don't be so sensitive," Greta quipped back. "Bea's fine! Aren't you?"

Bea offered a quick smile and shrug. "Of course."

"Besides, she knows her station in life, so bringing it up won't hurt her feelings."

"No." Bea's smile faded. "Not the first time anyway."

"Greta," I started.

Greta looked at me like I'd just scolded her. "Well, I'm sorry for speaking the truth. Bea's family doesn't have money. We all know it. You three can't always be so sensitive about everything. She said she was fine."

"It's starting to hurt a little, actually," Bea said. Mira and I glared at Greta.

Greta rolled her eyes. "I'll be fine in my T-straps; thank you kindly for offering what little you have." She pressed the door open. "If it won't hurt anyone else's feelings, I'd like to go climb a tree now."

I sighed and followed Greta out of the car. We'd parked the Model A under a patch of willow trees, which seemed drenched and drooping already, though the storm hadn't broken yet. Soon though. Even the air smelled of rain about to fall. I pressed down the silk chiffon of my flower-print day dress to smooth out wrinkles, lowered the brim of my cloche hat to cover my eyes, and adjusted my wool coat. My pearl earrings were too tight, but I tried to ignore the pinch. This wasn't a neighborhood I'd like to lose an earring in.

Greta opened the basket, looked both ways, and then pulled out her twin-barrel Beretta OVP Modello 1918. The gun was Italian, sleek as a pair of pumps, and could fire over a thousand rounds a minute. Greta was the best shot, so it made sense, in a way, to have her cover our backs, while Iris kept close to handle anything that got past her. Though it felt odd as possible to see the wealthiest of us climb up a tree with a rifle over her shoulder. Maybe it was because Greta and her friends liked to go on and on about how much money their families had, or about how *her* last name was on the new wing of the university I was dying to get into, or that my coat was from two seasons ago, and Bea's was homespun, and Mira's belonged on an old man, as if that made Greta and her friends better than the rest of us.

I grumbled some of that under my breath, but then I focused on our mission. The line of sight was good from the tree line, only about two hundred yards to the house. I'd seen Greta nail a can from farther.

"We need someone to cover the back route," Iris said, looking between Mira and Bea.

Mira glanced at Bea and then ducked her chin. "I'll do it," Mira said. "Whistle twice and I'll flash the rescue signal."

"Josefa is on relay," Iris said. "More Spinsters will be there if you need us."

The Spinsters usually handled dangerous men, but sometimes a man on edge was at the verge of violence against his family, and they've found Wives-to-be were the best to trim their fuses.

There's a privilege to being pretty and in a group.

If I was alone here, he might not tame so quickly. But if an angry man saw a group of pretty girls watching him, he'd stand up straight and uncurl his fists.

Sometimes anyway.

If he wasn't calmed, then the Spinsters handled it. They were our warriors. Our weapons. They did the work Wives-to-be like me couldn't stomach.

The society couldn't tell the future. Sometimes they missed a few bad men. Sometimes the man was angry but nothing would have happened anyway. Sometimes they send Wives when they should have sent a warrior. But in the last 111 years, we've learned to see a lit bomb.

And if the society couldn't stop it, at least we could get his wife and children out of his way.

That was what the First Ladies' Society was there for. That was why I signed my oaths. That was why the society had become my spine.

Mira threw me a weighty look, nearly a glare, before she took off. I nodded once to reassure her and off she went. Bea would be fine. I'd take care of her, and if my skills at charming didn't work, Iris would handle it. Our Spinster friend was one of the top fighters they'd trained.

Mira didn't care for many people, but she had a tender spot for our youngest friend. Not that she looked twice at Bea as she walked away. Mira thought that showing affection would be taken for a weakness.

And she wasn't wrong. Everything we did here would be watched by women from our society we called Gossips. And if we wanted the society's approval, which we did more than anything, then we had to be careful. As a Wife-to-be, the society could give me a life brighter than I'd ever dreamed of, if they liked me well enough. But it had to be clear that my loyalty to them was stronger than my loyalty to my sisters. Even though it was the society itself that gave them to me.

The air was damp enough it might as well be raining. I tugged my coat tight. I should not have worn the silk.

"You ready, Elsie?" Iris asked as she joined me, concerns shading her copper eyes. She was a trans woman a little older than me, maybe early twenties, her eyebrows shaved and then painted into thin arches, with a strong nose and lovely bowed lips that had smudged at the crease. The kindness in her eyes gave me something to hold on to that was stronger than my nerves about that car in our target's driveway.

If the husband was there, we weren't defenseless. We were trained to de-escalate violence, but if he wasn't calmed . . . Iris was close, and a group of Spinsters was not far behind.

I tried to force my nerves to calm.

Bea joined us, holding a basket full of something fresh baked that smelled like a patisserie.

"Ready enough," I answered Iris.

I glanced at Bea, but I knew bringing up Greta's ridiculous comments would only make their sting worsen. Bea was trained to put slights like this behind her. We all were. Every one of us was trained to become the wife of a powerful man the society would lift.

Forgiveness was our first lesson.

Being forgotten was our second.

Our heels clicked in unison as we walked toward the door, making a fine picture no one looked out the window to see—Iris tall and lithe with subtle curves, while Bea and I were round, and buxom. The two of us were the largest of our group, my body wide at the curves and soft at my stomach, while Bea was made of softness and size. The cold wind played with our skirts.

"What a quiet day," Bea murmured. She made a good point. Even on a stormy day, children should be playing in the yards, riding bicycles, tossing marbles. I didn't know how the Matrons had done it. Perhaps they dropped off new puzzles or indoor games the day before. Or perhaps they handed out free tickets to something in town. Days or even weeks of planning, all to keep this one street quiet enough that our clicking heels echoed as we marched up it.

I lowered my shoulders. If they could do that, then we could handle a car in the driveway.

The house at 127 Adams wasn't too different from others on the street. Weeds grew between cracks in the cement; a bicycle lay on its side on the lawn. Crocuses sprang brightly from the front bed, but the daffodils had lost their petals. All perennial flowers. Nothing freshly planted. Nothing that marked how deep the women's roots were.

Iris knocked twice, and I folded the advert in fourths and slipped it into my pocketbook. No neighbor eyes were watching. No one except Greta through her scope.

A babe cried from within the house, and a curtain fluttered, a small red-cheeked face peering at us as we counted under our breaths how long it would take their mother to open the door.

Seven seconds. Near enough we were welcome.

A white woman in a pale green housedress tucked a baby against her hip. The shine of sweat lit her forehead, but her cheeks were powdered to hide a bruise. She'd been hit. I stilled my face to not show a reaction, but for a moment I felt my seventeen years had not prepared me for what this woman was facing, what this woman had seen. I was a child here, out of my depth.

But the society was old, sturdy, and powerful. It would be enough to help her where girls like us alone could not.

"Hello," I said, not giving my name, and not asking hers in turn. She paused at the door, her fingers turning pale as she clutched the frame. My trained eyes were sharp as I peered around her into the house. I spied a Bible on her bookshelf and, tucked away between novels, the spine of the society's pamphlets. I noted the crack on the wall from an impact, and children hiding in the safety of the shadows. I saw the secrets of her marriage in one glance, though she still blocked the door as if she were trying to hide the truth from us.

"May we come in?" Bea asked with a smile. It was important to always ask permission. Mira would have walked straight in and scared the poor bunny into sending us away.

The woman nodded her consent, and we entered. Then she closed the door behind us and locked it. We removed our cloche hats. I tucked all three into my bag with our gloves while Iris peered into the darkened hallway.

"We heard one of your children had a cough," I said. It was a friendly remark, seeing as she didn't know our names, and we didn't know hers. And it was a safe-enough reason for a visit. It was always wise to offer to help the children first. Mothers sometimes could take help for their children before they took help for themselves.

The woman in green touched the door with one finger, but wouldn't turn to us. The moment stretching long enough I could feel her children wondering why we were here. I glanced to Bea.

"Would you children care for a treat?" Bea asked in a soft

voice as she held up her basket. "I baked a blueberry loaf with cinnamon and sugar icing. It's my grandmother's recipe and she used to make it for me every Sunday, but I miss her so much I make it nearly every day now. Can you tell?" She gestured to her large rounded stomach, and the children smiled warmly with her. "Would you share it with me?"

The youngest children waited for their mother's permission. Iris sent me a shadowed look.

She was right—the children were too quiet. Too skittish with strangers.

I glanced back into the shadowed hallway. Not a creak or a whisper of movement.

But a fresh-baked treat was a siren song even to frightened children. The youngest three followed Bea into the hallway. The eldest, a girl of eleven or twelve, stayed put and watched us with clear distrust, her small hands bound into fists.

In the hall behind me, Bea must have stumbled on something, sending a clatter and a crash, and then her own rumbling laughter accompanied by a child's soft giggle. I fought a smile. Bea could wield a pretended clumsiness like a knife, carving away distrust, until she'd worked her way into your heart. The children giggled again at another of her unseen antics.

The woman turned and handed her eldest child the babe at her hip. "Join the others, Anne. I'll be fine."

The girl, Anne, sent us a sharp glare before she fell to her duty and we were left alone to hear the story her mother couldn't tell to her children.

"Would you care to sit down?" she asked finally. Her voice seemed skeletal, like her throat was bleached dry. We followed her gesture into a well-scrubbed davenport couch. She knew of the society well enough to recognize this for what it was. Wives-to-be only came if she'd reached out already. She didn't seem to have questions about what we could do for her; she only questioned whether or not she wanted it.

"Is your husband home?" Iris asked with a soft high voice. The woman startled at the mention of her husband.

I smiled to soften the moment. "We saw the car."

"No. He had engine problems, some gasket or plug or something. I don't know. So our neighbor picked him up for work. Won't be home for hours."

Thank heavens. My neck muscles relaxed as Iris moved to the window and flashed a signal for Greta.

"Do you happen to know how to drive?" I asked.

The woman crossed her legs and turned to face the window. "I've been practicing."

Fascinating. That explained why the car was here, and why they had sent for us. Mira could fix that car as quick as any mechanic. I wondered, Were the Spinsters responsible for the car breaking down in the first place? They were so clever. Some battle plans were as simple as a note, or a midnight unwiring.

While I was distracted by my wonderings, the woman must have lost her nerve. She stood. "I thank you for your visit, and for the cake, but we're fine here. It was a mistake to mention anything."

I closed my eyes. We could only offer what a woman could take.

"Do you have enough food?" Iris asked. Her expression relaxed, now that we knew there wasn't a threat. The light hit her freckles and with her bright eyes softened she looked much younger. I bit my lip. Iris wasn't trained to hear the finality in the woman's tone. "Are there any bills we could help with?"

The woman shook her head but didn't speak.

"We could bring you meals," I offered.

She smiled brightly. Falsely.

Three words about a woman's smile: *it conceals multitudes.* "We don't need any charity. I have fine children who can help with the cooking."

"Are you certain?" Iris asked.

"We'll be fine. We'll get back on our feet in no time at all."

She smiled again. My oaths taught me to believe women, but sometimes women were taught to lie in order to keep their husband's secrets. The clues inside the flyer were clear. Where it said, "Father's money on drinks," it meant the husband had been spending all their money on alcohol. And the cracks in the wall and the bruise on her cheek showed he was a mean drunk. They sent us here to look, and I could not ignore what I'd seen.

I would need to charm her into it. "I hear you are an excellent seamstress. Did you do these curtains yourself?"

"Yes," she said softly, "and the children's clothes." The pride in her voice was almost a whisper.

"Perhaps we could send you a few odd jobs, help build up a savings," I said.

"It won't work," she said. "He counts my money."

The truth. Finally.

So I'd reward her with truth of my own. "We're friends of Abigail," I said, eyeing the pamphlets on her shelves. "You know what we can do. We want to help you, and your children."

"There's no need," she said. "Save your resources for someone with a greater call for it. If you'll excuse me, I do have errands to run, so if you'd . . ."

I called her bluff. "Very well," I said. I stood and crossed toward the pamphlets. By the soft pink paper cover it was clear it was an older edition, printed before women had the right to vote. There were condemnations for the suffragettes printed in this edition; where in the latest copies the society almost seem to take credit for the whole Nineteenth Amendment. That was not a judgment on the society in my estimation. Instead, it was proof that they were willing to grow, to change, even if they'd probably pretend they had always been what they'd changed into.

I plucked the pamphlets from their spot on the shelf.

"These would only upset your husband if he found them. I'll take them for you." I slipped the pamphlets into my pocketbook. She watched them disappear, the side of her lip twitching inward, showing a flicker of regret.

But not enough. She was really going to let us leave?

Iris's cotton dress wrinkled as she shrugged and stood, but I wasn't ready to let this go. Not yet. I picked up the woman's Bible and flipped through the well-worn pages. "Mrs. Rose had a Bible on her shelf too," I said. The woman stiffened, but I didn't look up, I simply flipped from Romans to Galatians to Hebrews. "She told us she and her children would be fine, just as you have. And how I wish that were so." I slammed the Bible shut and met her eye. "But no matter how sacred, words and women burn so brightly in a man's fire."

I signaled with two fingers in front of the cover, and Iris moved quickly. "It was good to meet you, and we wish you the very best." She stepped toward the kitchen and called for Bea.

I didn't move, and only watched the woman as her facade crumpled, her hands twisted, and her eyes sent a sharp glance toward the window and a soft one toward her children.

I gestured three fingers, and Iris and Bea stilled at the front door.

"I need safe passage," the woman whispered.

"You didn't need to bully her into it," Bea said softly with rain dripping from her light eyelashes. "Kindness counts."

Rain had begun to fall, seeping into my hair, pulling my curls straight and as drooping as the willow branches, and my dress was positively ruined. Perhaps that was why I was in a mood. "Kindness would have left her there," I said as I pulled on my white cotton gloves. "Kindness would have taught those children that how their father acted was permissible. My words were not kind, but they were right."

Bea touched my arm. I glanced through the rain to the car. The children watched my raised voice like I'd raised my hand with it.

I sighed and ducked my head.

Bea lifted her arm to block the rain from striking her face. "You're right. I'm sorry. I just can't help but feel for her." She handed me a letter and a recipe card. "Can you check this for me?"

I looked the message over quickly.

Mrs. Allen,

We've had a Request for your delicious blueberry loaf recipe. Please double-check that my memory has recalled the Passage Safely.

Blueberry Loaf Cake

INGREDIENTS
— *½ cup butter, softened*
— *1 cup sugar*
— *Five Eggs, One Hen*
— *½ cup buttermilk*
— *1 teaspoon vanilla*
— *1¾ cups all-purpose flour*
— *1 teaspoon baking powder*
— *1 cup fresh or canned blueberries*

"Is it too clear?" she asked.

Five Eggs, One Hen? Couldn't be clearer if she played it on a gramophone.

I gave it back. "It's perfect."

Truth was, most men wouldn't look twice at the recipe, no matter how clearly she'd hidden the secret message. It wasn't hard to keep secrets when no one finds your words worth reading.

I crossed through the rain and handed the note to the mother tucking her children into the family car. "You're doing the right thing," I said. She wouldn't meet my eye, but her oldest daughter's eyes lit with a gratitude that made me feel like this rain had painted me golden. She looked at me like she'd never forget my face.

The engine roared to life, and Mira clenched her fist in a celebration. Grease streaked her nose and darkened her fingers.

Iris glanced at her grandfather's pocket watch. "Three minutes."

Mira had fixed the engine in less than three minutes, with only a few curse words and grumbling moments where her feet dangled out of the underside of the car.

She grinned and Iris rolled her eyes. Iris had bet Mira that she couldn't do it in less than five. Now she owed Mira a quarter.

I slipped the mother a fold of cash.

"Thank you," the woman whispered as she took her place in the driver's seat.

We stood back and they drove away, a quiet car on a quiet street heading toward a safety net of women. My sisters and I waved goodbye until those taillights faded. A group of Spinsters would be by soon enough to pack up all they could. But for now, our task was finished. All in all, the Chat had taken less than an hour.

"Nice work, ladies," Iris said with a grin.

"Race you!" Mira shouted, because of course she did.

Iris took off, but Bea and I were wearing impractical shoes for the rain, so we held each other's hands and rushed as quick as our slippery soles would let us until we reached the car. A victorious Mira ran circles around Iris and inside the car a rain-soaked Greta waited in the back seat, her rifle tucked away inside the basket.

Unfired.

This time anyway. We climbed back into the car with a simmering satisfaction and a quiet rumble of conversation, and then we left behind us the house with the cracks in the walls and the fine curtains, which by the time the husband was home would be empty of everything but dishes covered in cinnamon icing the woman would not be washing.

A rebellion so quiet we'd left no room for a response.

When the day comes

when I hold a babe in my arms,

I'll see round cheeks and twilight eyes.

I won't see a gender.

I'll see hunger.

I'll see need.

So I will wrap the thing in white dresses,

and all my hopes.

Cotton bonnets, and all my love.

I'll sing quiet songs and give my milk.

And one day that babe could hit his wife.

Or one day that babe could be shoved

against a wall.

Such a simple difference

could lead my child

so well loved

down two very different paths.

CHAPTER TWO

Footsteps sounded behind me as I walked down a drenched street I'd thought was empty.

I tugged the handle of my bag of library books higher and told myself not to look behind me. It was probably nothing, not a large man hiding behind that azalea shrub I'd just passed, or a mobster with a tommy gun who would try to hold me hostage. My imagination jumped ahead of me because I'd simply read too many adventure novels, and I'd seen too much in my society work. But while even simple footsteps could send a chill up my neck, I could also remember my training and slow my breathing. Whatever it was, I could handle it.

Then a large splash sent me spinning with my fists raised and my thumbs tucked inside my fingers even though Iris has told me time and time again the correct way to punch someone.

And it was only a little girl, perhaps eight or nine, in a bright yellow wool coat and too-large galoshes.

Oh. I pressed my hand to my chest. *My cursed nerves.* Always alerting me to danger that wasn't there.

The little girl smiled coyly back at me and then jumped from her curb into the rain drainage. Water of a questionable cleanliness drenched her stockings.

I smiled back and then continued my trip through the drizzling rain toward the library, when the footsteps sounded again, but now I could hear the squeak of wet galoshes against the pavement.

I peered back, and the little girl was hunched over, gripping one shoulder as she walked like a caveman. Or . . . *like me*, I suddenly realized. I corrected my posture and loosened my grip on my shoulder strap, walking how the society had trained me, and behind me the girl's gait changed as well. This time she pushed out her bony hips from one side to another, like a sheba from a nickel movie. I grinned and then bowed my legs like a cowboy and walked forward for a few feet. I glanced back, and she copied me and then pinched an invisible brim to a hat in a *how do you do.*

Oh, she was a hoot. I laughed full out, and I switched to standing on my tippy-toes like a ballerina. She mimicked me, and we twirled together. Then while she was still spinning, I curled my fingers and snarled my lips and turned into a fierce T. rex. She shrieked with delight, became a dinosaur, and pounced on all fours into the puddle.

"Ruby!" Her momma stepped out to her front porch and called the little girl back inside, ending our fun, but possibly saving those stockings.

I folded my hands sheepishly as I recognized her. "How do you do, Mrs. Jackson," I called.

She looked me up and down and smiled as recognition dawned. "Oh, you're that Fawcett girl. Nathaniel's sister, right?"

I swallowed. "That's me."

"You tell him to come on by next time he's in town. I've got some cobbler waiting for him."

I noticed that invitation forgot to include me, but I was used to that. "Will do."

"He's a great man, your brother."

I smiled. "Don't I know it?" My painted smile faded as I turned away.

It's not that I wasn't proud of my brother, or the work he was doing as a lawyer fighting for poor folks who were swindled into making bad mortgages. I was so proud of that. And of him.

I just wanted to be a great person too.

And that was never going to happen.

As I meandered down toward the library, I slunk my hands into my coat pockets. Pockets that I knew for certain were empty when I'd started this journey, and now the right one hid a paper card. I searched down the house-lined street. I hadn't heard a single step that didn't have a squish in it, and now the trees and flowers lining the street showed no sign of the Gossip who'd left the message for me. She'd slipped away like she was made of shadows.

I'd not caught a Gossip since I was nine, and even then I was pretty sure the young woman had let me catch her to ease my overactive imagination. She'd had a kind face and thick glasses. I'd often wondered if she needed those glasses to see, or if she needed them for people to see past her. Gossips were the spies of the society, and they were extraordinary at their job. They were almost the Fae from my stories, slipping through shadows into the fairy world.

Their training must have been even more difficult than my own.

I pulled out the card. A simple recipe for Pretty Duchess Potatoes handwritten on a lined card with small roses printed along the bottom. The kind of card no one would look twice at, not when it was coated with specks of flour and smelled of vanilla.

No one would notice it hid a secret message.

PRETTY DUCHESS POTATOES

INGREDIENTS
— *2 pounds potatoes (peeled, chunked, then boiled)*
— *salt*
— *¼ cup heavy cream*

- *4 tablespoons unsalted butter, divided*
- *¼ teaspoon nutmeg*
- *½ cup raisins*
- *Dash vanilla*
- *½ teaspoon black pepper*
- *3 egg yolks*

Mix, mash, pipe into stars, and bake at 450 degrees for 20 minutes.

Though why would vanilla go anywhere near potatoes? The first rule of the society was you never actually cooked following the society's recipes. This recipe contained raisins (with potatoes?), which meant to come to Mrs. Allen's house; the mention of royalty meant this was a romancing mission; the capitalized *Dash* meant right this minute; and the three roses penciled in at the bottom of the card meant bring only what you could carry.

I grinned. I so loved an assignment. Most of the time anyway. But what kind of assignment could it be? It was difficult to know what to expect from the information on one recipe card; this could be fifteen minutes if I didn't want to romance their target, or a week if the attempt at romance failed, or even a lifetime if I won the romance. But I'd gone on missions like this one before and left without a ring, so there was no telling how long to expect.

Mrs. Allen's home was only a few blocks away. The first time I'd ever gone there I was twelve years old, holding my mother's hand as she introduced me into the First Ladies' Society. In the parlor there had been dozens of girls around my age waiting to enter the dining room and leave with a title. Some of these girls would grow up and then would take small children and mold their minds with the right words, the right books. They would decide what history would be taught. They would decide who could be the heroes and who would be the villains.

They'd be called Teachers.

Some would be trained in fighting, and in administering tonics. We all were taught to fight back, but these girls took to it with genuine talent. Some excelled in medicine and nursing, some in punching bad folks right in the teeth. Some of these girls weren't looking for a love between a man and a woman, and they found a safe place with our stronger fighters. And some just really liked fighting. They would be our warriors.

They'd be called Spinsters.

Other girls were to be trained in espionage. In correspondence. They would watch from the shadows and from behind opera glasses, and report back. They kept eyes on those we elevated. They watched those men and decided when they'd gone high enough. They'd be the ones who decided when to bring them back down.

They'd be called Gossips.

When it was my turn, the Matrons checked my blood

pressure, my bone structure, my head for numbers, and my willingness to take an order, and that was it. I was pronounced quality. Scared and pretty and smart. My family was well respected, my mother well trusted, and I'd figured out the message they thought to test me with in record time. And they found I had a real gift for Matchmaking, seeing through people to find who would make a fine pair.

I was twelve when they decided that one day I would marry a powerful man of their choosing. And then after we married, I'd become the influence that would change his decisions and history itself. They'd given all the Wives-to-be dolls dressed in white, and smiled as we all planned our future weddings. I would be trained to charm, and to turn myself into a wave and a smile behind the man we'd lift up. I'd be the beautiful woman you didn't look at twice.

And they called me a Wife.

I glanced to the north toward Mrs. Allen's house. The recipe card did say to dash over right away, but . . . these books were due tomorrow. I'd rather risk the wrath of Mrs. Allen for tardiness than let a library book be overdue. I hesitated for a second before I sprinted down the street and round the corner to my favorite building in my hometown. I ran up the steps, threw open the door, and dumped my books on the front librarian's desk. Mary flinched back from my rain-soaked bag and shielded her hot-combed hair with her hands. She was a Black woman, maybe in her early thirties, and as the source of all my books, she was one of my favorite people.

I leaned forward. I did not have the stamina I'd gained during training. "So sorry, Mary. I'm in a rush." I pressed a muscle cramp at my waist.

Mary knew me well enough to laugh and not shush me like she would have when I started coming here. "I'll take them to the back."

"Thank you! You are positively berries. The bee's knees. But now I've really got to go." I glanced at the clock. Only seven minutes late if I hurried.

"The new Sherlock Holmes has come in," Mary teased. "Twelve short stories about our favorite detective."

I stopped. It was as though my love of books were a cage I'd been trapped inside. I shook at these invisible metaphorical bars and tried to make them see sense. The society was expecting me, and what if the mission was an urgent one where someone needed me right now or they would die?

But Sherlock was so smart and grumpy.

"Really?" I turned.

Mary grinned. "I'll grab it for you."

In for a penny . . . "And the next of that Rosebound series, if you could. It ended on a cliff-hanger, and I need to know if Dora survives."

"I just shelved it. You know where to go . . . that is if you have the time."

I glanced at the clock. Ten minutes late. But it was no use. "All right, but I'll be as quick as possible. I really am in a rush."

"While you're up," Mary said, "do you mind taking these to returns?"

I laughed. I knew exactly which charming technique she'd used on me, and while Mary was not a member of the society (that I knew of anyway—they kept our numbers under a strict need-to-know basis and women of all races were accepted), she might as well be for how well her technique worked on me.

"On it." I picked up the bag of books I'd just dumped on her and ran it back to the return desk, where Carla, who has never liked me, looked up from her round glasses and shushed me so hard I could see spittle erupt from her lips. I lowered my shoulders, properly shamed. I knew the rules of libraries; these were sacred hallowed spaces, and she was 100 percent correct that I needed to be quiet to preserve the peace of my fellow patrons, so I made my steps as quiet as possible as I walked—no, *rushed*—quietly into the Adventure section.

A wave of peace sent me still. I traced my fingers across the bindings of the Jules Verne novels I'd read so many times that just seeing them felt like coming home, grabbed the next Rosebound, and then the next one just in case it too ended in a cliff-hanger, and then because I was already late I grabbed a book that had a stunning cover without even reading the synopsis, and then okay maybe one more just in case, and then raced back to Mary's desk.

"I pulled you a few more," she said as she showed me the cover of the first one. Langston Hughes.

Poetry. Glorious. I raised both hands. "I'll take them all."
I didn't have time today for our usual run-through, where
we chatted about each book. Besides it didn't really matter
what they were. I've never met a book I didn't like. Large
tomes of dry history, that, truth be told I actually loved reading; law books, which were complex, dull, and endlessly
fascinating all in the same sentence. Poetry, pamphlets, and
prim readers. And of course the words of our First Lady
Abigail Adams. She founded the society, and her words
were the quiet melodies to which the society danced.

I should have left right away. No matter the length of the
assignment, the society would have all the books I would
need. My heels bounced against the ground as she stamped
each card and slid it back into the sleeve. If only there was
a way to make this go quicker.

Stamp. Close.

Stamp. Close.

Mary looked up, her stamp hovering above the Sherlock
I could not leave behind. "Any new poems?"

I shook my head and pushed her hand holding the stamp
down on the card. "Please move faster."

She chuckled, and I looked at the clock without really
seeing it.

I had actually written several new poems, but none were
ready for anyone else's eyes. I'd only ever showed her the
one, but then once I got back home I lit that poem on fire
because it was nowhere near good enough, no matter her
kind words.

She slid me my stack.

Eight books in less than eight minutes. "Thank you!" I swept them back into my bag and hoofed it out of the library, my T-straps slapping against the wood floors so loudly I made Carla shush me all over again and Mary laugh so hard she had to cover her mouth.

"Sorry," I shouted.

Outside the gentle drizzle had turned to a full pour, so I stuck the bag under my coat to protect the books, and I grinned. That might be the record for my fastest-ever library visit. This visit was so quick it was an absolute triumph. I should write a poem about how perfectly well this went.

But I was now fifteen minutes late.

And I'd have to run through the rain.

***

Mrs. Allen's home was filled with elegant coiffed girls I've known since we were children, sitting in perfect rows reading stapled stacks of papers. I entered soaked as a wet rat dumped from a hurricane; just completely out of breath and fighting the rising acid of a good upchuck, about twenty minutes late. I ducked out of my wet coat and hung it on the coat stand, checked to make sure my books had made the journey without damage, and then I shook out the rest of me like I owned the place.

Bea waved from her chair near the window, and Mira put her legs down from the seat they'd saved for me. As I crossed the room, some of the girls shot me worried looks or said hello, but Greta muttered something about my clinging dress to her friends, and from the look in her eye, I knew it wasn't the dress she was mocking; it was the body beneath it.

I stopped in front of her fancy friends and glared. We'd just worked together not a month ago at the Chat, and now she sat with her friends like I hadn't trusted her with a Beretta aimed at my shoulders.

"Oh good," I said. "It's just you all. I thought there'd be some real competition." I wrung out my wet hair and dripped all over her papers, and then I smiled as I stepped over the ankle Greta had stuck out to trip me as I made my way to my friends.

I dumped my bag under the chair and sat. "What'd I miss?"

"It's a lifelong," Bea said. She handed me my own stack of papers.

"Yeah? What's his name?"

"They don't say."

Odd. I glanced through the papers. It was a questionnaire all about our likes and interests, and how we'd handle different charming situations. We've taken assessment tests before, but *this* was massive: eight pages front and back, including questions about Shakespeare, world economics, and long division.

"They're being all hoity-toity about it too," Mira said. "Matrons popping in to watch us answer the questions."

There were maybe twenty girls in the room. As I studied them, I noticed who among the Wives-to-be had not been invited, and who was here. They'd brought in girls from different chapters across the country. Girls I'd only seen once or twice but knew by reputation. Girls of all races, religions, and socioeconomic status.

All the top-tested Wives.

Each of us would one day marry a man the society would make influential. A good man, worthy of the title. Someone smart and charming. Someone who would listen and fight against injustices as he led business empires or media conglomerates. Someone we would encourage to be braver, calm if we needed to, and change his mind if circumstances demanded it. We were to be the voice and the chance of representation our founding fathers wouldn't give to us.

These girls were the only ones who understood my life, and they were also the only ones who could keep me from it.

"And it's timed," Bea said. "We've got ten more minutes."

Jeepers. I grabbed the pen, and I raced through the answers like I was running down the street, but even as I frantically tried to catch up, a small part of me kept thinking of what this could possibly mean. My friends and I had charmed many young men the society would one day help place in positions of power, but we'd never been assigned someone above a priority five. My own brother had been a priority four, who, by his own compassion and a few of my mother's machinations, had made himself a priority three. He was on a path to becoming a justice one day.

And *wouldn't* I be so proud then?

But this test had to be for someone higher.

I did my absolute best, as quickly as possible, with adrenaline racing through my veins. My friends might tease me for this, but I've always loved a test. It felt so good to be challenged, to use every aspect of my thinking and capacity.

This could be my shot at something more for my life. I would fight to prove my life could matter. Mira lowered her shoulder so Bea and I could check our answers on the math; Bea glanced over our recipes, correcting how much flour I'd need for cookies and scratching out yeast on Mira's; and I made sure they could read my answers on Shakespeare to tweak theirs in their own voices.

And then it was over. A Matron collected our papers, and I sat damp and shivering in the window draft. One by one they called girls in, and then one by one those girls either returned to the chairs or they collected their coats and left.

When Bea was called in, Mira and I waited with fingers crossed until she came out smiling. Mira strutted to answer her called name with more confidence than any other girl here, only to return a few minutes later trembling like a mouse as she walked back to her seat.

And then they called me.

I swallowed and walked into the same dining room where they'd once given me my title.

Three Matrons sat around the table, while the woman at the center of the table studied a picture of my face and my test marked in red. I took the only spare chair. I knew Mrs. Allen and Mrs. Alvarez of course, but I'd never met the woman holding my assessment. She was white and plump, with light brown hair twisted into a bun, and she looked down at my assessment like I wasn't sitting in front of her. I recognized her as one of the Matron heads from the Midwest chapter. Mrs. Brown if my research was correct.

I tucked my rain-ruined hair behind my ears.

"She's a stout girl," Mrs. Brown said, referring to the larger size of clothing that fit my body.

"And proud of it," I answered, refusing to duck my chin. "Although I prefer the word *buxom* actually. Or *voluptuous*. Like a romantic painting. *Statuesque* is another word I enjoy . . ." I trailed off when they glanced up at me.

"Prone to speeches," Mrs. Brown said.

"You get used to it," Mrs. Alvarez said with a slight teasing smile that I returned. Mrs. Alvarez was the most compassionate of our two chapter head leaders. She looked great in her light tan wool dress, it set off the deep brown of her skin nicely as she handed Mrs. Brown my best photo from the file.

Mrs. Brown still didn't look at my face. "Quite pretty."

"Thank you," I answered, though it wasn't a question.

Mrs. Allen tapped the papers. "She's Nathaniel Fawcett's sister."

Mrs. Brown collected my papers like an answer had been

reached. She looked up and smiled at me. "Go retake your seat, Elsie."

I should have been grateful, dutiful, and obedient like I'd been trained. But my emotions were rumbling like a storm in my chest and I didn't move. "You don't want to ask me any questions?"

Mrs. Brown was already moving on to the next girl's file. "We know enough."

"I could quote Shakespeare if you like? Or demonstrate a flirtation, or I could tell you the history of our society, name all the chapter heads from Abigail Adams on down."

"I'm sure you could. But with your family—"

"—I am more than just my brother's sister."

They were quiet.

But I couldn't be. "I need my life and my brain to matter as much as my brother's will. Do you understand?"

They were quiet. Mrs. Brown wrote something she wouldn't let me see on my file.

"Go sit back down, Elsie," Mrs. Allen said. "Before we change our mind."

I stood reluctantly and left the room. Bea and Mira stared at me. I nodded and retook my seat next to them, but then I couldn't speak. I felt like I had said something true. Something important.

And yet it was like they forgot me already.

When there were only seven girls left in the parlor chairs, Mrs. Brown entered the room with the Matrons following behind her like baby ducks.

"Where is she from again?" Mira whispered.

My friends didn't do research quite like I did. "She's one of the heads of the Midwest chapters."

"Long drive," Bea said.

She was right. This was a long way to come to meet us. Bea had a talent for noticing things that I'd missed. I clasped both of their hands tight.

The flickering sconce lights traced Mrs. Brown's face. She was dressed in a blue embroidered work dress, her hair twisted up and her expression warm but weighted as she examined each of us like she was checking the price of groceries and found us marked too high. Mrs. Allen and Mrs. Alvarez hovered behind her, their faces not giving any sign of how we'd done.

"This assignment is a priority one," Mrs. Brown said without preamble. My stomach dipped. "And as such, this will be a responsibility not only to our society but to the world. It will be high risk, and high stress, so before we go any further, I need you to search your own feelings and capacity to ensure that you can handle such a role. If not, leave now with our blessing and highest regards. Leaving will not affect any future placement, of that I give my word as a Matron. I need to know that you are ready, not only for the task, for the responsibility of the life, but for marriage itself."

My fingers grew numb and my chest buzzed.

She paused, and we all looked at one another as the weight of her words settled in. A girl grabbed her bag and left silently. Another sat with tears down her cheeks, her knee bobbing. Mrs. Brown watched her as Mira's hand in mine began to tremble.

"I don't know," Mira whispered. "I don't know."

Mira was the bravest girl I knew, and this terrified her.

"Am I too young for this?" Bea squeaked at my other side.

They were both terrified, but my heartbeat was steady and my nerves were electric with excitement. Priority one. This was what I wanted. This was the opportunity I've always hoped for, but never thought possible. This wasn't a choice for me—this was a chance to breathe when it sometimes felt like I'd been drowning. This was air. This was the promise of every fairy tale I'd ever read. I didn't ask myself even for an instant if I was ready. I felt like I'd been waiting for this my whole life.

But I knew I couldn't do it by myself.

"You stay put," I said. "Both of you. And we help each other. If we work together, one of us can win and then we lift all our stations higher."

Bea and Mira both nodded, and we clutched one another's hands tightly to keep us steady as the crying girl slipped out. And then another girl left.

Until there were only four of us still sitting in the room. The three of us.

And Greta.

Of course it had to be Greta.

Mrs. Brown nodded, and the Matrons locked the doors and lowered the window shades. "His name is Andrew

Shaw. Eighteen years old. He's marked to become president of the United States."

I leaned against the seat back, my mouth gaping. This was . . . This was more than an assignment. This was more than meeting my future husband. This was a chance at the most powerful position for a woman in the society. In the world.

And Mrs. Brown had just given it to four of the most ambitious girls I've ever met.

I glanced at my friends. My sisters. Bea's eyes were glistening, Mira let out a sharp laugh and then covered her mouth. Across the room, Greta's eyebrows lowered, already scheming.

My competition.

Any one of us could have a life more impactful than I ever dreamed.

All we had to do was make one man fall in love with us first.

CHAPTER THREE

The rain had cleared by the time the Helpers dropped me back home. I had an hour to pack before someone was coming to drive us all to our target's hometown.

Before the priority one, my friends and I would have walked home, Mira stopping in the wealthiest section of town, Bea and I moving farther, and then Bea walking the rest of the way home on her own. But now, the night was deemed too dangerous for the woman whom we might become. We were now precious to the society, much more than before. So now we needed to be protected.

I was going to charm a priority one.

How positively nifty was that?

The only thing that soured my excitement was our Helper Elizabeth's slumped posture and heavy sighs. A few gentle questions later, and she'd opened up to us. Poor thing. Her mother was ill. Bea and I were able to talk through her feelings for most of the drive. It must be so difficult to carry all her mother's heartbreak and illness, when she was already holding up from her own struggles.

If I wasn't leaving so soon, I would have stopped in on both Elizabeth and her mother in the next week.

The car hit a bump, and Bea and I jostled into each other. Bea stared out the window.

"What's wrong?" I asked. She didn't have an ill mother too, did she?

"Nothing." Bea shook her head, and I knew it was because she didn't like the attention centered on her. Bea preferred to be the one who helped others.

I just looked at her, and the silence turned into the prompting she needed.

"It's just . . . It feels like you all are so much better at this than I am."

"That's not true. I've seen your scores; you are brilliantly charming."

"I know. Still . . ." The car's tires crunched through pebble road as Elizabeth pulled into my neighborhood. "It sometimes feels like you all are leaving me behind."

I took her hand. "Oh, Bea." She was quality. She knew it. I don't know how she could doubt the society saw her. We have scores and training, and how could she doubt something quantifiable?

"I don't know. It's silly. It's fine. It's just . . . I feel like I'm always trying to keep up," Bea said.

"Youth is a strength here. I've never heard a man complain about not wanting a young wife."

"I have." She shot out a breath, her bangs bouncing in her exhale. "They always see me as a little sister. I thought that would change as I got older and grew these mighty bosoms." Elizabeth and I laughed, and Bea smiled.

Our legs brushed. "You're everyone's favorite, Bea. I'm sure it will be fine."

The car turned, and I could see my house not a minute away.

Her voice caught. "But what if the Matrons were wrong about me? What if I'm nothing but potential I didn't meet." She stopped, her face scrunched up as she fought back tears. "What if I'm not good enough for this?"

"Oh, Bea."

"I'm sorry," Bea said as she wiped her cheeks. "I didn't want to throw my feelings on you and make you feel conflicted. I'm glad we all have this chance. I'm proud of all my friends. I just . . ." She looked away, her eyes glistening. "I want my turn. I want . . ." She drew a deep breath. "I want the stars and the sky, but . . ." Her wistful smile turned mournful.

"I feel that same want."

"But you have so much." She looked at me with shock, a line cutting a crease across her forehead. She turned to face my house, two stories tall and shining stone, the landscaping free of any weeds. "How can you want more when you have everything?"

I did. I know I did. Was it ungrateful to want more when your stomach was always full?

Bea ducked her head. "I . . . I have this sky-sized hole in my heart that will never be filled enough, not with sweets or baked goods, or fancy dresses, or handsome men. I want more. I want so much more. But I want to earn it. I want people to think I am the most special person in the entire world, and I want it to be true."

Bea said the words, but I felt them in my bones.

"I will do everything in my power to help you, Bea," I said. "You deserve a chance to earn that sky. I believe in you."

"But I won't." Her eyes glistened, and her voice grew so quiet I'm not certain even Elizabeth could hear her. Silent tears slipped down her cheeks. "I won't. I'm going to be barely good. I'm going to be forgettable. I'm never going to be as big as my wants."

I pulled both of her hands into my lap, and I made her look at me. "That's all right too. You are a light to everyone who knows you. And kindness and cakes is every bit as important as signing laws or being a doctor or some fancy title. You make everyone around you happier. That's enough. You're enough."

She wiped her cheeks. "But what if that's giving up on what I could be? On what they expect me to be?"

"You matter, Bea. No matter the size of your influence."

She swallowed and I saw her put on the smile she used for charming. She turned to face me, streaks from the streetlight brightening her freckles. She'd shown vulnerability here, but now she was shielding it, and I was going to let her. "But now we have a chance to influence the whole world. I never dreamed this big."

I grinned at her and her smile turned real. "Start dreaming, Bea. Because this is just the start of what we'll do," I said. I squeezed her hand one more time and then I left the car, leaving Elizabeth in Bea's most capable hands.

But as they drove away I had to pause for a moment. I didn't want our celebration to cause us to miss a need. There was more I could do for Elizabeth and her mother. I didn't want to forget them. I pulled out the recipe card from my pocket, turned it over, and penciled in a quick note for the Gossips with Elizabeth's mother's information on it. I placed it in the mailbox with the flag at half-mast for a Gossip to pick up. They could add her to the watch-care rotation. They'd make sure she wasn't forgotten.

Because now I was leaving. I had a mission. A chance for the brightest possible life.

Now it was just me and the moon and the path toward my front door, and finally I could celebrate without an audience.

Priority One. I could do so much good. Jeepers. *Mrs. Elsie Shaw*, First Lady of the United States. History would remember my name, I knew it. I knew I could win this. I felt like a princess, and fairy kissed and so full of optimism and cheer and an all-consuming longing to write it down in my journals that I flew on angel wings up my steps and into my house where my mother waited up with her knitting.

She looked up with a start as soon as the door opened, the shadows under her eyes deepening in her lamplight. "I was so worried! Do you have any idea how late you are?"

I tossed off my coat and dropped the bag of my library books. "I stopped in at Mrs. Allen's, and before I knew it, night had fallen." My mother knew everything about the society of course. When my mother had received a similar testing to my own, they'd given her a different title. She wouldn't wed a powerful man, she would raise one. She'd be a Mother.

But my mother never seemed to know what to do with me.

A son was proof of a job well done. A daughter was a question.

A question I'd fought to give the right answer to every day of my life.

"You could have warned me," she said. "I've been so worried. All that rain. You know you have a frail constitution."

"Didn't they leave you a message?" The Gossips always let her know where I was.

"They did, but they didn't say anything about the hour. I wish they would leave more information in the recipes."

I understood her then. This worry wasn't 100 percent about me. "Is Father here?"

It was nearly eleven at night on a Thursday. I wouldn't have asked the question if the answer wasn't often no.

My mother clenched her hands together. "He's gone up to bed. It's an important day for him tomorrow."

I lowered my hands to my sides. "It is an important day for me as well."

Mother stood. "Let me get you some food. You must be starving." She crossed into our kitchen, and I followed behind her, noticing every hung photo or sparkling surface like I was saying goodbye to it for the very last time. Mother put the kettle on and pushed through the well-sorted pantry for cookies. "The tea will warm you up, but I want you to grab a blanket, dear—the last thing you need is to catch a cold. Put socks on and sit by the fire."

"There's no time. They're picking me back up in an hour. It's a lifelong, Mother. And this one I'm going to win."

"That's nice, but you will not leave this house until you're fed and I'm certain you're well. Go put on some wool socks."

I stood my ground. "I need to pack. I need to make a plan for how I'm going to win. Mother. This is a priority—"

"—You'll win nothing if you're sickly or dead. Go do as you're told."

"It's a priority one."

"What?"

I grinned and walked back to my room with my mother tight on my heels. "You are right," I teased. "It would be difficult to charm a *future president* with snot running down my lip."

"*What?*" she repeated.

I laughed as I raced to my room.

Mother called after me. "Elsie. Do not run. I've just mopped, and I don't want you slipping and breaking an ankle."

I opened my bedroom door and danced about my bedroom, pulling the quilt off my bed and wearing it like a wedding veil. My mother sighed as I dropped pillows and sheets to the floor. My room was clean, of course, because my mother's nerves could not abide a mess, and covered in bookshelves and dolls I still loved but never played with.

I was sickly a lot as a young child, and then I'd caught the influenza when I was only nine. It took my grandmother and my father's sister and so many other people, but somehow I survived what should by all rights have killed me. My mother had been overprotective ever since, and my father spoiling, so I received every doll I'd ever pointed at, and any book I could carry, but I also had to drink tonics, and sit by the fireplace, and I was always subjected to whatever newfangled health plan was touted by my mother's magazines.

But part of me had always wondered if maybe I was saved for a reason. That perhaps I was born to do something great, even though God had seen fit to make me a woman.

I peeled off my stockings and rain-stiffened clothes and dressed in wool slacks and a sweater that would be warm for traveling. My mother went to fetch a pair of my brother's old socks. I sat on the bed with the quilt wrapped around my shoulders like a queen's cape.

"A priority one," my mother said with an even voice as

she collected my dirty clothing and placed them with her washings. "Now that is exciting."

I pulled a packed bag from under my bed and opened it. They never gave enough warning, and after I was caught underprepared for my first mission, I stayed ready to leave for the next opportunity.

Like this one. *This one*. My heart was positively goofy! I was so thrilled. This one I would win.

Only Greta really would stand in my way.

"Your brother is only a priority three at present. Though I think it's possible for him to become more than a justice; perhaps he could one day become Chief Justice Fawcett, can you imagine?"

My smile felt forced. "That would be wonderful." Priority one meant my standard pack wasn't enough. I reached into my wardrobe for extra ammo in this fight. Greta was so wealthy, I was certain she'd bring forward any advantages she could to leave us all behind. Mira had mostly garçonne suits, which were well enough, but Bea? She'd only be able to use whatever the society provided, and lovely though those dresses were, they were always donated or came secondhand and a few seasons late.

"Oh, I didn't tell you the news," Mother added with a smile. "Nathaniel made partner today. Can you believe it?"

"That is exciting," I said as I held up a dress so sparkling and full of moving fringe that it could pull the attention of any man in a crowded room.

But it wasn't enough for my mother to look my way.

"Partner before his second child even comes. I'm planning on heading to Chicago to celebrate, and I'm going to make the most delicious cake recipe I just clipped from my *Modern Priscilla* magazine; pineapple upside-down cake."

I put the dress into the bag. I was one size smaller than Bea, but we could let these out, I was certain of it, and take them way in for Mira. My family wasn't extraordinarily wealthy, but we'd always had enough for our needs, and now my brother was making such a solid income taking from those greedy bankers that we had more than enough to share.

Mother straightened one of the glass figurines on top of my dresser. I swallowed hard.

"And now you'll have two children to be so proud of," I said softly as I turned to face her. "A future chief justice and a future First Lady."

She met my eyes. "I am very proud of you both."

I smiled so hard my cheeks hurt.

"I'd love to hear more about your future husband. Have you received the dossier yet?"

Some of the air nipped from my lungs. "Not yet," I said.

"Well, you'll have to write and tell me all about him." The kettle wailed in the kitchen. "Oh, your tea."

She left, and I stood still for a second, all the light and optimism that had been holding me up dimmed, and all at once I could feel every inch of exertion from the day, and the pull of the late hour.

She hadn't asked me about what I'd do with that title.

She hadn't mentioned anything about the ways my life and my influence would create change in the world. She hadn't said anything about all the ways I could help now.

She went straight to asking about Andrew.

I tucked my notebooks full of poems on top of the clothes, and then I packed my favorite books. I wanted my life to matter as much as my brother's, but even if I married a priority one, no matter what power and influence I could wield in the society and in the world, would my life ever matter as much as my husband's?

Would this just be choosing a taller shadow to stand in?

I hesitated and then went back to packing. In a shadow that large, I could do so much good.

I crossed to my jewelry box. The society jewels were better than mine, and I'd prefer to borrow than bring along, but there was one thing I'd take.

My grandmother's hair clips.

Soft silver moons with pearl-dusted flowers. They were the loveliest thing I owned, and since I inherited them at nine years old, part of me held this romantic notion that I would be wearing these art nouveau clips when I met my future husband.

I'd never worn them before.

I don't know why. Perhaps it was because I never felt old enough for marriage, or because whenever I looked to the future it felt like a fiction someone else was writing. It never felt like a possibility. It was never me standing at the end of the aisle or holding those babies, or making those meals. I'd prefer to go and support my fellow Wives-to-be as they found their happy ever after. I'd go and play as Matchmaker.

It was safer that way.

This was the first time I wanted to win. This was the first time that my future looked like a blank page and I was the one holding the pen.

I held those clips in my palm until they felt too heavy to carry, then I tucked them into a safe pocket and closed the luggage.

Then I made my way to the fireplace and let my mother cuddle me like I was still her little sickly baby, as she told me stories about my brother's amazing future.

Until the car came, and it was time for me to fight for a chance for my own.

CHAPTER FOUR

A dark green truck pulled to the curb where my mother and I stood with my bags. The baker's truck parked on the corner with its headlamps off and its engine idling, the words FRANKWORTH AND SONS painted on the side, circled with painted roses in a crescent-moon shape. The driver Helper took my bag, and I turned to say goodbye.

"Good luck, my darling." Mother picked at a hair that hung over my eyebrows and tucked it behind my ear, the side of her lip clenched in a subtle grimace. "If this doesn't work how you wish, know you always have a home with me, and there *will* be more men you could marry."

I didn't need a safety net, like a trapeze artist in the circus. I was going to win this. I knew it. I kept my face still. "I'll write."

"Or someone will. You needn't bother if it is a distraction from your mission. They always keep me updated. I'll be fine." It was an excuse in case I forgot about her. Which I would never do.

On purpose anyway.

I swallowed. She'd be so alone without me now.

"Make us proud," she said, for my father who wasn't ever here.

I stilled. *This*. This was what I wanted more than anything. I wanted to make my parents proud, but more than that, deeper than that, I wanted my parents to see me as someone who *could* make them proud. "I promise I'll try my very best." I kissed her dry cheek, and then crossed to the back of the truck. Pausing, I turned to say goodbye to my home.

The moonlight hit the drive and our carefully manicured lawn, and the lights in my home made a halo around my mother's faded brown hair. She waved me goodbye, and the sparkle and excitement in her eyes made me feel like I was her hope, like I was a maiden from a story waiting to be rescued by a handsome prince and she couldn't wait to read the rest.

Though was that story the one I'd hoped to pen?

I turned the handle and opened the back double doors of the truck to see rows of bread and flour on metal shelves, a false back of the truck painted on canvas. I slipped behind the canvas screen and into the truck cab, where lighted mirrored vanities lined the truck walls and velvet benches were placed back-to-back. Bea sat deep inside the truck bed with her carpetbag tucked under the vanity. Our friend Iris sat across from her with her own bag held in her lap. My arms tensed with a sudden burst of nerves at seeing a Spinster protector. Was this going to be dangerous? I kind of skipped over that part of Mrs. Brown's warning.

I sat next to them and the truck took off toward Mira's.

"I'm glad you're here, Iris," I said. I dropped my bag of books and slid it under one of the vanities. I sat next to Iris. "But why are you here? Exactly how dangerous is this mission? Don't get me wrong, I'm so glad to see you, but also . . . should I have brought a weapon?" They were sneaking us into the town in the cover of night, and we had a Spinster protector, and I really should have paid attention to what this was risking, not just what I could gain from it.

Iris squared my shoulders with both her hands and looked me straight in the eye. "Don't spiral, Elsie. It's all going to be fine. Priority one missions always have a Spinster companion, just in case."

"Oh, good."

Iris looked both ways, leaned forward, and lowered her voice to a whisper. "But what I didn't know until about an hour ago is that the Spinster protector of a priority one fights for her own priority. This mission is how Spinsters decide who will become the Head Spinster Matron. If I do this well, and one of you gets engaged, then I will begin training to become the Head Spinster." She glanced at Bea with a touch of a smile. "If this goes the way I hope, I could be in the future First Lady's cabinet."

"That's wonderful," Bea exclaimed.

"Congratulations," I filled in a second late. If this went well, Iris could earn the right to become a future Matron. Her name would be written down, and society girls would be quizzed about her. Each Matron was the highest-ranked woman of her title of her chapter, but the Matron Circle was even higher than that. The women in the Matron Circle were the top in the country and would reign for as long as their First Lady was in the White House. Iris would be able to work firsthand with the inner circle of Matron Leadership, and as a future Head Spinster she'd be in charge of all military planning and keeping us all safe. If she were a man, this would be equivalent to her being accepted to become a future general.

But we didn't use such language.

"Thank you, my sweet friends," Iris said, her eyes sparkling. "I'm poso-lutely gobsmacked, to be completely honest. I thought they would have sent Vera or Edith! Someone older and more experienced." She shook her shoulders in glee. "But I'm so glad it's me. Oh, and I wanted to tell you! Elizabeth's mother is going to be all right. Her fever broke, and the Gossips have included her in their watch-care list."

I sat back. "Good. I'm so glad they got my message."

"I'm glad you sent one," Bea said. The side of her lip dipped down quickly.

I opened the vanity drawers and fiddled around inside. They had left us a comb and hair clips. I took some pins and started waving my hair. "I'm glad we could watch out for her. Those retired society women deserve so much of our kindness. Especially when they're all alone. I . . ." I pinned a curl back. If it wasn't just Bea and Iris, I might have stopped there, but they were as big of romantics as I was. "I wonder if there are any sweet old men we can set her up with once she's recovered."

"Oh, can we play a game of Matchmaker?" Bea asked with a grin.

"I'm in. But we'd be looking for a woman, actually," Iris answered.

I glanced over.

"I had a similar thought." Iris bit her lip. "The Gossips told me the partner who just passed away was a sweet old woman. The poor little bunny."

I returned to my pinning. "Who can we net in? One of the retired Spinsters perhaps?"

Iris's cheeks were glowing. "I was thinking Janie."

I gasped. Our dear trainer. She'd just retired herself. "That would be perfect."

Bea cooed and clapped her hands. "We'll have to start some Matchmaking schemes when we get back." She looked away. "I mean when one of us gets back."

It wasn't going to be me. Least I hoped it wouldn't be me. But somehow I'd forgotten that that meant my friends would leave disappointed.

"Don't worry. I set a few plans in motion before I left." Iris tucked some hair behind her ears as she lost her smile. "It's strange to think that if this goes well, I won't be coming back home for a while. At least not as a Spinster. I'll stay with whichever one of you wins the priority one. Go to college with you. Then follow your new family around during campaigns. And then I'll move close to the White House." She shook her head. "It's so strange that the next forty-some-odd years could be set now. If I can just keep you all safe. If I can help . . ." When Iris looked at me her eyes were wet with tears. "I can't . . . I can't believe they chose me."

"Of course they chose you," Bea said. "You're so strong and smart and kind."

"We trust you completely," I said. But still something about her future life being so set in stone, but set back in the shadows behind one of us didn't sit right with me. I leaned forward. "But don't you want a life of your own?"

Iris shook her head and her hair brushed her cheeks. "Honey, this is my life," she said. "What we do for women and families in need, and for girls like me? I want to be doing this for my whole life. It's lonely out there without our society. Isolating. Being someone different, never knowing who I could trust with my real self, never knowing if someone might try to hurt me for being who

I am. But this society taught me how to fight back, it gave me vocal coaches, and gave me access to some of the most incredible patternmakers. And it gave me all of you, and so many people who will fight at my side. This society gave me so many sisters and friends. All I want is to work with one of you dear girls to make positive change for kids who don't have this society. We're going to make a better future, if I have to punch the present into submission."

I reached for her hand and squeezed. "I know we will."

Bea nodded. She held her bag to her lap like a pillow.

"How are you doing with all of this, Bea?" I asked.

"Honestly, I'm excited." Her face lit up with a smile. "I think I have less pressure than the rest of you. There's no way he's going to choose me. I'm only sixteen and a half years old." She lowered her voice. "I'm not ready for marriage."

"Neither am I," I admitted. "And neither probably is he. He's only eighteen. But it's always a long engagement. We wouldn't actually be married until we're both eighteen or nineteen at the youngest."

"It's still so young," Iris said. "I don't hardly remember what I was doing at nineteen, and that was only four years ago."

We leaned into one another as the truck stopped.

A moment later, Mira slipped around the painted canvas, lugging a pair of plants with long leafy spines, that scattered dirt as she slid them under the benches. Then she leaped onto the velvet bench with her hands held out as if she were sliding down a snowcapped hill. "Hello, you gorgeous dames, who's ready for an adventure?"

I laughed.

"Oh you know I'm in," Iris said.

It did feel like one of our escapades. When we charmed Livingston, the four of us had run off in the middle of the night and hopped onto a train to the next stop over. And then we held on to the back of a bakery truck through dawn. We barely made it back to slip into our beds before the Matron knocked to wake us. We didn't have a destination in mind that time. We just wanted the journey. Or the time before that, when we were charming George Weston, we'd escaped to watch a vaudeville show, only to find the show we'd hidden in the back of was a burlesque, and our giggles got us kicked out by a woman who wore a painted mole and not much else.

The truck door slammed, and the engine started.

"Bea doesn't think he'll choose her," I tattled.

Mira sat down in a leap. "You take that back. You are a stunning, lovely, brilliant woman. Anyone would be happy to have you."

"And you all as well," Bea said.

"Don't we know it," I shouted.

"Bully for us!" Iris said. We all laughed, and then nearly as one, our laughter softened into a silence we all tried to ignore. All of our futures hung like a question in the air. And as much as we built each other up, not one of us knew if we'd be able to secure this.

"I'm glad we're all together," Bea said, breaking the silence. "Poor Greta doesn't have you all as her support."

"Didn't you see her glaring at her friends?" Mira made a face. "I think she was trying to make them give up their chances."

"We'll support her through this," I inserted for Bea's sake. "It's a mission. Our vows say we need to play fair, and help each other."

"I do feel kind of bad for her," Bea said. "We have each other, but she's all alone. But you're right. She has an equal chance at winning him." She shrugged one shoulder.

"Bea you are such a tender heart," Iris said. "But I'm here for all of you girls, including Greta. I don't play favorites."

"That's a lie." Mira said.

"Okay fine, Greta's my favorite." Iris said, her eyes sparkling with mischief.

Bea didn't smile. I swallowed hard. "I'm sorry if I made you stay on. If this isn't what you want, I'm sure the Matrons will support you if you choose to go home."

"No," Bea said. "I'm here, and I'm excited. I can't wait to be somewhere my little sisters aren't stealing my old clothes and a Davy and Michael aren't yelling over some jacks or little Suzie doesn't need me to read to her while her little sticky fingers brush my cheek so softly." She cleared her throat. "I mean I'm grateful to come along. And I'm grateful for the mission pay. This priority means twice the monthly allowance, and after my father hurt his leg, my family needs the money now more than ever."

Mira's shoulders pressed back. "Don't worry, Elsie. You didn't force us to come. And don't think I'm going to go easy on you. I've got even higher marks on charming than you do."

"And I happen to know my cookies will make any man fall in love," Bea said.

"So that's what we're calling them now," Iris said with an arched eyebrow.

I cackled as Bea shimmied her massive chest.

The truck stopped again, and we settled a little. Mira shoved her bony behind on the bench between the two of us.

The undercarriage boomed as luggage was packed in beneath us, and then another bag slipped behind the painted screen. One suitcase. Then another. Then another. And finally Greta climbed in, holding a plate of truffles I know she didn't make herself and giving us all a smile I'd seen graded and judged.

"Isn't it exciting?" Greta said with a polished charm I knew better than to trust. She placed the plate of truffles on the bench next to us. Then she turned her back to us and the chocolates, opened her handbag, and began powdering her face in the mirror. "Priority one. Positively berries."

Mira glanced at the tiny painted balls of deliciousness.

Bea and I shook our heads in warning. I didn't trust those truffles for a second. Of course I didn't think they were poisoned, Greta would never go that far, but maybe she happened to use an ingredient that had "accidentally" spoiled and then we'd spend our first meeting fighting a rumble in our stomach.

"It's a long drive," I said. "Perhaps we should figure out how we're going to sleep back here."

The screen opened, and someone slid in a stack of papers with a photo of a teenage boy clipped to the top.

The dossier was here.

"Or not," Bea said.

The back doors closed and locked. Mira dived for the papers, and Greta took off after her, just an instant behind as they tussled over them.

I stood. "There's plenty of time," I said. "No need to fight. Let's share notes. Compare strategies. We need to treat this like we would any other priority assignment. We work together, and we let him make his choice."

"Fine," Greta said as she took the dossier and held it to her chest. "But I'm reading first."

"Age before beauty," Mira said as she sat back down.

Iris pressed her lips tight as Greta glared, her pouty bottom lip trembling for a second. I knew Mira's barb had hit its mark.

The truck started, and we all swayed as it turned again, this time toward the highway.

Greta studied the photograph carefully and then tucked it away with the blank side toward us as she moved on to the next page, like we all weren't dying to see what he looked like. Any sympathy I'd begun to gather for her floated away. She was insufferable.

"What do you think he's like?" Bea asked.

"Stuffy and boring like Livingston," Mira said, rustling a blanket from her bag and wrapping it around her shoulders. She bent down to make sure her plants were well settled.

I pressed my lips together. "I liked Livingston."

"You would," Greta said. "What did you always go on and on with him about, the life cycle of ants?"

"That was one conversation." He was a scientist who valued intelligence in his partner. Our friend Nora snagged him, and she has the most remarkable mind. Such a good pair.

"That went on for hours." Greta complained, but I'd liked trying to charm someone who let me be smart.

Mira made a face as she sat down on Greta's side of the truck. "Least he didn't kiss like Mr. Weston."

Greta snorted and then came after Mira with her mouth wide open. I laughed when Mira shoved her over.

"Was George Weston a bad kisser?" Bea asked. "He was so young and handsome."

Greta and I shared a look, but I decided to be diplomatic. "Kissing is a skill that can be taught to improve."

Greta smiled at me, despite herself, and then she handed me the photo. Mira scooted forward and Bea leaned into my side to study it.

Andrew Shaw was handsome enough, in a boy-next-door kind of a way, with light brown hair that scooped to one side, circle wire-rimmed glasses, and tan skin with a layer of padding that made it clear he'd never been one to miss a supper. There was intelligence in his expression, or a sense of concern, as if he were secretly wondering if I needed any help.

He looked like the kind of man I'd want to vote for.

But did that mean I found him attractive?

Mira bit her lip like she hid a similar question, but Bea was staring at the photo with her eyes and pupils wide, a soft smile tipping the corner of her lips, her cheeks pink and glowing.

She closed her eyes tight. "What if he's mean?" Bea asked with sudden energy. "What if he has an angry streak that the Gossips missed; what if—"

"—Don't worry," Iris interrupted. "You're not forced into anything here. And the society isn't going away. They'll support you if he turns out to be a disappointment."

"I'm more worried that I will be the disappointment," Bea said. "There's no chance for me here. I'm the youngest, the plumpest, the poorest . . ."

I grabbed her hand. "Plump is not a weakness."

I hoped.

Mira took Bea's other hand. "It's not."

Greta took my other hand. "It's really not," she said, though I knew her well enough to know this was a tactic to try to make us trust her, and not something she stood behind as strongly as she should.

Still, for a second, we faced one another, our gaze and our responsibilities shared. I took in the line of Greta's nose, the length of Mira's neck, the steady confidence in Iris's gaze, and the unmasked terror hiding behind Bea's expression. These girls, each one of them, were my family. And even a priority one wouldn't change that.

I wrapped an arm around Bea's shoulder and tugged her in tight to my side. "Maybe he'll be more than a handsome fellow," I said. "Like a lost prince raised in America, clever and likable, and maybe, Bea, when he sees you for the very first time, he'll forget how to speak because you, beautiful lovely you, are the most precious dream of a girl, and you will have all the right words, and all the right smiles, and by the end of this summer we'll be planning your engagement party. We'll be laughing and waving you off as you go find your happy ever after."

Bea leaned against my shoulder. It was easy to tell this story for her, but as much as I wanted it, I still couldn't see myself on that road with my hand held by this stranger, waving goodbye to my friends.

My friends had always been here for me. Sometimes they were the only ones who saw me. And by the end of the summer, if everything went to plan, I'd be leaving them. I've always known the end of our friendship would come eventually, but now it would be here before September.

"What did you all pack?" I asked quickly to not get stuck in my feelings.

Greta spoke up first. "Three new haute couture dresses, a Schiaparelli sweater, and cologne made with sheep pheromones. The saleswoman said it was scientifically proven to net a man."

Goodness. How on earth could I compete against that? "You really want to win this one, then?"

"I always do. That's the problem." She turned around, her hands clasped in her lap. Her expression softened. "I fall in love too easily I guess. And the men always want to kiss me, but they always choose somebody else to make their bride."

"Men are the worst," Iris said. "I have been in that position so many times. But why don't they just find a girl they like and commit. It's not like it's hard."

"It's not," Mira said. "It's science. There are steps and tricks and words you can say to get them to commit."

"Words you will teach me?" Iris asked with a flair of the hand.

"Of course!" Bea said quickly.

I was still watching Greta. She stilled, like she was waiting for our attention to swing back toward her. That restraint was how I knew this sudden show of vulnerability was a tactic.

"You know what I've been wondering, though?" Greta's eyes were dreamy, her smile engulfing. "All those times before when I had my heart smashed into itty-bitty pieces, what if it was because I've been saved for this one?"

We didn't answer. I'd seen Greta hide tears before on the drives home after we weren't chosen. I knew her truth as she said it.

Which didn't mean it still wasn't an attempt to charm us.

It's strange to think how the steps to charm a person into a romance was simply a psychological manipulation. I didn't like thinking that way. Love was romantic and magical, like a fairy tale. But what we did was plotted. It was like a recipe really, and if you combined the right steps, baked at the right temperature, and included the same ingredients, then the cake came out the same every time.

And for a second, I really analyzed the ingredients the society had put into this charm. They'd given this choice to four white girls, and gave the priority to a white man. I knew that part of the decision of who to give a priority future to would depend on the ability to win an election, that there were places in this country that wouldn't accept anyone who wasn't their certain image of an ideal. I knew that we had to work with the world the way that it was in order to create change in our future.

But I couldn't help but wonder if all this work, this opportunity I was so hopeful for, wasn't just an attempt to maintain a status quo that set one race above all the others.

And worst of all, I knew that even if it did, I was too ambitious to ever turn it down. That for all my speeches on inequality, I wasn't going to turn down something I knew they weren't giving to other Wives-to-be from different races. And now, even as the storm in my thoughts wouldn't stop berating me for that, my friends were talking about flirtations and admiring the length of Andrew's eyelashes.

These were the girls I loved more than anyone in the world, and I felt so alone. They seemed safe and warm, and I was being rained on.

Greta wiped under her nose. "So what did you bring, Bea?"

"I . . ." She glanced at me, her eyes concerned. I put on a soft smile and she continued. "I mostly brought cakes, to tell you the truth. I found a few new recipes, and you know what they say about the way to a man's heart, don't you?"

Greta arched her thin eyebrow. "I'm mostly concerned about something a little lower."

I pressed my fist to my mouth to stop a laugh.

"Greta," Iris said, her mouth wide open in shock.

"What? It's not like we haven't all been trained—"

"—I didn't know you had that in you," Mira said.

"You should have told me you wanted sheep phero-mones," Bea said. "I could have brought a lamb to spray all over you."

Mira slapped her knee, Iris fell over giggling, and I snort laughed.

Greta couldn't suppress her distaste. "I'll use my own tactics, thank you very much." She held out the dossier. "Here, meet my future husband. It's clear you three are going to need as much help as you can get."

Bea grabbed it first. Mira moved over and I leaned in.

"Oh," I said, reading over her shoulder. "He has a little sister. I've always wanted a little sister."

"Good family too," Greta said as she nestled back. "His parents are the leaders of the local prohibition group. Educated at an excellent school."

"Swell grades," Mira said. "Though Elsie's are higher in history and diplomacy, and mine are higher in math."

"What are his political leanings?" I asked.

"It doesn't say," Bea answered. "Though it does say he's open minded and compassionate. His racial bias test shows a strong desire and acceptance for inclusivity and equality, but his ideas on free market and a robust military might need to be guided."

"Or it's a strength," Greta answered, because of course she did. We've clashed on politics before, so if we were both invited, then it meant Andrew must be somewhere in the middle. "I believe in a free market. Too much regulation can hurt business growth and—"

"—On the backs of its workers," I interrupted. "Regulations are necessary in order to protect worker rights."

Greta raised her eyebrows. "Regulations only hurt the wealthy. A strong upper class means a strong economy, which trickles down to help the poor. You can't help anyone if they don't have jobs."

I shook my head. "If you really want to help the poor, then we need to talk increasing taxation on our wealthiest—"

Greta scoffed. "Didn't realize I was in a truck with a communist."

"Oh, here we go," Mira said, taking one of Greta's truffles as she settled back. Iris grabbed one as well to watch me like I was a picture movie.

Well, I did feel a speech coming on. "I'm not a communist, but it is simply not ethical for a small percentage of our country to hold the majority of its wealth. I think—"

"He bakes," Bea said softly. My voice trailed off as I saw her, completely engrossed in the dossier in front of her. She met my gaze with glistening eyes. "I never for a moment imagined that he would like to bake."

Bea was absolutely mooning over this dossier.

I slumped back down on the bench.

My passion for proving Greta wrong was less important than one simple truth.

Andrew was a real person, and what we were going to do to him meant working in real feelings. It wasn't about winning, or being right.

Not completely anyway.

If we were going to make him fall in love with us, then in order for us to be happy and successful in our lives, we had to *actually* fall in love with him back. We had to be in this for the right reasons. For the possibility of love. For our future family. For our own happy ever after.

And it looked to me like Bea had quite the head start.

A Word on Love

I've felt the remains of love
fade like a bruise upon a cheek.
I'd seen love make fools
of women and men and daughters.
I've felt love rip through me like a storm and
when it passes
I've rebuilt my own self differently.

All I've seen of love is destruction.
But all my stories tell me it's joyful.
Is it possible it's both?

Joyful destruction,
Build me into something new.

CHAPTER FIVE

Early morning, before the sun crept over the mountains, the bread truck finally stopped. We gathered our bags and our blankets, and exited the truck to find we had parked at the end of a long winding road that led through a large patch of trees up toward a two-story house.

Mira wrapped the blankets over her shoulders. "It's too early for walking," she grumbled.

"Time of thieves and criminals," Iris said, studying the woods around the path as she stood sturdy while Greta leaned on her to fix her shoes.

"Or mothers," Bea said.

"Or me," Greta answered with a grin. "You forget this is my time, and you all are my Helpers." She smiled, but I wasn't sure she actually meant it as a joke.

"I'll go set up a perimeter," Iris said. "Stay close to the house until I'm back."

We nodded and she took off.

"Speaking of Helpers . . ." Greta turned with a smile. "Bea."

"Don't do it," I muttered under my breath.

Greta ignored me. "I have a job for you."

"Just say no." Mira picked up her luggage and started walking toward the house.

"I will pay you an entire dollar if you take my bags up to the house."

"Oh, an entire dollar," Mira said over one shoulder.

"I won't take your money," Bea answered quickly.

"Good girl," I answered.

Bea bit her lip. "But . . . I do only have the one bag . . ."

"Stay strong," I said.

Bea winced, but it was no use. "And you have so many, so I'd be happy to carry one in for you."

"Thank you," Greta said. She pointed to the largest bag. "That one if you don't mind." She picked up two bags and left three in the dirt.

Bea heaved the largest bag onto its side and pulled it down the pebbled path.

"You made an attempt," I said with a smile. "That counts." I started down the road after her, tugging my bag full of books over one shoulder, and lifted my other bag by the handle. The trees were dappled with a soft orange hue that would brighten as the sun woke, nearly as light as our future.

"Well, if I didn't do it, she'd make Iris. And it's not like I haven't lifted bales of hay that were heavier." She groaned and lifted the bag over a rock in the road. "I think Greta packed a safe in here."

We slowed to a walk, our steps crunching under our feet. "I think Mira should have the first go at Andrew. I love watching Mira flirt," I said with an artificial brightness, desperate to change the subject. "It's like watching the Kraken crush the Nautilus. There will be no survivors."

I glanced at Bea, but her smile seemed to come late.

"What is it?"

"Has the society had a hand in every president being elected?"

"Not at first. It took us time to get organized." The Electoral College helped. Once that was established it was almost simple. The safety net of women moved the battered women and children we rescued into swing states, and then we created jobs and filled those positions with good men who would remarry those women and give them good lives and who voted the way we asked them to.

She looked at me like she was still interested, so I let my overresearched rambling fly. "And not every election. Sometimes a dark horse takes us all by surprise. When that happens, either we try to recruit his wife, or else we hold on tight for four years, or through his reelection. The heartbreaker was President Benjamin W. Eves. We worked so hard to have him elected, and then two months into his term his wife, Delores, died of a carriage accident. He was lost to us for years."

"Do you think we're doing something wrong? The Constitution says by the people, and of the people. If what we're doing is so good, then why aren't we doing it out in the open?"

"We're people." I made a face, but she didn't laugh. "When they started this, we didn't have the right to vote, we didn't have the right to own property after marriage, and we were entirely dependent on men. And we wanted to have a say in who we would make our leaders. We wanted representation. So the society decided to find and research men who we thought would make good leaders who might be sympathetic to the cause of women and help place them on a path toward leadership. Help give those men opportunities, make sure the men in charge were those who would listen. And we knew that the most influential woman in a man's life was . . . well, his mother, to be frank, but secondly his wife. So they educated women like us, to try to charm them. It's mostly just Matchmaking."

"But isn't it lying?"

Sometimes it sure felt like that. "All it means is a method to try to have a voice where for so long we've been made voiceless. And we are definitely not the only group trying to influence America by selecting her leaders. At least our oaths are ethical."

"What if the man doesn't care for women in that way? Do we not let them be leaders?"

"Franklin Hobbes and Vice President Jeffers were very much in love. As were their wives."

Bea shot me a look. "Really? They didn't teach us that in training."

"There are some secrets that are not ours to tell. They're not alone either. Lots of our forefathers had romantic inclinations of that nature, and you can find them if you read through all the footnotes. Some marriages find loyalty is even stronger than love. There's a lot of different ways to make a marriage. They aren't all romantic."

I could see the house through the trees in front of us.

"It really is a shame," she said at last.

"What?"

"That you were born a woman. You'd make a great candidate yourself."

My heavy arms held me tight. "If it is, it's not my shame. I love being a woman. If America can't see me as a leader because I was born a woman, then at least I'm in good company. America has a habit of missing out on brilliance because it doesn't look the way it expects."

I immediately wanted to take back the implication that I thought I was smart, or that I was referring to anything other than other people's brilliance.

But why couldn't I claim my own?

I grew quiet, because Bea's questions had given me a few of my own. Did the society make things better for us, or did it make us live in the shadows? We've always drawn power by weaponizing the invisible work of women.

But it never changed the fact that we were still invisible.

"I wish we didn't have to do this all in secret," Bea said. "I wish America would let us live and lead out in the open."

"That's the future for which we fight," I said with a smile I didn't feel. Bea's words had swirled up some memories. When I was young, before I knew better, I wanted to become the president of the United States. I used to look into my mirror and answer imaginary reporters' questions, and often I'd stand outside and give speeches to the trees in my backyard, until the neighbors noticed and my mother brought me back in. I had such ideas too, like how the president should send a note to every citizen on their birthday and include a quarter, so they could get a treat or take someone to the movies. I just wanted everyone to know that they were important. I remember my brother debated with me on that one, and that's how I learned words like the deficit, or economic stability. We used to hold mock debates all the time, debating serious things like the economy or civil rights, and frivolous things like was it time for me to put away my dolls, or why if I did his chores it would be good for my developing work ethic. He'd always let me win, and it wasn't until later when my parents and I watched Nathaniel do oratory debates in high school that I realized he'd been holding back. Part of me loved him for letting me win.

But part of me didn't.

And as I grew older, the debating stopped. It was always,

Christmas isn't the time for such conversations, or sometimes my father would tell me it wasn't ladylike to speak so loudly about opinions that were not for me. I should talk about ribbons or recipes. I should talk about curling my hair, or painting my lips.

Or better yet, I shouldn't talk at all.

Bea and I reached a large brick bungalow with a wraparound porch and flowers in the sill. We left the heaviest bags at the base of the stone front steps, which we climbed. The front door was unlocked, but I knew the house would be empty. They always let us get our strategies and things settled before they brought the husbands back home.

I fluffed my hair and climbed into the entryway and into the front parlor, where Greta sprawled out on the floor with Mira on her back holding her in a headlock.

I swear we were only behind for about five minutes.

Greta was squawking like a duck while Mira flicked her hair out of her face. Part of me went immediately into my training in de-escalation. But the other part really wanted to see Mira give her a good wallop.

Bea entered behind me, pink with exertion. I reached for her hand.

"Pay Bea her dollar," Mira said calmly.

"You don't have to pay me anything," Bea said quickly. Her cheeks were red and her eyes pleading. "I'm fine."

"Mira, stop." She wasn't just hurting Greta here. Bea was already raw, and being defended only served to make her feel small.

"I said I would pay," Greta said. Mira pulled her arm up higher. "Ow! I'm going to tell the Matrons."

"No you're not. And you won't say another thing about Bea's poor family, do you hear me? You don't talk down to any of us again."

I winced as Bea's hands tucked into fists.

"Mira, let her go," I said. Mira finally looked at Bea's expression. She sighed as she realized how she'd made her feel, and then she climbed off Greta's back.

Greta stood with as much dignity as she could muster and rubbed her shoulder. "I swear, if this bruises . . ."

Bea let out a small huff of a sigh. "Let me take care of your arm." Her lips pressed together like a smashed sandwich, and she turned her glare on Mira. "I can't believe you."

They walked out of the entryway and deeper into the house.

Mira stood with her eyes closed. "You didn't hear what Greta said when we got to the house."

"I understand the impetus completely. But that doesn't mean it helped."

"I know." She slumped into a chair next to the front fireplace and placed her head in her hands. "I bungled that up so badly."

Floral wallpaper covered the walls above the dark wood wainscoting which ran down to marble tiles making checkerboards of the floor. No, a chessboard. That's how difficult this might be.

I sat down on the floor next to her. "You did."

"It's just that Greta makes me so . . . Ugh! And then Bea never says no, so she thinks she can just . . . *Ugh!* I'm so mad I can't even form sentences."

I chuckled softly. "That's okay."

"We gotta protect her," Mira said, her eyes feverish. "She's going to give up everything she's ever wanted."

"Like Andrew?"

"Did you see her face? She's half in love with him just from the dossier, and now we've got to flirt with him?"

"I know. It's never felt quite this complicated before. It's because this is for more than just a man. Or a family. This is a chance to mean something."

Mira let out a long exhale. "And the worst thing is I really want this. I was scared at first, but I want to be that person at the center of the society, making all those plans, figuring out what's right and who should go where, and pointing the ship. It seems like the greatest puzzle ever. Like an engine you constantly have to rebuild. I want that."

That was exactly it. I loved the society and I believed in the mission, but I saw so many ways it could go wrong. And I knew historically the impact of a weak or wicked First Lady. I wanted to be at the head of it, to be able to make decisions for how it would run. I didn't trust Greta to run it—she'd lead us into selfishness. And I had so many ideas of how I could take us into the future. I wanted my hand on the helm. "Me too."

"But how can we take it away from Bea?"

I leaned into Mira's knee. "We can't think about it like that. We've got to be there for each other," I said. "We play fair, we be honest, we be gentle with feelings and support-ive when he makes his choice, whoever is chosen."

"Of course. But if it's not me," Mira said, "I want Bea to win. We'll be fine, but this is the best chance Bea is ever going to get. She wants love and children, and I want to see her happy. No matter what."

For a second, I swallowed back my hurt. If she didn't believe in me yet, then perhaps it was my responsibility to change in order to prove I'd be worth backing as a First Lady. But Bea would be an excellent First Lady too, and I knew I could trust her to lead us with compassion. I held up my little finger, and Mira wrapped hers in mine and we made a pact. "If it's not me, then it's Bea."

We dipped our hands together in a solemn vow, before Mira grinned. "Did you just finally share one of your poems with me?"

I laughed and stood up. "If it rhymes it's sacred." I shook my shoulders like a vaudeville clown. "But never cook naked."

We both laughed, and then Mira stood. "I'm going to go claim a room before Greta knocks down a wall and decides we can sleep in the garage." Mira suddenly got a far-off look, and she peered toward the front window.

"You know you're going to be sleeping in the garage any-way."

"Probably. But not tonight. I'm looking forward to some goose down pillows." She picked up her blankets and her plants. She shot me a look.

"I'll talk to her."

"Thanks, dollface."

I made a kissy face. "Sure, sugar."

She winked at me, then climbed the stairs up to the second story.

I left my bags behind and made my way into the house. The place was massive. The entry foyer emptied into a long hallway with a large wallpapered dining room on one side and a series of locked doors on the other. Old family pictures and paintings covered the halls, a testament to the large family that once lived here, but now the Brown children had all grown up and moved on and Mr. and Mrs. Brown live alone with all these extra rooms. They looked happy together.

Of course they did. Mrs. Brown was trained as a Wife. She was trained to be happy like this.

Next to the pictures, I saw Mr. Brown's diplomas, articles written about deals he made, pictures of him with his powerful friends, and a retirement announcement framed like a trophy. The walls told two stories. Two lives. Mrs. Brown gathered children while he gathered accolades.

No matter how cherubic those cheeks, my dreams looked more like Mr. Brown's life than the one I was supposed to want.

The end of the hall tucked straight through into the kitchen where I could hear Bea slamming pans as she angry baked.

Greta walked back in with her elbow wrapped and her chin upturned.

"I'm sorry about Mira," I said.

Greta smiled. "Don't be. It's forgiven."

We'd been trained to forgive, but I know that Greta wouldn't forget.

"Where is she?" she said with a painted smile.

"Maybe she's out in the garage?" I said, though I knew perfectly well she was climbing up the stairs.

Greta narrowed her eyes and brushed past me.

Oh. What a bony shoulder.

I followed the sound of cooking and the smell of fresh-baked something. Bea was in her element in the kitchen, wearing a yellow apron freckled with flowers. She matched the yellow subway tiles that covered the walls, cut through with a soft green tile in a subtle geometric pattern. The kitchen windows, lined with cotton embroidered curtains, were open to the backyard, and I could hear birds and crea-tures chattering outside, and taste the cool fresh air of the morning. The cabinet trim was painted green, and the glass centers showed clean and well-organized shelves full of plat-ters, cups, and canned goods. All my friends seemed to have a place to belong here. Like one day a house just like this one would be their own.

Something inside me twisted. For a second, I was alone

staring at a massive home that didn't belong to me. I knew my place. I knew my future. I would be a wife of a powerful man. I would turn his head in the direction the society led me toward, and that was enough.

That was more than enough. I was grateful for everything they'd given me.

The front door opened, and a woman's voice called from the foyer. "Girls?" Mrs. Brown was back with Iris in tow, and they weren't alone. A group of five or so Beauty Makers rolled in carts and paints and curlers. I stood tall.

The Beauty Makers' training and world were separate from our society. They were more like allies let in on our secrets than sisters. Cousins, maybe. But we trusted one another with our secrets, and sometimes one of ours would move to their society, and sometimes we'd bring in one of theirs to ours. The Beauty Makers were men and women and those in between, who played with beauty and gender until there were no labels that would stick to them. They were beautiful and handsome in the same breath. Their weapons were the artist brush.

Both societies knew well the power of observation. Sometimes it was best to fade away into a crowd, but other times you'd need to stand out. It was almost a magic trick really, the way clothes could turn a girl invisible, or make her the center of attention. Misdirection. A wave of the hand. If Harry Houdini could use a woman to distract, then why couldn't we use ourselves?

It was an honor to have them in. But I lowered my

shoulders and raised my chin. If we were already in the Beauty Making stage, then I knew what came next.

Next we'd meet the boy.

My stomach twisted, and I closed my eyes. I thought of the eight-page assessment, of what I'd studied for, of all the plans and hopes I had. I thought of my brain, my life, my future.

Then I opened my eyes, painted on a smile, and let them turn me into a doll with a perfect face, hiding dreams no doll should have.

My father gave me a collection of dolls.
One for each birthday he missed.
One for each mistress.
One for each time a business venture failed.
One for each time he came back home
with his arms wide and he was welcomed by
my mother.
They stood untouched on a shelf.
Painted smiles, perfect silk, collecting dust for my
mother to clean.
How could I curl their hair or touch their cold faces
when they were made to silence my storm?

The storm has always been inside me, rumbling
inside my bones.
Asking questions when I should be silent.
Climbing trees when I should be still.
Ruling my dreams of a life my best friend doesn't
think I deserve.
The storm pattered against my brain
when I should've been silent.
The way all dolls were.

CHAPTER SIX

We made plans while they rid our bodies of hair. Mira won first go, because Bea and I ganged up against Greta and voted for her. I chose to go last because from my research, the last chosen had statistically the very best chance of winning. Going last would mean the most lingering feelings when we moved into the second stage. But my heavens, was it ever going to be hard to wait!

The Beauty Makers slathered creams to make our skin brighter as we spoke of where we'd like to meet him. Bea insisted on meeting at a bakery, which was an advantage I'm not sure any one of us could fight, but at least we'd eat well as we assisted her. Mira chose to meet him at a mechanic's shop, Greta at a fancy restaurant, and I'd meet him in a library. They painted our hair with masks made of oils to repair the damage of the irons they'd use to fluff our hair up to stylish, as we chose which jobs we'd take to assist. Giggling and planning and arguing just a little as the Beauty Makers played with paints and powders for lips and eyes and cheeks.

Before I knew it, it was time for Mira to meet the man who I hoped would become my husband.

I wished I didn't have to speak so much about the clothes she wore, or the hours of preparation that made her eyes brighter and darker, her hair slicked back and curled at the side of her ears, or the way her soft white jacket made her bronzed skin shine like sunshine, or how her white high-waisted slacks made her legs look miles long, or her cream heels clicked like tiny drums marching her to her future.

I wished I could speak about the thoughts in her head, or her dreams, or the kindness in the way she touched Bea's shoulder before she followed the Matrons out to the car. I wished I could focus on the way Bea and I received our instructions and stood at the outside of a car shop, as we worked to redirect any other patrons from walking into the mechanic's shop. I wish I didn't have to speak about the matted wig that made my scalp itch, or the way the loose brown dress made me nearly invisible to the men and women walking down the street.

Beauty didn't equal worth. I believed that down to my bones. Worth was intrinsic.

But those walking past me would have looked twice if I'd been the one done up, and now their eyes skidded right beyond me. Beauty made a microphone.

And without it I was as silent as a shadow.

I heard the splutter of Andrew's car before I saw him turn up the street.

Andrew's jalopy of a car ran, which was about the only good thing I could say for it. The fenders were covered in rust, the seat cushions had been carefully patched, and the engine left a trail of smoke that sputtered enough to be taken for Morse code.

I caught a good look and then turned my back as he pulled his car into the shop.

Iris flashed me a signal from her spot on a park bench next to the road that she would take over this task as I moved on to my next objective. I ducked inside to intercept the mechanic, in order to give Mira extra time to meet Andrew.

I pulled off the wig that had kept me invisible for Andrew's entrance as I made my way through the back hallways toward the office. I flicked open my hand mirror and fixed my hair, and blended my makeup into my sweaty hairline. I needed every ounce of my beauty now. The mechanic, my target, was an older man with a soft gut and dark grease lining his knuckles. He sat in the back of the shop cleaning parts as the spluttering car entered the sun-streaked garage. A cloth tag on his work jumper uniform said his name was John, but from the Gossip's report I knew it was actually Juan.

I blocked Juan's path toward the open garage right in front of a glass window separating the halls from the open workspace. Mira lay on the trunk of Mrs. Brown's car with her hat tucked over her eyes.

"Hello," I said softly to the mechanic, careful to stand out of Andrew's line of sight. It was important that Andrew knew where the mechanic was so he didn't come looking for him. But the last thing I wanted was for him to see me too soon and dressed like this. "I'm so sorry to bother you. But could you help me with something?"

Juan glanced back toward the shop where Andrew and a future paycheck waited. I pursed my lips and pressed my shoulders back, holding my eyes as wide and innocent as they went.

"What can I do for you?" he asked with a soft and subtle accent.

I pulled a map from my purse. "I'm new in town, and I'm afraid I'm completely turned around. I can't find my aunt's house anywhere."

His lips curled up. "It is hard to be new in a place. I will help."

"Thank you so much." I opened the map to block his view into the shop, but I could still see through the glass as Andrew climbed out of his car.

"I'm looking for Lilac Grove Lane," I said. The mechanic focused on the map, but I watched Andrew put his hands in his pockets and look around. I watched him as he noticed Mira. I saw his neck bob, and he looked away.

Andrew Shaw seemed younger looking than he was in the photos. He was only a few months older than I was, but his face seemed too innocent compared to everything I'd seen. His brown hair was trimmed and parted in the same style he'd had since he was a child, thick glasses not obscuring a rounded nose, and lidded brown eyes. Something about him reminded me of a puppy, like he needed to be protected.

Or trained.

His nose seemed wider in person than it looked in the picture. He wore his weight well, with a thick neck and rounded arms like I expected, but the photos didn't show the way the light warmed his skin, or how veins made rivers up his wrist, or his height. I thought he'd be taller. Maybe that was because the stack of information in my head about him was taller than a skyscraper.

He turned back to look at Mira. Really looking, now that he was certain she wasn't aware of him.

I narrowed my eyes. Why him?

His test scores were higher than average, with a real head for numbers. Well liked by his peers. Small romantic history with age-appropriate girls planted from the society. But . . . what marked him different from the other men we'd charmed? My own test scores were as high as his, higher in history and diplomacy. Who decided he'd be the one to have a glowing life?

What did he do to earn all of this?

What had he done to deserve us?

"I like your car," Mira said.

Andrew startled a little. Mira lifted her hat from over her eyes, and I saw him stand taller.

He rubbed the back of his neck. "She's great, isn't she?"

"*She?*" Mira said. "Why do men always insist that cars are women? I don't enjoy being compared to property you can ride."

Andrew's ears flushed pink. "Sorry, I didn't . . ."

Mira climbed off the car and walked closer. "So what's wrong with her?"

"Is that it?" the mechanic asked me, pointing at the map.

Oh drat. Was there actually a Lilac Grove Lane?

"Yes," I said with a false happiness. "You're wonderful. So I know we took three or four streets from Lilac Grove, and then we turned onto a street that had Ivy in the name, though I can't remember, Was it Ivy Field? Ivy Avenue? And then it was either 52nd or 32nd?"

He took the map and held it closer.

Andrew turned to his car and opened the lid thing. "Well, she needs new tires, a fan belt, and a bit of polish. But I think there's something wrong with the starter."

Mira leaned forward, peering into the engine. "I can help with that."

Andrew reached for her hand to stop her. "I couldn't."

She turned and gave him a look. "Why? You don't think girls know anything about cars?"

He flushed again. "No, that's not it."

"Then what?"

He looked at her like he had no idea how to deal with a girl like her. "You're wearing white."

Mira glanced down and then she pulled off her jacket, revealing a light gray vest and a light blue collared shirt that showed off an ample bosom she did not actually have without padding. She grinned her *I DARE YOU* grin. "Now what excuse are you going to use?" She dug into the engine like it was one of her toys.

Andrew glanced over for the mechanic. I ducked behind the map.

"Can you grab that torque wrench," she asked with her hand outstretched. Andrew looked about, then grabbed it for her. He leaned over to see what she was doing with his car.

Their fingers brushed against each other's, and they both seemed so invested in the engine, they didn't know how perfect they looked together. Standing side by side like equals.

"How much did you pay for this car?" Mira asked.

Andrew's eyes lit up. "Seventy-five dollars."

"You overpaid." Mira wiped her nose with a grease-stained hand.

"I know."

I was impressed. A lot of men would have been angry or frustrated by Mira's challenging tactics. Andrew reached for a clean cloth.

"My dad hates this car," Andrew said, his voice quieting as he wiped the grease from Mira's nose. "Calls it a flea-ridden bag of bolts." Mira raised an eyebrow, and Andrew laughed, free and easy. "He's not exactly wrong. But I paid for it with money I earned myself. I fixed it with my own hands."

"That's actually quite impressive," Mira said, her voice quiet from the door. "I love a man who can use his hands."

Andrew grinned and leaned against the car.

"Oh, there it is," I said suddenly. I folded the map and stepped away from the window.

I was supposed to give her more time alone without the mechanic. I knew that.

But she was winning now.

"Do you need help finding the exit?" the mechanic asked gently.

I glanced back and Andrew was smiling as Mira made a joke. "I can find my way out of the shop," I said.

He pointed toward the door anyway. "It's that way."

I blushed as prettily as I'd been trained and then took slow steps toward the door. I reached into my pocketbook. If Mira was fixing the car, then weren't we stealing a job from Juan? I placed a five-dollar bill on a workbench. "For your help."

Juan waved his hands, but I turned and wouldn't let him refuse my money.

I should be happy for her. I was trained to control any feelings of jealousy, but it wasn't just that she was winning Andrew. It was that if this worked, if she won him, then she'd be married and gone and our friendship would be over.

I'd seen it happen, time and time again.

Bea and Mira were my whole heart. My sisters. My home. We'd always done this together, but I never really worried about the moment we'd lose one another to a white veil and a life behind that happy ever after. Bea was always too young, Mira never seemed to fall for anyone because her standards were always so high, and while I'd fallen in love often enough, I always let the love fall apart before it could change me into someone I didn't want to become.

I stepped out the door and into the glaring sunlight of the street. The door closed behind me, and Mira's and Andrew's voices disappeared behind the shut steel.

I wasn't going to get out of this assignment without losing something.

The game had started, and no oath, promise, or history of friendship would make this simple.

My heart twisted as the people on the street walked past me, toward their homes or jobs or lives. They walked with purpose. With greatness. They walked like they knew exactly where they were needed.

And I just stood still as a shadow, watching as they all moved on.

Perhaps feeling small was what brought on that attack of my nerves. Perhaps it was fear of losing my sisters that made my eyes burn. I took deep breaths as my heart raced. My nerves would not stop, and my heart pounded so hard I could feel pain at my chest. *Breathe, Elsie. Breathe.*

My shoulders lifted nearly to my ears as I forced out hard short breaths.

Iris joined me like she saw the inner battle I fought and she'd protect me from it. "Want to play Matchmaker?" she asked as she leaned against the brick wall.

I wiped my sweat-soaked cheeks and nodded. I stood still and fought to slow my breaths.

My eyes burned as a woman in a wide hat walked past.

"Any ring?" Iris asked.

My mouth was full of saliva, and I couldn't think clearly.

She walked past too quickly for me to see. I didn't respond; I just searched the street.

Another woman walked past. Not wearing a ring, and walking with pride and a purpose to her step. I shook my head and let her go.

Iris met my eye with a gentle kindness. She'd seen a few of my nerve attacks, and she always stood so steady at my side.

Another man walked by

"He doesn't seem lonely," I said with only a slight tremor in my voice. We turned and watched the man walk and turn into a grocer.

The street was too quiet to be full of lonely hearts waiting for their chance to find love.

After a few minutes, as I focused on taking even breaths, and the panicked, painful chill of an unearned adrenaline rush finally subsided, I saw across the street a dapper old man in wool pants, a carefully tied bow tie, and a worn knit vest enter a small restaurant with large windows. He waved at the waitstaff and sat at a table by a window like it was a regular thing. A waitress brought him a coffee and a plate without him looking at a menu.

I lowered my shoulders. "I caught one."

Iris rubbed her hands together. "Where?"

"The window at the restaurant. That's a widow who doesn't know how to cook for himself if I've ever seen one."

Iris grinned. "So who do we set him up with?"

"I don't know yet. But I will." I glanced back. "Can you cover?"

"Yeah, no problem. Look for the signal."

I pressed my hand to my chest. "Thank you."

I meant for more than just taking over my assignment. Iris tugged on one of my curls and grinned.

I crossed the street quickly, my bag banging against my knee, as I followed after this man with the confidence I'd gained from a new Matchmaking game. When I looked at other people, I looked for their heartache. That might be selfish, but when I saw other people struggling, it made me forget about my own difficulties, and it also helped me put my own struggles into perspective. And then, when I fixed problems for others, it relieved some of the pressure. It's like . . . if I could help other people, then somehow it tricked my brain into thinking I'd helped myself.

So when I saw a lonely man eating a sandwich with a slice of lemon in his water, a pickle, and a clump of grapes to the side, I knew his loneliness was a problem that could be solved.

And if I had the power to do that, then maybe I wasn't completely powerless after all.

I entered the restaurant with the subtle jingle of a bell, but I didn't move past the hostess station. Instead I searched the booths and tables for someone who could keep that old man company, some new second act for this man whose name I did not know. There were a few promising candidates sitting at the tables, but one woman—a woman alone, reading a book at a table, eating a slice of apple pie—fit the mark the best. Shining gray strands peppered her brown hair, wrinkles lovingly set into smile lines, and her fingers showed sagging skin that were never once indented with a band of metal.

The only problem was that she sat with her back to the gentleman.

I grinned. There was the puzzle I'd been looking for. But how to solve it? Drafts worked sometimes, or perhaps I could have the waiter bring her something and say it was from him? I searched the restaurant for a solution, then I saw it. I moved to the window and pulled a string to lift the blinds sideways. The sun's glare shone in the woman's eyes. It took a second to draw the woman from her story, but finally she squinted toward the window, sighed, and then moved to the other side of the table.

Success.

A waiter approached. "Hello, miss, table for one?"

I smiled. "Sorry, I'm still waiting for someone."

"Take your time," he said.

I glanced through the window. Iris held up three fingers. Oh fiddlesticks. I didn't have any time to take.

When the waiter's back was turned, I walked to a table and stole wilting yellow daisies from a chipped vase. I slipped into the gentleman's booth and held out the flowers.

"You could give her these," I said quietly.

He startled and pressed his hand to his jacket pocket, where I believe he hid his wallet. "What? Who are you?" he asked gruffly. "Do I know you?"

Perhaps the direct approach was a mistake. "I'm Elsie, and no, you don't know me. But do you see that woman right over there with the book? She's lovely, isn't she?"

He followed my subtle pointing, his bushy eyebrows still pressed together. "She's reading *The Secret Garden*."

I turned back. "Oh, is she?"

"I would never make a pass at a grown woman reading a children's book." He took a messy bite of his sandwich.

I gasped. "That is an insult. There are a great many children's books that are excellent literature. Though I'm not certain that book qualifies. I found several lines appallingly racist, and the treatment of India was very othering. Can you imagine how exoticism can affect the view of an entire populace? Especially a populace currently struggling under the effects of colonialism."

His eyebrows would not stop pointing. "You are a strange girl."

I leaned against the table. "But wouldn't that make a fascinating conversation? I think you should go over and talk to her."

"Are you related to her?"

"No."

"But you must know each other from somewhere. Or is there a wager you're playing?"

"No. I just saw that you were lonely, and she was lonely. And I only thought you both could use a slight push in order to find love. With each other."

He sat back and then took a bite of his sandwich. He took a long thoughtful chew. "I'll have you know that I have found love."

"Oh."

He raised his index finger. "But one does not need love to be content."

"Of course." I pressed down my dress. "Sorry. I just thought . . ." About myself. I let go of the flowers. "I didn't think. I'm sorry. She's reading. Why would she want to be interrupted? I'm sorry to bother you." I slid to the edge of the bench.

"You're not a bother." He smiled behind his bushy mustache. "You remind me of her actually."

I stilled. "Who are we talking about?"

"My great love. My wife, Anne. She was our neighborhood matchmaker. Responsible for eight weddings, and thirty-two children. Before she passed."

That compliment felt like a warm hug. "She sounds lovely."

"She was."

"Well . . ." I lifted one shoulder and scooted back to the center of the bench. "Perhaps it's time for you to have your second act?"

He glanced at the woman and then brushed a crumb off his lip. "There are some acts you never get over, I'm afraid."

I glanced out the window toward the mechanic's shop and the task I was supposed to be working on.

The man slid a card across the table. "I'd like to hear more of your thoughts on *The Secret Garden*," he said. "We're always looking for a few good reviewers."

I flipped the card. "We?"

Frank Groeing, Editor in Chief, *Park Village Gazette*

"Are you offering me a job?" I asked incredulously.

He shrugged and took a sip of his coffee. "I like strange." His eyes twinkled as he smiled. "But no, I'm not offering you a job. I'm offering to look at your pages. It's not the same thing."

I took the card and held it to my chest. "Thank you," I said quietly. "And thank you for telling me about your wife, but I don't think I sh . . ." My voice trailed off. Something in me wouldn't let me say no to this job.

I glanced back at the woman, who turned the page with a soft, content smile.

My heartbeat settled. I didn't know if it was my romantic nature or that I'd just always been taught that a person was a half of a whole. But that woman seemed full enough to me.

There was not a problem here that needed me to solve it. Not really.

"Thank you," I said again, and then I stood, holding tightly to the card.

I slipped out of the booth and left the restaurant.

Just in time to see Andrew and Mira drive off together in a spluttering car.

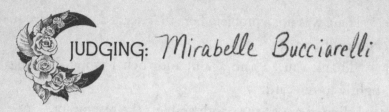

JUDGING: Mirabelle Bucciarelli

CATEGORY: First blush

Amount of Bloom:

Three florets, two soft, one lingering

Quality:

Bold and challenging

Physical appearance at time of judging:

Appealing well-groomed, slightly masculine, but used to good effect.

Creative arrangement:

Well matched, playful after a challenging beginning Perhaps too focused on skills shown.

Faults:

Failed to pick up on three clues. Missed cues lead to missed opportunities.

TOTAL SCORE: 17 out of 20

Judge initials: MB

CHAPTER SEVEN

When it was her turn, Greta insisted on wearing her Schiaparelli sweater, no matter that seven out of ten Beauty Makers insisted she looked better in the blue silk, no matter that the dark knit colors seemed more suited for someone with paler skin. But *Vogue* had bought forty copies of this sweater, so *that* was what she was going to try to sell him. That plus the beadwork collar she paired with it, which cost more than any of us could ever afford.

Money was the one thing with which we couldn't compete.

That and being completely impossible. No one could hold a candle to Greta on that.

Then, of course, there was the selection of venue, the time of day to create the best lighting, and was it possible for her to make an entrance from the back of the restaurant, since her best angle was from the right, and wasn't it completely necessary to make the most perfect impression since this will be Andrew's future wife, and didn't we owe it to him?

She was ridiculous, and of course with her family connections she also got everything she wanted.

Which meant I was the one tasked to run interference if his friends tried to take up too much of his focus. It would be my job to flirt with his friends, but also to look less attractive than Greta, so as to not steal her spotlight. Which meant there was a very good chance that Andrew's first impression of me would be with my hair flat and my dress loose around my waist, flirting with boys for whom I had no interest.

And I was so mad that I was so mad about such shallow things.

I touched the card from the editor I'd hidden in the pocket of my coat, and I entered the restaurant with my chin low and my eyes sharp. The place was ritzy as any place back home. Art deco pendant chandeliers hung around the tin ceiling with painted trim, and white-tablecloth-covered tables dotting the shining floor, all filled with men and women dressed as fine as the china. Silverware chimed, and electric lights fizzled from new sconces.

Andrew and a couple of friends were taking dinner here to celebrate his friend's graduation, and with the city dry due to Prohibition—and thank heavens for it—any bar or club was out. At least for respectable candidates. I'd known a few men to inhabit a speakeasy, but no man I'd want to marry. I'd charmed enough drunken men. I'd prefer to live with someone sober.

A live band was setting up their instruments. If all went well, Greta would get Andrew to ask her to dance.

If he wasn't too distracted by his friends to notice her.

Part of me wished I wasn't so good at my job.

But I was. And if I couldn't outcharm Greta with my hair straight, then what were all those years in training for? So I made a plan. I knew each of Andrew's friend's names and had read a few paragraphs about them in Andrew's dossier. I liked the idea that Harper and Johnson were possibilities for future matches for the other girls. Perhaps even future senators. Men often succeeded in groups.

Not Richards, though. The man couldn't pass an exam without cheating, just a dimwitted bully with all the right connections. People like him were one of the reasons the society existed. Without it, any fool could be president, and then where would we be?

Perhaps there was a way I could keep my friends close after I won. Maybe Bea would marry Harper, and Mira could marry Johnson. Then we could summer together, raise our babes close.

That'd be positively spiffy.

Bea sat near the kitchen, wearing a scarf around her hair and shades. She was assigned to be a lookout for any other girls looking to flirt. Andrew could choose any of us four, but if a woman outside the society got to him first, then all those years of training and preparation would be wasted.

Mira stood by the band setting up in the back, her hair tucked beneath a man's hat, wearing an ill-fitting man's suit and a glued-on mustache. She'd request the band play Andrew's favorite song when the time came for Greta to dance. And Iris was taking cover inside the kitchen dressed as a waitress to help us all escape if anything went catastrophic.

It was a good plan. A good trap. Andrew would still have a choice, never knowing he'd chosen a card from a stacked deck.

But the men weren't here yet. I moved toward the soda fountain and sat down on one of the bar stools. The soda jerk, a young man with a paper hat and a bow tie, smiled at me. "What'll you have?"

"Egg cream, please."

A bell jingled and I turned.

And there they were. Four young men entered, all of them with the clothes, status, and the tilt of the chin that proved they knew they'd be pronounced quality. Johnson was the one who'd just graduated, and he walked at the center with a pink paper crown around his brow, his friend's arm slung around his shoulders. Andrew walked one step behind them, his smile hesitant, his eyes darting around the room like he needed other people to confirm that he was actually with them.

Greta hadn't made her entrance yet. She was taking her sweet time.

The soda jerk slid me my drink. I took it with a nervous smile he didn't seem to notice. His eyes were on the same men mine had been, and he studied them entering the restaurant and sitting at their table the same way I had earlier, like he was casing the room.

There were dozens of people in this restaurant. Yes, they were the loudest, but why was he watching those teenagers?

He penciled in something on a small pad of paper. I spied Andrew's name.

My bobbing knee stilled. What was he looking for?

I took a second look at him. Where Andrew was handsome, this boy was beautiful. Roman nose, light blue eyes, and cheekbones that seemed crooked, one higher than the other, like a break had not healed correctly. His dark brown hair was long for a soda jerk, sharply parted yet hanging almost to his nose, the thick pomade fighting and losing to his hair's desire to curl. And his shirt wasn't right. The other waiters' shirts were starched and bleached, with two buttons on the collar, while his seemed almost soft yellow in comparison, like he'd brought it from home, with a single button obscuring his long neck.

How odd. I nursed my drink and turned away, but I watched him from the corner of my eye. He was younger than Andrew, maybe sixteen or possibly just turned seventeen like me, with night dark hair and fingers so long and pale and thin I could almost see the bones.

I touched the counter with my index finger and traced a circle, and the movement drew his eye. I cocked my head to the side, and I gave him my very best smile with the straw clenched between my teeth. The smile I'd practiced. The smile that had been graded.

The soda jerk's neck bobbed, and the poor boy dropped the glass in his hand. He cursed under his breath, his cheeks flushing red as he hurried to mop it up.

I sat taller.

I wasn't powerless.

The boys at the table began to sing, and Johnson lowered the paper crown over his eyes to hide. Andrew glanced my way, as that bully Richards held up five fingers.

I sucked in my stomach. But the signal wasn't for me.

"Right," the soda jerk said behind me. He served a bubbly pink drink to someone else at the bar, and then, answering the signal, put out clear glasses and mixed five identical drinks. Lemon juice, simple syrup, quite a lot of simple syrup, and what was that? He moved too quickly for me to see. He slid the glasses to the edge of the bar. "Prohibition sour?" he called out, his voice lower than I expected for one so young. Andrew stood from his table, and I reached for one of the glasses.

The soda jerk gripped my wrist quick. "That's a man's drink, miss. Much too sour for someone so sweet."

I caught the smell of alcohol, bright, buzzy, and strictly forbidden. I raised an eyebrow, and he saw me then, not as a pretty girl but as a threat.

Was it wrong to say I liked that better?

He still held my wrist in a hard grip. His hand was warm and calloused. I glanced down and he let me go.

Andrew approached the drinks, and I had two choices, I could turn away, and save my first impression for my turn, or I could break my oaths.

And fight for my future.

While Andrew approached the bar, I slid off my coat. It was simply too good an opportunity to make an impression. Greta was taking her time making an entrance, and I know it wasn't my turn, and that my hair was too flat for this, but I stood directly in front of the drinks and turned to face Andrew.

I lifted my chin and held my body in its most appealing pose. The pose that had made strangers stop and stare since I was twelve years old.

Andrew blinked long brown eyelashes, a crease cutting a line above his eyebrows. He picked up the drinks, perching them between his fingers, a frown at the corner of his lips.

Say something, Elsie. "I . . ."

"Excuse me," he said, his voice full and rumbling and low, causing others at the bar to turn to hear him, as though even his voice had a gravitational pull. He ducked past me.

I couldn't answer. I couldn't even smile. He smelled like a library. Like dust and oak and stories. How did he smell like stories?

Come on, you've trained for this, I thought. I flicked my hair. "It . . ." My mouth opened but no further words came out. He kept walking away. *Think of something to make him stop. Say something. Anything. Ants. No, not ants. SOMETHING.*

The moment was as open as a vacancy sign, and I, the girl who loved words more than any other thing, could not find a single one. I've discussed window casings, and the Romanovs, and though my friends didn't know it, I once had a remarkable discussion about the life cycle of a beetle for an entire evening, but at this specific moment I could not remember my training. I couldn't remember my name.

Andrew made his way back to his table.

He hadn't even noticed me.

What if I failed at this? What if he never saw me? What if I had to go home empty handed and hear my mother sing the praises of my brother, knowing that I could have had a better life and I was the one who failed to claim it? What was the point of breaking my oaths if it didn't even work?

I slumped down in my bar stool and reached for my egg cream. And in that second, I realized that I had drawn the eyes of one person.

The soda jerk.

He couldn't seem to look away.

Not while Greta made her entrance. Not while she fell into Andrew's lap. Not as her laughter and flirtations made everyone else turn toward her. Not when every penny and every measure of her family's good name made every person in the restaurant watch her like she was a starlet right out of a moving picture.

His gaze traced my shoulders like Greta wasn't even here.

I arched my neck and felt him casing me, like I'd studied him earlier. I closed my eyes for three seconds, which turned into five and then ten.

I still had time to fix this. My turn was coming.

And there was more than one way to distract Andrew's friends.

I leaned back on my elbow and gave the boy a look. The soda jerk turned away quickly. No blush, though I know he knew I'd caught him staring.

I took a deep breath and then gave him my very best smile again, the one that had got me top marks back in training, the one that has softened angry men and charmed my way out of many a predicament. This smile was my favorite weapon, and it was well aimed.

"May I refresh your drink?" he asked, his neck bobbing like a lure.

My glass was half-full. I leaned my shoulders closer. "Not unless you've got something stronger?" My expression was friendly, but I know he heard the threat anyway.

He stood taller and cleaned a glass. "Hank's is a law-abiding cafeteria, not a speakeasy. You'll find no devil's drink here."

"But would a man? Say, those men?" I started to point, and he grabbed my hand again. He'd touched me twice now, and I didn't know his name. I didn't know a single thing about him.

His grip was rough. "Please," he said, his voice low. "I got a family."

My smile faded slowly. If the restaurant was reported, I knew Andrew and his friends would never be indicted, and the owner wouldn't either. Money made charges like this slide right off. The only person I could hurt here was him.

"You're safe with me," I said, softening my tone as he let me go. My wrist tingled at the touch. "But jeepers you're awful young to have a wife and children to support."

He smiled. "It's the grandchildren who've been stiffing me." I laughed a little, and he leaned forward on his elbows. "I'm Patch," he said. I must have made a face because he amended quickly. "Patrick Elliot Villipin, but you can call me Patch, if you'd like."

"Elsie," I said without thinking. "But you can call me Clara Bow if you like."

He grinned back, and I realized with a start that I liked his crooked face. He had an open smile, like he hadn't practiced it often in a mirror. Unabashedly real, like a meadow in sunshine or something.

Oh no. I was thinking in metaphors again. Poetry was right and good, but people weren't meadows, or sunlight, and I definitely didn't have a storm inside me. I was a girl, and he was a boy, and he was not my target. The band began to play a slow waltz, nice and respectable. Waitresses cleared empty tables near the stand, and couples were gathering on the floor to dance.

I turned my back on the patchwork boy and studied the room to make a battle plan. Greta held all of Andrew's friends' attention as she held court. Andrew's glass sat untouched, where his friends' cups were drained, and he looked around as if looking for someone to talk to. From all indications, he was waiting for Greta to notice him again.

Nothing made a man readier for love than if he thought all his friends had found it first.

He was trying to keep up with them, I realized. He thought himself the underdog. This meant he'd need her to be his trophy. And she was playing it perfectly.

But it was my turn to get into the game.

I turned toward Patch. He'd taken off his little paper hat and looked much better for it, though his overpomaded hair stuck together in clumps. But there was a warmth in his eyes, almost a hunger.

This might even be fun.

"Elsie, huh," he said. "You got a last name?"

"Bow. Have you forgotten?"

He grinned. "That's not it."

"Why do you care about my last name?"

He licked his lips and lowered his voice. "A good last name is like a bottle of wine; a fine label will cost you more, but the taste is worth it."

Bold. He held my gaze for a long second. Villipin. Villipin. His last name didn't come up in the dossier, but Andrew's friends clearly knew him well enough to trust him with a drink order. Hmm. "You new in town?"

"How'd you know?"

"I'm smarter than I look."

"Oh, you look quite smart to me."

No, I would not smile at that. My lips betrayed me. "Where are you from?"

"What's your last name, Elsie?"

I swallowed. Once he knew, this conversation would be different. "You didn't answer my question," I said instead.

"Neither did you."

"Then ask me a new one."

"Dance with me," he commanded.

I tilted my head to one side. "That's more of a statement than a question."

He offered his hand. "You got an answer for me anyhow?"

"Maybe." I lowered my voice. "You got to do something for me first."

"Anything."

"You see that boy in the glasses."

"Andrew Shaw?"

I fought back any show of concern that he knew his name. "Is that his name? That poor child looks so miserable with that drink in front of him. Can you send him a milkshake or something?"

"Why'd you care?"

"I don't," I lied. "He just looks kind of sad, and I've never been one to be happy when sad people are around. Besides, I'd hate to leave your *very* important job undone."

His eyebrows lowered like I'd insulted his pride. He pressed his tongue against his cheek. "And then you'll dance with me?"

"Sure. Why not."

Patch mixed an egg cream, then he hopped over the bar and raced across the room. "On the house, Mr. Shaw."

The glass shook on the table, and Andrew reached forward to steady it. As he did, his gaze followed as Patch ran across the room, grabbed my hand, and yanked me onto the dance floor.

I laughed loud enough to be heard as Patch spun me a little when we got to the dance floor and then tucked me into his arms. Andrew's eyes met mine.

He looked at me like he cared about me, even though we were strangers. His expression wasn't one of instant attraction, or like he wanted to claim me as his possession. He looked at me like he wondered if I needed his help, like I'd called his name and he was there to bring me whatever I needed.

And for a breath, I couldn't look away. Because there was a white house in Andrew's eyes. Not the presidential home. Not yet. I couldn't see roman columns or specks of light hiding inside the limestone. I saw a white clapboard house with flowers on the sill, and a path that led to a picket fence. Exactly the same as any other house on a street, yet hidden in his eyes was also the home I'd been taught my whole life I was supposed to want.

Patch pressed me tighter, and I looked at him as he pushed me about in a quickstep. Up close he was taller than I expected, all legs, and dark hair, and hands on my waist. The band's music was a cacophony of the wrong notes in just the right places, sweet and smooth and surprising. The other dancers around us were laughing raucously, their elbows too pointed, and their kicking feet pressed me closer to my partner for safety.

The song had ended before my thoughts had lined up in a row and the next song shifted to a slow waltz. Patch didn't let me go between songs, and now he pressed me tight against him.

Maybe too close. My heart had begun to race.

"Where are you hoping to go to school?" I asked, my voice tight from the heat of his arms.

A strand of his hair had fallen over his eyes, but Patch didn't let go of me to fix it. "I'm not. Working in the family business."

I gathered he didn't mean Hank's. I smiled anyhow. "All those grandbabies to support."

"Little brother actually."

"Oh." He was being honest.

"And it isn't really a family business, so much as it's the only family I got, and the only way I know to keep my brother fed and warm."

I went quiet. I wasn't expecting honesty. "He have a name?"

"He does."

I waited, but he didn't fill in the answer to my question.

"Do you have a last one?" he asked again.

I didn't answer. I rested my cheek on his shoulder. Why'd he care anyhow? It wasn't that I was ashamed of my family. But I couldn't bear it if he knew my brother's name. I wanted him to know me for me, not because I was the little sister of someone impressive. Besides, once he knew it he could track me down easy as pointing to a map. This had to stay here on the dance floor, in this cafeteria. There was no way that this conversation could continue for more than a few songs.

Because I liked the way his hands felt on my body. I liked the way he spoke so quickly. Not every man could keep up with me. And I liked the way I knew nothing about him.

I knew too much about Andrew. The balance of power was heaviest on the side of the scale I was not on.

Patch sighed, his breath stirring my hair. "So I figure if you can't trust me, then I probably can't trust you."

Fair enough. But I didn't need him to trust me for this to work. "What's your favorite book, then?" I asked with a bright smile.

He narrowed his eyes. "Who says I read?"

"A good name is like a wine label . . . ," I said loftily. "What penny novel did you rip that one off of?"

He tossed his hair backward. "I thought that one up myself."

"Really?" I lowered my voice. "Well, if you can think of metaphors that quickly, then you must read plenty. What's your favorite?"

He sighed, and his breath, smelling sweet and lemony, hit the sweat at the nape of my neck. Every bit about this boy made me feel warm.

"I'm sorry, miss, that's too personal," he said with a teasing grin. "I believe a person's favorite book is like a glimpse of their soul. It's best we stay strangers, ain't that right?"

It was. My, but he was good at reading a situation. Still, the not knowing felt like a challenge. And it was an innocent-enough question. "*Moby Dick*?"

He snorted. "Call me Ishmael-no."

I laughed with delight, and he spun me away. When I was back in his arms I tried again. "Charles Dickens?"

He leaned forward. "Please, sir, may I have a no."

Oh, he was trouble. I loved when a boy liked books as much as I did. What could it be? Andrew's favorite author was William Shakespeare, though I didn't know if that was something he decided in order to show the world how smart he was, or if it was his honest answer. Not yet anyhow. Sherlock Holmes? Patch was curious enough to like him, but he didn't strike me as a man who liked something just because it was popular. Not that I really knew anything about him. Why did it feel like I knew him? Instead, I looked him up and down and decided on picking the author I'd suggest he read.

"Jules Verne. *Around the World in Eighty Days*."

His grip tightened, and a genuine bloom of joy in my chest made my feet feel light.

"Found it," I said triumphantly, my T-strap shoes dancing beneath me.

"Fine. I will admit to that one thing. My favorite author

is Jules Verne. You've seen my very soul, so tell me, Elsie, what else would you like to know?"

Honestly, everything. I met his eye, and I didn't see a white house hiding there. I saw nothing but a stranger, and a mystery, and a boy involved somehow in the distribution of something of which the society would never approve. Something of which I couldn't approve.

Something that could threaten this mission.

"How do you know the Shaws?"

"Don't really," he answered. "Just by reputation."

Their stellar reputation seemed shaded from a rumrunner's point of view. I met him at his expectations; let him think I thought the same as him. "The lot of teatotalers. What a bunch of wet blankets."

He looked at me in surprise.

"What?" I asked. Now he'd trust me enough to let any true thoughts free.

"Nothing. I just pegged you for a book-reading do-gooder."

He wasn't wrong. "You don't know me," I lied.

"I'd sure like to."

I couldn't help the smile that earned, and he looked at me like I was a trophy he'd won.

"How 'bout you," he asked. "You know the Shaws?"

Only every single thing. "Never met them. I just noticed you wrote that name down, and I was curious, is all. You writing a poem?"

"No . . . ," he said quickly, like his ego was bruised. "My employer's gathering information on them. That's all."

"On the Shaws?"

His warm breath heated my neck. "You never know when a little blackmail might come in handy."

Jeepers, had I flirted with the wrong boy.

Or the right one.

The Matrons needed to know about this right away.

A splash and an angry yell divided my attention. That egg cream Patch had given Andrew hit the ground and glass shattered.

"I'm so sorry," Andrew said with both his hands out. His friends all laughed.

And chocolate egg cream dripped down the beading of Greta's Schiaparelli sweater.

Oh.

She looked as if she was about to cry, and then her face turned into the ugliest scowl. In one show of anger, I knew Greta had just blown her chances.

Girls like us didn't get to show anger.

We didn't get to let people see the storm inside.

So we hid it, buried it deeply, and only let it out on innocent people who couldn't strike back.

I turned to Patch, to the worrying distraction of his arms, and I chose my sisters. My back stiffened. "This was awful fun, but I need to go."

He didn't release me. "The song's not over."

I lost my warmth. "I said I was done."

He should have heard the finality in my tone. He should have respected that.

His hot hand stayed at my waist. He leaned back, studying me, before he bit his lip and looked away, his eyes hurt. "This because of Shaw?"

"No," I lied quickly. I changed tactics to gain his sympathy. "This has nothing to do with those stick-in-the-muds. I just need to go help my friend."

He removed the hand from my back, but his other hand still held mine up like we were still dancing. "So you'll be back?"

I didn't speak or look at him until he released my hand. Once he did, I gave him a soft smile to soften the moment. "I'm sorry." I stepped away.

I followed Greta to the ladies' restroom. Bea followed after, but Mira just watched.

I touched Bea's hand. "Can you send for the Beauty Makers?"

"I will, but be kind to her in there," she told me. "I don't think we know everything about her family's expectations." I saw my own reflection in her glasses before she turned away.

I would have been kind without the warning. I was certain of it.

I took a breath, and then I pressed the door open.

Greta stood over the sink, splashing the sweater to try to wipe off the chocolate. Her tears revealed sharp lines of her real skin under the powder cake.

"What?" she shouted, turning on me. She scrubbed her beaded collar until those crystals broke and fell like a sparkling rain against the floor.

And for a second, I saw beyond the painted porcelain of her perfection. I saw only a raw nerve.

I stepped closer and wrapped her into a hug. She stood stiff in my arms. "It's not over," I said. "It's not over yet."

Her stiffness melted into me. "It is," she whispered. Her shoulders shook. I held my hand to the back of her head and let her lean into me.

Let her feel how soft this body she often mocked could be.

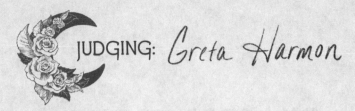 JUDGING: *Greta Harmon*

CATEGORY: First blush

Amount of Bloom:
Five florets, one soft, one aggressive

Quality:
Firm and long stemmed

Physical appearance at time of judging:
Appealing, well groomed. Spectacular.

Creative arrangement:
Twenty-minute conversation, bright and balanced, impressive, yet overshining.

Faults:
Subject to slight bruising, sloppy-followed-by-grimace not a softening smile.

TOTAL SCORE: ~~15 out of 20~~ 17 out of 20, per adjustment by FH

Judge initials: MB

CHAPTER EIGHT

After Greta's meetup ended, my friends and I marched up the stairs toward our respective bedrooms, each of us bone weary from the work, and from shouldering Greta's anguish. Her *very* noisy anguish.

Mr. Brown, a well-dressed man with a large sculpted nose and thick gray hair that swooped over his eyes as he looked up from his chair near the fireplace, seemed puzzled, but not particularly intrigued by the heartbreak of single women.

I wasn't sure he understood why Mrs. Brown was hosting us at all. Bea was some "lost relation," and we were her friends from boarding school, hoping to help Mrs. Brown with some woman's fair or something. He never cared enough to ask for specifics. We were supposed to call him uncle, and not enter his study, and that was that. If Bea won, it would become far more complicated, but that was a path I couldn't look too far down.

"I know what you're doing," Mira said from the hallway after Bea took a still dramatic Greta to her room.

I turned to face her. Mira's eyes were unusually serious.

"What are you talking about?"

"You left your post early at the mechanic's shop during my turn. I was supposed to have a good fifteen to twenty minutes. I could excuse that, because no plan goes off without a hitch, but then you tried to poach Greta's meeting, and then soured her whole chances by making some large show with that soda jerk."

"Patch."

"I don't care what his name is!" Mira always said exactly what she was thinking without much fear. Her voice lowered to a sharp whisper. "Just because we made a deal doesn't mean you should try to sabotage me or Greta to meet it. That's not fair either."

"I didn't."

She poked my chest. "Well, don't you do it to Bea." Mira's face was serious like she never was.

"I won't." I ran my hand up my arm. The hall sconces fizzled with a wavering light that made my eyes ache. "I had an issue with my nerves, is all. That's why I left my post on your day. And I know I messed up with Greta, but he walked up to me; was I not supposed to smile? She would have done the same thing, and you know it. Not that it worked. My nerves shut down any chance of poaching him."

Mira pulled at her vest. "You can't use your nerves as an excuse for bad behavior."

Mira shot me a look, hard and harsh, and I saw the end of our friendship coming. I didn't know if we would survive if Andrew chose me.

And I'd deserve it. "I'm not."

"You have to take responsibility for your actions. At some point, not today, mind you, but soon we're going to be grown-ups, and if you're the one who wins this priority, then you need to stay stalwart and true to our oaths and to the people we'll serve. I need you to not turn selfish."

I'd thought that . . . She was right. I'd done every bad thing of which she'd accused me.

"I'm sorry."

Mira ran her hands through her hair. Something was still bothering her, but she didn't trust me with it, like she normally would have. And I couldn't think of a single thing that could charm her back to being my friend.

She turned and left me alone at my open door.

My heartbeat surged, and my throat felt like fire that scorched up to my eyelashes.

I closed the door to my room and locked it tight.

"Get yourself under control, Elsie," I muttered as I bent and gripped my knees. I didn't usually have nerve attacks twice in one week. It was just the pressure of this whole thing. That's all, but I could handle it. I . . .

All the thoughts in my head felt like a rumble of thunder. My thoughts were cycling, spinning around and around, one phrase repeating itself.

I was a bad person.

I let out quick breaths and tried to plant myself in my surroundings. This room was small, but at least it was my own. Mira and Bea shared. Because they were the closest. Maybe they were best friends and I was just their lost cause, their third favorite. The one they'd be happy to leave.

Focus. My room was small and quaint, with richly polished wooden floors, a single window covered in lace curtains, a quilted bed with a white metal frame, a writing table, and a small bookshelf.

My brain was lying to me. It did that sometimes. But it was just my nerves acting up. That was all. A bad person wouldn't have noticed our driver Helper and left a note to leave Elizabeth and her mother under the watch care. A bad person wouldn't have aced the moral exam, or any of the other quantifiable times I've chosen to be a good girl and do what I was supposed to do. I made a mistake, but that was okay, because that means I could fix it.

Through my fogged vision I spied a letter waiting for me on the bookshelf with my name elegantly curled on the top in my mother's handwriting. If I was her son, she would have information for me, her tips and her ambitions written out in her instructions.

I placed the card from the editor on the bookcase next to it. What would my mother say if I got a job at an actual newspaper, if I could write out all those speeches in my head and have people read them?

She'd probably want me to write about Nathaniel.

I opened the letter, and my eyes brushed through the words.

But I couldn't read more about my brother. I couldn't bear to hold my mother's hopes for him on my shoulders yet. My mother's letter didn't correct the thoughts in my head, or even acknowledge the struggle inside me. I was lucky that she asked about me at all, and even so it was just an inquiry after my health.

I paced that room, my steps heavy strikes and my fists tiny tempests.

My mother would hate Patch. When she found out I'd danced with someone else, she would never understand why I did. She wanted me to marry someone with a good last name. She wanted me to become just like her, but she was the only one who was pretending that her marriage was a happy one.

Why did she want me to copy her life when she had to pretend in order to be happy in her own?

And why did Patch need to know about my last name? Was my family in danger, like the Shaws were?

I pressed the side of my head. What were his employers going to do to Andrew's family? We were going to elevate Andrew because we knew there was nothing bad hidden that someone could blackmail.

Nothing except for the society. Nothing except for what we were going to give him.

I sat at my writing desk, hoping to pull together my thoughts, to start making plans. But words pulled at me, falling like rain. My heel bounced. I put my pen to paper and let them pour.

If I was a storm,
my mother was a glass bottle.
Amber. Lovely.
With a fine label and an elegant slope to
    her neck.
No one looked close enough to see how she
clouded in the light.
No one looked close enough to see she was empty
on the inside.

Drunk dry.

When men see me, they see my mother in me.
They tabulate the slope of my neck,
the label and fine vintage stuck to me by my good
    last name.
When they see me, they look close.
Deep through the glass.
They see clouds swirling.

And they are thirsty.

I didn't reread the poem after it ripped from my pen. Instead I stared at my bare face in the mirror. My eyes were bright, my cheeks soft and round. I was beautiful. Quantifiably so.

Why wasn't this enough?

I let out the breath I'd been holding and felt the release of my nerves. Writing my poems stilled my thoughts like nothing else could, but now the storm was gone and my hollow glass bones were exhausted.

I slipped into a fresh nightgown and pulled back the covers of my well-earned bed.

A note rested on my pillow. I unfolded it.

The Marisol Hotel was written in careful handwriting. I turned the paper over to see it was written on the back of an advertisement.

Andrew wasn't staying at the Marisol Hotel. He had a grand home to match his grand family. This note was about Patch. The Gossips must have trailed Patch.

I knew it, just like it was clear that the Gossips had noticed our flirtation, and the Matrons needed me to end it.

I lay down deep into my covers and held the blanket over my eyes. The Gossips couldn't have been close enough to listen to our conversation. I could stay away from him and end our flirtation just as successfully. He didn't know anything about me, nothing real anyway. All I had to do was avoid that part of town, and make sure Andrew wouldn't head over there. It'd be easy enough. I could warn the Spinsters, and they'd keep a watch over him, keep him away from us.

But Patch had answers. Patch had more questions.

I pulled the blanket off me and placed my bare feet on the carpet.

I should stay away. I knew it.

But I didn't listen.

I was thirsty too.

The Marisol Hotel was in the less respectable part of town, so the knife tucked into my garter was a comfort as I replayed the fighting training the Spinsters had given us every time a man looked my way.

But the streets were clean, the glowing lamps warming the sides of the faces of the people milling about. It was late, far too late for a party, but the streets were full of strangers, most of the men with scars of the Great War still showing in their eyes, or in their lack of limbs. A lone trumpet played something mournful, but the crowd moved to the sound like it was lively.

I've never sneaked out this late at night alone before. I didn't know the night could be a living thing without my friends here to enchant it.

The air was muggy and sweet with fog. With each step I took, I felt more drawn toward the answers I needed. Toward Patch. It felt almost like a dream my mother would not want me to have. I saw Patch before he saw me, leaning near a railing, his pants buttoned high, his thin shirt missing, wearing only a sleeveless white undershirt, his bare arms lithe and strong as he juggled knives like a showman. He tossed those knives so fast and so sure that his hands seemed like blurs to me. He wore a black brimmed hat on the back of his head, and he'd assembled a small audience. His eyes were wild as he caught that crowd in his performance, as he tossed those blades higher, faster, and flickering in the streetlights. He seemed alive in every inch, and all at once I wasn't tired. If walking toward him felt like a dream, seeing him woke me up.

When his wandering eyes found mine, I glared.

And the knives fell.

Thud.

Thud.

Thud.

Point down. Into the street.

His small audience laughed, and he grinned back, both

hands spread wide as he bowed, then pulled his hat from his head and offered it like a sacrament cup. Bills and coins slid inside his pockets as soon as they touched the brim.

I pulled my coat closed as he walked toward me.

End it quickly.

"You like the show, Elsie?" he asked, his long neck bobbing as he swallowed. And then his pale blue eyes met mine and I knew at once that he was scared. Scared of my beauty. Scared I'd walk away. Scared I'd see right through him, like he was the fog that tasted so sweet on my tongue.

His fear made me bold.

"I've got questions for you." I grabbed his wrist and pulled him through the crowd past an open doorway and into a darkened alley at the side of the hotel, where we were all alone, where the Gossips might miss me. All alone and I didn't have to live up to someone else's standards of quality.

"What do you want to know?" he said, a shadow running across his face.

I folded my arms. "Everything," I said, and all at once it felt like I'd cut myself open and laid bare the most honest thing about me. The Matrons always tried to tame my curiosity. My mother told me that asking too many questions was unladylike. My father told me to be quiet more times than he told me he loved me. But I didn't care that Patch knew. "I want to know everything." I tightened my fists. Don't be foolish. "Who is your employer, and what dirt have you found out about the Shaws? And why do you care about them? They're just a bunch of do-gooders; they haven't hurt you a bit."

He tapped a finger to the edge of my eyebrow. "You know when you're angry you get a crease right here. It's gonna turn into a wrinkle when you're older."

Rude.

"There it is again."

"I asked you a question."

"You've asked me several questions, and earlier I asked you questions, and I believe that's what they call a conversation." He stepped closer, brushed my curls off my face. My breath hitched, and for the briefest of seconds none of my questions seemed to matter except the one my thudding heart kept shouting.

Why won't you take me away from all this?

Ridiculous. I shoved his chest. You foolish girl. You don't even know him. "I need to know everything, Patch."

Repeating it made the words more important. He saw my anger, he saw my future wrinkles, he saw my bare face. I was ignoring every inch of my training. And he still looked back. Honest to goodness, it felt like I was offering one of those bits about me I was supposed to hide, like unbottling myself and letting him take a sip.

He inched closer, smelling sweet.

"I need . . ." Focus. To know more, to . . . Jeepers.

He touched my neck. We were all alone. His hot hands pulled me against him, and I liked it. I liked him.

I needed to get as much info as I could and then end this.

I shoved him back. "Tell me what you're planning."

"Nothing," he said with a smile. "Nothing."

"Liar."

"I'm not the one who's lying. You obviously care about the Shaws."

"I don't," I lashed back because it felt like an accusation, like I was siding with his enemy. But it was an empty anger, because why else had I come all this way? "I'm not the one who's breaking the law."

"It's not a just law. Prohibition has created more criminals than it has saved the world from drunks. It's making criminals richer, and the wealthy still keep getting drunk anyhow. It's not a law if it's only illegal for the poor. It's a wealth tax. And why shouldn't the poor have something to dim the pain of being poor?"

I couldn't breathe. "Was that a speech?"

"So what?"

"I love speeches."

Our hot breaths circled, and all at once I noticed how close we stood next to each other.

"How'd you know my favorite book?" he asked with his eyes closed tight.

I arched my neck up. "I didn't," I said. Honest. For the first time honest. "It's my favorite book too."

He swore softly. And then he kissed me hard, and heaven help me but I threw my arms around him and kissed him back. His hands were like fog—moving so fast it felt like he was juggling knives. Like I was the dangerous one, the one who would cut him if he dropped me. His mouth on mine had turned my thoughts into metaphors. Into poetry. He kissed like he was thirsty, but I was not drained by him, I was filled.

It was nothing. It was nothing. My heart thundered. Sparks arched between our fingers. It was nothing. I couldn't breathe. It was nothing. I pulled back from his lips. I stepped back from his fog, I saw him through the darkened alley.

"Wow," he whispered, his voice hallowed as if it was a prayer. I didn't move, and this hymn of silence sang between us, the pounding of my heart a drumbeat calling to gods or devils.

"Wow?" That was all he could say? What about *I'm sorry?* What about *I shouldn't have done that?*

What about *want to do it again?*

He cocked his head to one side. "I was not expecting—"

"Me neither."

"I can't . . . ," he said at the same time I spoke up, "Patch, you gotta know something."

"What?" he asked, his broken eyes already distant.

I shook my head. I . . . How could I possibly explain what was going on? I couldn't tell him about the society. I couldn't tell him about Andrew. I wouldn't want to.

This was the point I should have ended it. I had to end this.

"Nothing," I said. "It's nothing."

Nothing was all that that night could have been. It was nothing. So I couldn't have pulled him into shadows again, or recited him passages from my favorite poets, or laughed until I snorted at his stories, or climbed to the rooftop of that hotel and searched the stars with his arm behind me, my hands clutched to a fire escape I could have taken at any moment. I couldn't have fallen asleep on his shoulder during a nickel movie, his hands on my skin, fingers brushing my cheek like a thousand stolen kisses. This boy calmed my storm and made a circling eye at my center. A respite. A peaceful tropical holiday, hiding between thunderclouds. He couldn't have been real.

I wouldn't have done that.

That would have been foolish. I've made vows bigger than a boy with a crooked smile. And it was nothing. Just a dream and untouched skin.

Because I knew better.

CHAPTER NINE

It was nearly dawn when Patch dropped me off in a truck hiding smuggled liquor in the back.

Mrs. Brown's house was as dark as the night that had slipped away without me noticing. I crept up the path and tested the door. Locked.

Of course.

"You need help?" Patch asked, his voice too loud.

I shushed him hard and motioned for him to go. It was not my finest look, I could admit it. Leaving a strange boy's truck, angry at him for making noise, after spending a whole night collecting kisses.

The same day I met my future husband.

No, miss, that was not a good look at all.

Oh jeepers, I was in trouble. It was far too early to already have Andrew's voice inside my head.

Patch's engine roared to life and he took off with a squeal and a hum, since of course, he didn't have to hide, finally leaving me alone, to be caught or punished on my own.

I slumped to the front steps, gripping my knees tight.

But no one in the house stirred.

Maybe if I could get back inside Mrs. Brown's house, this night could become the nothing that it had to be. I crept around the brick house and tested the windows. The bottom floor windows were all shut tight, and the back door was locked, and, my heavens, I was in a load of trouble.

The whole house was locked.

Maybe one of my sisters would help me. I counted the windows at the back of the house. Mira's room was the farthest away from Mrs. Brown's room. She'd understand why I'd been so reckless. I palmed a small pebble and tossed it against her glass.

It took three more throws, but finally the curtains swayed.

Mira popped her head out.

I moved to wave, but dropped my hands and glared at the trees that surrounded the house. I couldn't lie to myself any longer. People had seen me with him. I knew Gossips were watching the house, just like I knew they were watching as I didn't end things like they told me to. What would the Gossips do with this information?

What had I just done to my chances?

A few moments later Mira opened the back door. I rushed inside the kitchen, my shoes too loud against the green and yellow tiles.

"You have fun?" she whispered with a grin.

"You'd like that," I said under my breath as I slipped my shoes off.

"I would." Mira leaned against the deep farmhouse sink. "We could all use a pinch of fun now and again."

"Why don't you believe in me?" I asked.

"What are you talking about? Of course I believe in you."

I unbuttoned the back of my dress and walked up the stairs. Maybe it was because of how tired I was, but my tempest was full-on raging. "You just want Andrew for yourself," I hissed as I climbed up the stairs, "and if I fall for some no-good rascal, then that's one less girl standing in your way. Is that what you want?" When I reached the landing where the stairs turned the other way, I tugged my dress over my head, standing in only my slip. "We made a promise, but it just meant that you placed me third."

She gripped my arm and shushed me. "I don't care about the competition. I just want you and Bea to be happy."

Happy? Who on earth got to be happy? I turned and took the rest of the stairs up. We had our duty. We had our oaths. Happy was never a guaranteed part of our ever after; even when I was a child I knew that. I hoped for someone kind, and nice, who I could make fall for me. Someone safe for me to fall in love with, who wouldn't change me into someone I couldn't recognize. But even my most romantic thoughts knew that my loyalty had to be to the society before anyone, before my husband, or my heart, or even myself.

That's what reaching my goals would take.

I folded my dress over my arm as we reached the hallways between our rooms. I spoke with a voice so quiet it wouldn't wake anyone. "I can't help my nerves."

"I know. I'm sorry. I shouldn't have said that. And I do believe in you. I think you're incredible. You'd make a great First Lady. Honest."

I swear it was exhaustion that sent tears to flood my eyes. "But I won't, because I just messed everything up." What had I just done?

"Elsie. Nothing is unfixable." She grinned wide. "Let me get my wrench."

I glared. I wasn't ready to joke about this. "I haven't even met him yet, and I'm already so far behind, and now this? I just made a fool of myself with a no-good boy when they told me to break it off. He was tall and handsome, and I lost all sense. Oh, I am a Dumb Dora. The Matrons are going to send me home. They're not even going to let me try."

"You're going to get your chance at Andrew. No one is going to send you home. I won't let them."

I covered my face with both of my hands. "I just want my life to matter."

Mira pat my head. "It does, sweetheart. It does."

Ugh. I was being foolish. This wasn't over. I could make this better. I could find my way out of this mess. When I looked up Mira had a far-off look in her eye.

"Do you like him?" I asked.

She startled. "Andrew?"

"Yeah. I know he likes you, but do you like him?" I didn't know why that mattered so much to me. I didn't know why my heart clenched as I waited for her answer.

"I don't know," she answered. "I think it's still too early to tell. He's nice, though."

"That's good."

"For Bea," Mira said. She met my eye and amended, "And for you."

And for her. She was leading the race: Why was she backing out like she wasn't? "What aren't you telling me?"

"You know me," she said with a shrug. "I don't really like anyone until I get to know them. I've never been one to fall for good looks. I have to find an emotional connection—"

"—in order to get all romantical."

She rolled her eyes. But her lips bunched in an expression I couldn't catch. "In theory anyway. I just have exceptionally high standards, but if a priority one can't meet them, then . . ." She cleared her throat. "We should sleep. It's Bea's turn in the morning. She deserves our best efforts."

I cleared my throat. "Will you be happy if Andrew chooses you?"

She didn't even stop to think. "I'll be grateful. That's close enough."

"But it's not. You deserve to be happy too."

"I will be. Get some sleep, you vamp," she said, shoving me into my room. "Take your well-kissed behind to bed. We'll solve this puzzle in the morning."

I turned, and she closed the door right on my face.

"Ow," I called.

"Liar," she said back.

I grinned. Then I and my lips that should have stayed unkissed leaned against the wood door, drinking in the solitude of my small room. I pressed my hand to my mouth and closed my eyes.

Mira was right. I needed to catch as much sleep as I could.

My room was peaceful in the dawn light. I knew what I wanted from my life.

I just didn't know what had possessed me to want anything different. I grabbed my leather-bound notebook from my writing desk and sank into my bed. I lay back against the feather pillow, and I opened my notebook, flipping through my collection of poems and thoughts, each one sacred because they existed fully formed outside me. They were pen inked on paper, but to me they felt like etched stone. Like something permanent. Some monument I built word by word, my thoughts made too solid to blow away in a wind. I couldn't feel so lost with who I was inked in, sentence after permanent sentence.

But as I flipped through poem after poem, I realized something that sent me searching. No, *ripping* through the notebook.

Hundreds of poems. All my thoughts.

And I never signed a single one.

I climbed out of bed and sat down at my writing desk. I flipped to the first page where I'd written the words *Poems and Thoughts* in my very best cursive. I palmed my pencil, and then with vision blurred through tears or exhaustion, I wrote three more words.

By Elsie Fawcett.

I glanced up at the dawn streaming in through my window, and I knew, down to my soul I knew, that I'd just done the most dangerous thing I'd ever done in my life. I'd declared something, sure as setting my foot on the first step of a new path.

My name mattered.

My thoughts mattered.

And I could never forget that again.

CHAPTER TEN

Sunlight streamed through my window onto my open notebook as I woke up to the sound of cooking from downstairs. Or perhaps it was the smell of bacon and of baked bread rousing me from my rest.

They'd let me sleep in. Heaven above, they'd let me sleep. What did that mean?

I opened the large maple wardrobe tucked by my door, and I chose my most innocent of dresses, washed my face with the water from the porcelain jug that had been tucked on top of the wardrobe. Then I paced behind my door. This was the first assignment I'd ignored. This was the first time I'd chosen to do the opposite of what they had asked me to do.

I was not a coward, and they would never hurt me. I could handle whatever punishment had happened, and I hoped it was strong enough of a punishment to ensure I never wanted to do something that foolish again. All I wanted was for the society to shove me back on a path I did not want to leave, not for nothing.

As much as I'd loved every second of that nothing.

It was over.

And now I had to face the repercussions.

My sisters' rooms were all empty, and as I crept down the hallway and toward the stairs, a poem I didn't dare write down ripped through my thoughts.

Patch's hands

Patch's hands were too young
to be so creased in lines.
A scar across two fingertips.
A freckle near his wrist.
His palms were rough like they'd known work,
but they smelled of oils and smoke
and coins he earned for himself.
Patch's hands hid a line I would not cross.
It was a line reserved for husbands, not for fog.
But on that night that was made of nothing,
I tiptoed to that line like my toes were in sand
and that line was the ocean.
Soft waves up to my ankles, not deep enough to

have felt the undertow,

but far too deep for a girl who knew her

husband's name.

Far too deep not to drown.

I flapped my shirt to create a breeze to cool the heat rising up my cheeks. It was a hot morning, was all. I was not getting all bothered by a poem I didn't dare write down.

Bea stood in front of the mirror in the dining room while Beauty Makers curled her hair and lifted dress after dress to her dimpled chin.

"The pink one?" I said.

Mira turned. "Right?" she said. "That one's as sparkling as pink champagne."

"And I said it's much too fine for me." Bea made a face.

"It's just a dress, Bea," I said. "Let yourself be beautiful."

She ducked her head. "But we're going to a bakery, not a dinner party."

"Well, how about this one?" A Beauty Maker with sharp cheekbones, a thick brow, and painted pink lips pulled out a soft yellow scarf dress that turned Bea's brown hair into chocolate, the warm color brightening her cheeks and her eyes.

"Bellissimo!" Mira shouted.

I clapped. "Perfection."

Bea herself made a cooing sound like she'd just seen a tiny baby fawn. Even she couldn't walk back from the face she'd made. And no kind of protest could fight the fact that she wanted this dress.

Even Greta looked at it without saying something nasty.

At least to her. "There you are, Elsie. I thought you'd never get up." Her gaze was sharp. "Mrs. Brown is asking for you."

I swallowed hard. Both Bea and Mira gave me a supportive look.

"You look beautiful, Bea," I said. I looked at both of them like I was saying goodbye.

I made my way through the halls and into the kitchen, entering as if summoned to the gallows. Mrs. Brown's hair was down, soft to her shoulders, and her checked light blue dress hung at a drop waist. But instead of handing me my head, she had me sit at the small breakfast nook. She placed a plate down in front of me. Blueberry muffins, well-salted scrambled eggs, two pieces of bacon, and a tall glass of freshly squeezed orange juice.

"I'm sorry," I said.

"Don't say sorry to me," she said as she sat at the only other chair. She tossed her hair back and unpeeled the wrapper from a muffin. "You are not the first girl to run into a stranger's arms when meeting a future husband, and you will not be the last." Her smile was brief, but it unknotted some of the tension between my shoulder blades. "Although you might want to apologize to him."

"I'm not engaged yet, and Andrew has—"

"Not Andrew, love. This boy. What you are doing is not kind to him." She took a bite of her muffin.

How was it rude to Patch? "It's nothing."

She lifted her eyebrows.

"It's over," I insisted.

"Um hmm. That's not what the Gossips say."

"I didn't hurt him, it was just kissing. Nothing wrong with a little kissing." I'd practiced my kissing plenty during training. A kiss meant noth . . . it didn't have to mean anything.

"You weren't hurting him," Mrs. Brown allowed, "but you were using him."

I waved a hand. "That's not true."

"You've been trained, Elsie. You could have any man. And while this is not all on you, because he did choose to be used, it was not really a fair fight. You were scared, and you used him as a way to run away from your future."

"That is not even remotely true." I hadn't used my training on Patch. If I had it would have felt like pretending. If I had, then I'd be safe from these feelings that kept picking at me when I knew I needed to let them go. I gnawed at a piece of bacon and wouldn't meet her eyes.

"If you want this Patrick fellow, you could have him." I met her eyes, and she reached forward and took my hand. "Elsie, sweetheart, you get to choose your own life. This assignment is not a trap, or a prison. It's an opportunity. But no one in the society will force you into an unhappy match."

I met her eyes and swallowed without registering the taste of bacon. Bacon. Oh jeepers, was I ever in trouble.

She let me go. "If this boy makes you happy, we will not stand in your way."

I could have him. I could be with Patch. A rumrunner. Who'd told me he didn't have a home or a family except his brother, who slept on the roof of a warehouse as he spied on a good family, who stole the book he'd taught himself to read, and the small library he'd built for himself. I could feel those sparks and that peace and get lost in those kisses.

But is that what I actually wanted for my life?

I stared at my eggs and thought of Patch's wandering eyes searching strangers for me. He'd said he hoped to see me again. He'd stared at me whenever I'd glanced away as if I was a daydream he didn't want to lose. What would he do after I slipped into the life I've trained for and become nothing more than a question he won't find the answer to until the day he votes against my husband?

My throat tightened.

I wanted his wild eyes, and his long rough fingers and crooked smile, but did I want a place in his rumrunner life?

That wasn't me. I didn't want that.

I wanted something safer, something so much bigger than him. Mrs. Brown was right. It wasn't his gentle hands and witty jokes I craved. It was his fear. It was the way I could walk in and out of his life and claim his heart without trying. I could steal his kisses and he'd smile gladly, like

I had lowered myself to be in his company. I liked that I could treat him like he was nothing.

Because it made me feel powerful.

I sat back in my chair. I was the one who had called him nothing. I'd judged him long before the society ever would. Before my mother could have.

When I looked through my own eyes, I didn't want to sleep on rooftops, or be subject to his employer's whims. I didn't want to be a blackmailer's wife. Not even for all the sparks and poems and speeches in the world. Not more than my oaths.

I just wanted the power I held over him.

Who wanted that?

They must have been mistaken when they called me quality.

I looked Mrs. Brown straight in the eye. "I want more for my life. We need the Gossips to look into Patch's employers. They sent him here to spy on Andrew and his family. They're trying to blackmail them. They're dangerous."

"My goodness." From her expression, I knew I'd shut the door on Patch like I should have done last night.

Whatever we could have had was over before it could even really begin.

I lifted my chin. "I want my chance at a priority one, and I want to keep my oaths."

Mrs. Brown stood and crossed around the table, and then she pulled me tight into her soft chest. She held me like I needed comforting, but I didn't deserve it.

"We'll take care of it from here. Well done, Elsie. Saying no is the right of a woman. A right that is so often denied. And I know it hurts so much to say no, when you could have said yes so easily, and made that boy very happy. But that yes would have caused pain to your own self eventually." She squeezed once more. "I'm proud of you for recognizing that, Elsie."

Those words nearly did me in. How could she possibly be proud?

I hadn't done anything yet to earn her pride.

But I would. I would keep every oath. I would help my friends. And then I would fight for a future that was as big as my ambitions.

No matter that the shadow of Patch's touch still tingled my nerve endings.

———◆———

Bea was as radiant as the sun. Mira and I walked with our arms interlocked, each of us sharing proud looks because our Bea just seemed so grown up and beautiful, and we were both bursting with a giddy pride that we could not share out loud or else she'd feel self-conscious and probably mess up her hair or smudge her makeup in order to dim the light that shone from her lovely eyes.

We let her go as we entered and a tinny bell chimed. The bakery smelled like heaven and fresh-baked bread, so basically heaven. Checkered curtains opened to sun-drenched windows left the shop bright and warm and filled with treats and people in fine clothes. The high ceilings dripped hanging porcelain lights, and the walls were covered in shelves full of flours and loaves of bread, including a stack of Frankworth and Sons loaves on the back shelf. The society provided those to bakeries across the country, and any woman in need could nab a loaf a day for free, or for a lower price if they preferred to still pay.

At the center of the room, square glass containers hid piped and flourished baked treats. The men and women at the counter wore white bonnets and long aprons, and from behind a closed door I could hear the hum of an industrial mixer.

A few round tables with wrought-iron chairs were tucked at the side of the open space, and that's where I sat. The frumpy coat I wore made me look older, especially with my hair twisted up like someone married. The Beauty Makers had drawn subtle wrinkles to the sides of my face and placed a sparkling ring that weighed down my left finger.

It was another way to turn invisible.

I sat with my back toward the front entrance, but Andrew wasn't here yet. Bea sat on a bar stool near the counter, with her lip tucked under her teeth, her fingers tapping on the glass. I gave her an approving smile, and her hand stilled. She was going to be splendid, I just knew it. If this place was a temple to baked goods, then Bea herself was like the goddess of muffins. She was a vision of warmth and softness and considerable size.

Andrew walked past the open window slowly, with a young girl at his arm. His sister, Rebecca. My target. Rebecca's golden hair fluffed like a cloud, her face cut through by a sharp nose and eyes so bright I struggled to look away from them. She was eleven years old, and a young and silly eleven from the dossier. She leaned on Andrew's arm as they entered the bakery and then stared up at the menu board with her mouth agape.

Andrew put his arm around her shoulders, but he wasn't looking at the board. Bea had caught him with one look.

She turned away as a baker handed her a slice of pie. Something crashed behind the door to the kitchen, and the baker left to be kept busy by our Mira. The door swung closed.

"Is that the lemon meringue?" Andrew asked Bea.

Bea nodded and then slid a hair behind her ear.

"You'll have to tell me how it is. I've always been tempted."

She slid the pie over. "You can try a bite."

"You sure?"

Iris stepped up to the counter wearing that awful white bonnet.

"Can we get two forks?" Bea asked her. Iris smiled warmly and handed the forks she'd already prepared.

Rebecca pulled on Andrew's arm and leaned against the glass counter. "Two slices of chocolate cream pie, please."

"Coming right up," Iris answered with a grin.

I opened my bag. I had a couple of books I thought

Rebecca might enjoy, and because the dossier said she liked art, I'd brought watercolors and several sheets of paper.

This was a tricky one. I needed to keep her busy, but also make sure Andrew knew she was safe, and do it all without revealing my face.

"How's the chocolate cream?" Bea asked.

Andrew's face lit up. "It's the cat's meow." I made a face I wouldn't show. Slang sounded so odd in Andrew's normally polished speech patterns. It made it sound like he was trying too hard. Andrew cleared his throat. "They add cinnamon to the chocolate."

"Cinnamon? How clever! I bet that adds a depth of flavor. Have you ever tried adding pepper?"

"With chocolate?"

Bea bit her lip. "Not like black pepper." She laughed. "I love to pair ancho or chipotle peppers with chocolate."

"And is it good? That sounds—"

"Rich and sweet and smoky. Chipotle peppers are my favorite. They go so well with a good dark chocolate. It's perhaps not for everyone; you need to make sure the balance is just right. But if it is, it adds another level of flavor."

I dropped a book and kept my back turned, using my teaspoon to look behind me.

Andrew hadn't looked away from Bea, even after that tremendous bang.

But Rebecca did. Iris handed her a slice of chocolate cream pie, and Rebecca took the plate and fork and glanced at the book I'd dropped.

It was the new Sherlock Holmes I'd borrowed from my library. I didn't pick it up, just pulled out a few coloring sheets and painted daisies as I sipped from a cup of hot cocoa. I wasn't an artist, but the paints were bright and before I'd painted a fourth petal, Rebecca placed her plate on my table. She picked up the book.

"Excuse me, ma'am," she said.

Ma'am. Ow, that hurt.

She tugged at her ear. "You dropped this."

"Ah. Like Sherlock from the falls."

Her eyes lit up. "Right? Wasn't that the most interesting ending?"

"Or was it a beginning?" I asked with a smile.

She slipped into my table. "Are these for me?" she asked of the watercolors and extra papers.

I faltered for a second, then I slid them to her. I hadn't needed to invite her to sit with me.

She licked her fork and then started painting.

"You know what's going on?" I asked quietly. I didn't need to bother lowering my voice. Bea and Andrew were positively captured by their discussion of different types of chocolate.

"My mom told me," Rebecca whispered. "I'm supposed to keep quiet and out of the way. I'm glad for the paints, though. Last time they did this, the girl just sat there and looked at me. Like she didn't even think I was worth conversing with. We like your batch better." She took a giant bite of her pie.

I reached for my pastry. "This isn't the first round of Wives?"

She laughed. Andrew looked over and then settled in once he knew that his sister was taken care of. "Not at all. There were the Grant sisters, and the Youngberg cousins."

"Really?"

"Yeah. You've got your work cut out for you. Andrew is really smart, but not when it comes to girls. Do you want some of my pie?"

I smiled and then took a bite. Oh, that was good. Chilled and thick and creamy. Chocolate with cinnamon, who would have thought? I licked my lips. "You know, I've been in your shoes."

She finished drawing five straight vertical lines and didn't answer.

"My brother was matched like this too. I was"—I did the math quickly—"thirteen years old when he met Doris and her friends. They were all so beautiful, and so old. I thought they were very sophisticated."

"I think most of you all are boring."

"Well, most of the time, sophisticated and boring are the same thing."

She made a face. "Then I hope I never get sophisticated."

"Me too."

I took another bite of my slice of an ice cream bomb as those sharp lines she painted turned into a building. No, it was a street.

I licked my lips. "Excellent use of perspective."

"Thanks." Rebecca painted windows and lights, and before my eyes that street shifted into a cityscape.

"Wow." I touched the corner of her paper. "You're quite the artist."

"I just paint landscapes," Rebecca said. "I can't do people."

"Well, that's still lovely work. Is this somewhere you've been?"

"Nah, just in my imagination."

I scooted forward. "You know, I bet you could become an architect one day." She looked up with a sharp look.

She shook her head. "I don't know."

"You could." I grinned. One of my talents was being able to see a person's potential. I used that skill often enough as a Matchmaker, but it was the same talent put to a new purpose. "Could you imagine designing buildings, setting up the lines in a night sky that could last for a hundred years? You could take these buildings from your imagination and make them real." Her buildings could be like my words, monuments that could never crumble.

"That's not for me." She lowered her voice like a co-conspirator. "The society already gave me my title."

"Oh."

"I'm going to be a Mother," she said softly. "Raise some powerful sons."

I sat back. She was smiling, but for me, it felt as though someone had wiped away the skyline.

And I didn't know why. There was nothing wrong with

wanting to be a Mother. I loved children, and I wanted to raise some of my own someday.

So why did this feel so wrong?

She went back to drawing, sharp straight lines, adding shadows to windows and birds in the sky of a world where she would never matter as much as the children she could create.

"Or daughters," I said firmly. "You could raise powerful daughters."

She gave me a puzzled look, and my comment wasn't the right words anyway. She wasn't my mother. She wasn't set inside her choices yet.

She was eleven years old. How could they decide who she would be when she wasn't nearly old enough to know who she was yet? Her whole life was in front of her, but the society I loved so much had decided that her life would never matter as much as her brother's. She was eleven, and she couldn't even imagine she could dream of a life where she could matter just for who she was and for what she could do. What she could create. She could create more than children.

She was eleven, and we'd already decided which men she would spend her whole life serving.

Bea and Andrew giggled over their shared slice of pie.

I wiped off the wrinkles on the sides of my eyes and untwisted my hair so it hung down to my cheeks.

I owed it to the girls who came after me to do everything in my power to make sure their lives mattered. I could change the society if I was at its head. Because what they'd done to this little girl was not right.

The society I loved was wrong about this.

And if they were wrong about this, then what else were they wrong about?

I slid off my coat and angled my chair so Andrew could see that the girl who was taking such fine care of his sister was the prettiest girl in the room.

"I'll pay you a dollar if you laugh right now," I said like Greta would have.

Rebecca threw her head back and cackled so hard that everyone turned to look.

And when Andrew met my eye I smiled the smile that the society gave me.

He swallowed hard.

I didn't have to look at Bea's face to know I'd just hurt her, but I didn't look away, and I did not wince.

When my turn at Andrew came, I would end this whole competition.

I had to.

That city Rebecca was drawing would not build itself.

And girls were too often forgotten in their brothers' shadows.

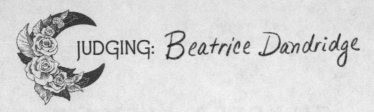 JUDGING: *Beatrice Dandridge*

CATEGORY: First blush

Amount of Bloom:

Soft and frequent

Quality:

Impressive, natural charm

Physical appearance at time of judging:

Plump and robust, stunning color

Creative arrangement:

Playful, natural connection,
genuine spark

Faults:

Wilted after being outshone

TOTAL SCORE: 18 out of 20

Judge initials: MB

CHAPTER ELEVEN

Getting a boy to smile at you was one thing, but convincing said boy to commit to you for a lifetime was an entirely different beast to wrangle. After the plans were finalized for my meeting with Andrew the next day, and the outfit chosen, I tucked into my blankets with the strict instruction to sleep so there wouldn't be dark circles under my eyes come morning.

If only my thoughts would stop making dark circles inside my mind.

I would fail at this, and I would deserve it.

They weren't exactly happy thoughts, or soft kind voices, that paced back and forth in my mind and twisted my ankles in the sheets. But I'd battled such inner voices before. Sometimes I sang songs to silence the flow of words in my head, sometimes I read until the words on the page were louder than my own thoughts, but since the Matrons would see the light, or hear my warbling singing, I used my favorite technique.

I cataloged my kisses.

There was a soft kiss from a man who married my friend, and a sloppy kiss with grappling hands that sent my body humming but later I'd joke about with my friends, a chaste practice kiss from a boy who would never feel romantically for me, but my goodness did he have great hair and soft lips, and an undertow-pulling kiss from a young and handsome boy I couldn't think about again. I couldn't get lost in Patch, not tonight.

The first time I learned how to kiss I was twelve years old. The room was full then of all the girls in my training class, taught by the lone single Wife from the class that came before ours. Ethel was a very pretty twenty-five-year-old with a waist corseted so tight she couldn't speak in long sentences. I've worn my share of tummy smoothers and have always found them quite comfortable once they're in the right position, so I don't know what her issue was. Might have had an undiagnosed breathing condition.

"Roll up your sleeves." She inhaled shallow breaths as we held our wrists, bare forearms horizontal, close in front of our lips. "Now, everyone, we start with a peck."

She kissed her arm and we copied her.

"This is called *the strawberry kiss*. Sweet and tart. The goal here is to prove your innocence and to leave a lasting impression." She breathed in. "Now, peck once more, but this time turn your head to the side as you pull away."

We did. My skin tingled, goose bumps bursting from my skin.

"Can you feel the difference between a press and a brush? Movement makes the kiss more tactile, and"—she drew in a long breath—"when you turn your head to the side it gives a demure look. Like so." She turned her head to one side prettily and lifted her shoulders slightly. "Let's practice."

I glanced about, but all the girls in my Wife Class did it so I kissed my arm again too.

"Add a smile, Nora," Ethel said as she walked down the aisle. "Don't look skittish. A touch of fear is fine, but you must"—she paused for breath—"look happy. This is a victory for the man. Make sure he feels it."

When we'd kissed our arms well enough that she felt satisfied, we moved on. "This is called *the peach kiss*." She demonstrated on her own arm. "Count two seconds. Not out loud. Not on your fingers."

We giggled, and Bea mumbled under her breath, "It was one time." She sat on the chair at my left side.

"Lips soft and puckered. When you reach two, smile and pull back. Again, the motion of your smiling makes the kiss tactile. Smiling leaves it as a victory . . . while also pulling your lips away. It's sweetness and makes a promise of more to come. Practice."

The girl on the other side of me, who I'd thought at the time was named Mira but I wasn't certain, opened her

mouth and shook her head back and forth in some passion-
ate mock display.

I barked out a laugh. The whole class looked over at us
as we lowered our arms.

The teacher smiled. "We'll get to that one soon enough.
But the way I teach it isn't quite so . . . enthusiastic."

The class snickered and Mira grinned with them, but I
saw her smile shift into a grimace, and from that point on
she stayed focused. Mostly.

"Next is *the blackberry kiss*. Also called *the Wife kiss*."

"Why are they named after fruit?" I asked.

"To report progress. We don't kiss and tell. But we do kiss
and bake." We giggled, but then silenced when she lifted an
eyebrow. "Now, pay attention. There will be a baking quiz
this Friday. You'll need to bake a pie and demonstrate the
kiss that it . . . signifies."

Bea raised her hand. "What if we don't have all the ingredients? Some of these fruits are seasonal and—"

"—The society will have what you need delivered to your
house. See me after class."

"Could I have my ingredients delivered to Bea's house
as well?" I asked. Bea's eyes seemed hurt, like I was offering her a charity. It was nothing of the sort. "She's the best
baker, and I want top marks." I grinned, and she blushed a
little.

Our teacher wasn't amused. "There are no shortcuts, girls.
You will each need to learn to be a passable baker. There are
many ways to a man's heart . . ."

"And how would you know?" a girl with shining blond curls asked. She'd been silent for most of the class, but it was impossible to ignore the fine tailoring of her dress. "My mother says it's a waste to be taught by the loser of her class. My mother says that we're dumbing down each generation of Wives by that practice. She says we should have the Wife who made the best match teach us."

Our teacher's face was well trained and didn't show any sign of that insulting wretch's diatribe affecting the line of her smile or the softness of her brows. "If each generation of Wives is dumber than the last . . . then what does that make you, Greta?"

We snickered, all except for Bea, who looked over at Greta with sympathy and compassion. I'd thought it strange at the time. Greta had been rude to our teacher. Teachers were the sacred holders of all new information. They should be revered and respected.

But now, I could see Bea's vision. The teacher was twenty-five years old. And she had berated a twelve-year-old child for asking a question and repeating the words of her mother. Quality needed to rise above petty hurts. Quality needed to regard our power above our feelings. Quality forgave a child for being childish.

Bea would forgive me. She was in all ways quality. But even if she wouldn't, maybe I could forgive myself.

I wasn't that far from the twelve-year-old girl who learned to kiss on my own arm.

I covered my head with the blankets and tried to ignore

the murmuring voices from Bea and Mira's room. They hadn't said much to me on the drive home. Mira wouldn't talk to me, and I did not blame her one penny. Bea would, but I couldn't speak to her. I couldn't apologize when I knew I'd do it again.

Did that make me a bad person?

Although when you think about it, they only came here because I made them. I made Bea and Mira take this assignment. And if it wasn't for my insistence, this would be a two-way challenge that I would have won already.

All I did was smile at him.

And I had a very good reason to do it.

Mira and Bea wouldn't help as I got ready, which was already far worse than smiling at a boy, when you thought about it. Which I did. Over and over and over again, my never-silencing brain making sure of that.

In the morning, I was painted and tucked tight, shining with my own light, and stubbornly determined to make this happen. I held my grandmother's hair clips, and I slid them snug on one side of my head. The Beauty Makers embellished my lips and eyes, curled my hair to glowing.

When I looked in the mirror, I saw someone crafted and beautiful and lovely. I did not see a bad person in that glittering white dress.

I saw a bride.

I saw a doll.

I saw someone who would make my mother proud. The only way my mother would let me.

But no matter how I looked, I did not see myself.

So I turned away from the mirror and thought about the cityscape Rebecca had painted in soft blue watercolors. She was going to throw it away, so I'd tucked it into my purse, and now it sat on my bookshelf next to the letter from my mother that I had not returned yet, the business card from that editor, and my own book of poems.

I was doing this for Rebecca, and for the girls like her. We needed to make sure that we could choose our futures based on what was best for us, not what was best for the men around us.

All I needed was for one man to fall for me in order to do that.

My friends would forgive me eventually.

They had to. I was doing this for them.

And I was doing this for me.

<hr>

The library had always seemed a sacred place to me. All these stories, all those voices hidden behind bindings, monuments to a person's thoughts, sitting on shelves ready to be taken. Just walking in was like visiting a friend, or coming home. But I think I feel more at rest in a library than I do in my own bedroom.

That's why I chose it as the place to meet Andrew.

Maybe libraries *were* my home. Though I'd never crossed the threshold of this building, even a new library felt familiar somehow, and that gave me strength. I'd meet Andrew, officially, in this place that filled me up.

My thoughts were still and steady as I walked through shelf after shelf, looking for Andrew. He wasn't on the first floor, and from Iris's signal, I knew he wasn't on the second floor either.

I walked carefully up the oak staircase to the top floor, and when I reached the landing, I paused and gathered my breath, pressing down my dress and making sure my hair clips hadn't slipped from behind my ear.

Here goes, I thought. *Let's go meet your future husband.*

It was bright on the top floor of the library, with plenty of large round windows letting in warm sunlight that shone on wooden shelves and softly bound books. The top floor of the library stored the periodicals, newspapers from decades and the century past, and important papers locked in files. It was quiet here, so quiet I could hear the sound of someone flipping pages of a book. The long shelves opened into empty tables, streaks of sunlight illuminating dust motes that floated as gentle as fairy wings. It warmed the bindings of the books and the air and my tense muscles.

I stepped forward, and there, sitting in the base of a curved window, totally absorbed inside a story, was Patrick Elliot Villipin.

My hand flew up to my chest, and I ducked back behind a shelf.

How? How had he sneaked past the Gossips? How had they missed him?

But for a single second as I took in Patch as he leaned against the curved sill with his knees up against the wall, with the book not five inches from his face, his simple tan-collared shirt with sleeves rolled up to his elbows, the black sweater folded carefully across his lap as he read Jules Verne's *Around the World in Eighty Days*, in that moment, his being there made a perverse kind of sense. He loved my favorite book. Perhaps this was a sign that he was there when I was made of nothing but nerves and need.

I slipped back behind a shelf.

This was not the time to get romantic. I had a mission. I needed to find Andrew.

Footsteps tapped closer. I hid myself better when a small boy about six or seven years old with dark hair trimmed in a line above his eyebrows ran up to Patch's side and flopped down on his lap.

"I'm bored," the boy said, his voice carrying to where I hid.

Patch adjusted his book on top of the boy's head but didn't look away. "Five more minutes."

"You said we'd go to the park."

Patch smiled and put his elbows on the boy's head. "Ten more minutes."

The boy shoved Patch's arms off him and stood. "But there's nothing to do."

"You have your car." The boy stomped his foot, and Patch sighed and looked at him. "Fine. Fifteen more minutes, and I'll buy you an ice cream."

The boy grabbed Patch's leg and yanked his ankles down from the window casing. "No, Patch. I'm dying. We've been here forever."

Patch chuckled, a gentle sound that drew me forward. "Just a few more minutes, bud. She'll be here."

The boy laid his head on Patch's shoulder, and Patch ran his fingers through his hair. Another book lay spine out from me, partially covering a drawing. A drawing of my face.

He was waiting for me. But how on earth did he know I'd come here? That I'd be here today?

My chest tightened. I've studied the stars and the planets, I've read about tides and undercurrents. I know about forces drawing objects together, but I was not prepared for the way I longed to jump into that boy's arms.

I clenched my fists so hard my nails left crescent moons in my palms. I took two steps back. My romantic heart was composing poetry about the softness of his lips, and the quiet secret moments when he must have taken pencil to paper and drawn my likeness with lines so faint they felt like fingers tracing the curve of my cheek, the line of my nose.

But my brain knew there was only one piece of art that mattered, and it was painted by an eleven-year-old girl.

Someone must have told him where I'd be. I ducked away on quiet feet. Unseen and unspotted, I slipped down those stairs as silently as I could. Greta waited on the landing in old-age makeup, with gray powder in her hair. Her expression slid into a satisfied smile as she folded her arms across her chest.

"What did you do?" I asked.

"Whatever do you mean?" She shrugged, but I wouldn't let her lie. She was too eager to put me back in my place anyhow. "All I did was tell a mutual friend where you'd be."

I grit my teeth. "He's not your friend."

"Oh, are you jealous that I talked to him? Don't worry; *I'd* never stoop so below my station. He's perfect for you, though."

"Is this because I saw you at a weak point? Now you need to see me broken as well?"

She flinched. "After what you did to Bea, your own friend, this can hardly be worse. After all, I don't even like you."

That was so rude. Everyone liked me. I needed them to like me; isn't that why the society chose me? I lowered my shoulders and said the ugliest thing I could back. "The feeling's mutual."

"Elsie?" Bea climbed up the empty staircase below us. My knees felt weak, and I had to look away. She cleared her throat. "Andrew is downstairs. Near the cookbooks."

Her eyes seemed glazed and distant.

I stuffed my hands in my pockets and couldn't meet Bea's gaze.

Greta was right about what I'd done to Bea. Greta's betrayal hurt, and I didn't trust her or even like her. I probably should have expected it.

But smiling at Andrew during Bea's date was so much worse.

"Of course Andrew's by the cookbooks," I said with a flush of guilt. "He's perfect for you Bea, I—"

"—Don't apologize."

"I'm *so* sorry. I mean it."

She gave a little shrug. "Don't worry about it. Why would Andrew choose me when he could choose one of you?"

Her eyes were clear. No tears or emotion clogged her vision. She said it like it was a simple truth, like the color of the sky, or the answer to a math problem.

But she was wrong. She was immensely lovable. Beautiful and kind and brilliant, and I'd made her feel like she was nothing.

"He'd choose you because you are wonderful," I said. "You are *so* worthy of love."

She winced a little and glanced down, as though my words had hit their mark.

I should have raced to find Andrew. I was already so far behind, and this was my chance. But Bea was everything to me. She had to know that.

"I'm not," she said. "I'm not."

I pulled her in tight. "Oh, Bea," I said. "If only you knew how easy you are to love." My heart hurt for her.

Mira stepped up the landing of the stairs and stopped as she saw us hugging.

Bea breathed thickly, and her voice turned small. "But men see me as a friend, not as a woman. I hate it so much."

I pulled back and looked her right in the eye. "But your

husband will love it." She let out a laugh that might have covered for a cry. I kept going. "I can't think of a marriage better than a partnership of best friends who like to kiss each other. If it's not Andrew, and I believe it absolutely could be, then it will be someone better."

"Than a priority one?" Greta said behind us.

I turned my head. "There are many lives better than being a footnote in someone else's history."

"Elsie." Now it was Bea's turn to look at me in concern.

I didn't say anything. I couldn't. Those were thoughts I saved for my storm. I would never have let them out if seeing Patch hadn't rattled all my thoughts. I knew what my life was going to look like.

If I could only earn it. "I need to go," I said as I pulled away. Mira met my eye and gave a nod. I knew she'd take over for me and help Bea.

I turned and took the stairs quickly, not knowing how to talk to my friends, or how to explain the storming thoughts inside my head. All my researching and preparations flitted in and out of my thoughts like birds picking at seeds. Greta knew exactly which button to push to mess me up.

I knew why she did it, but that doesn't mean it didn't still work.

But I couldn't think about Patch. I couldn't be distracted from my mission.

Damn Greta to bad hair and bad teeth. And wrinkles. And a stomach that grumbled every time she saw a boy she liked. If I were a witch I would curse her with dog's breath and empty pockets. I passed rows and rows of books that I'd always pictured myself as the heroines of, but now my brain lived in a house with chicken feet.

Iris and Mira both looked at me quizzically as I crossed shelf after shelf until I saw Andrew.

My spell of anger broke. He wore tan slacks and a wool vest, his glasses perched low on his nose as he studied a dessert cookbook.

He was handsome. He was. He was kind and good and safe. This was my mission. He was the one I'd chosen. I could be the damsel for him, I knew it.

But was love all that we were made for?

How much of our training was to train us to keep quiet? To keep small?

Sometimes it felt like we were on an assembly line moving toward a future that was designed to be invisible. We could have power and influence, but then we'd have to keep it secret. Perhaps that was why I loved researching so much; I needed to remember the names of those women.

Because it was so easy to be forgotten.

That was the fear that kept me up at night. I tried really hard to do everything right, but still, the closer I'd get to becoming perfect, the more invisible I became. And I worried that my name wouldn't ever mean anything, that I'll be just one more person, one more girl left behind in history.

Would anyone remember me? I passed Andrew and then slipped into the aisle behind his.

I didn't know how to proceed here. In all my stories, the

heroine didn't hunt for marriage, didn't care about her own love story or future until the hero proved themself worthy enough that the reader permitted it. I would dislike a character who chased after love, or who connived and scammed and tricked a man to be hers. Was that because we were taught that to want love was a weakness?

Or because we were taught that men are smarter and therefore impossible to trick? That love was something we had to earn but couldn't pursue. A fictional girl like Becky Sharp, who fought for love, was a scheming harlot, because ambition wasn't for us.

But why? My heartbeat had begun to race, and there wasn't any threat or problem to cause it, just me and my thoughts storming inside my own head.

Maybe it was because most of the fairy tales I'd read were written by men.

I adjusted my hair clips, sure at this moment that Andrew could hear me. I sat down on the hard wood floors and put both my hands over my face, let my bare shoulders shake as I made soft crying sounds.

My tears weren't hard to fake. My heart was still racing, my thoughts still swirling. Andrew turned and peeked through the open shelves. I met his eye and thought the words *Help me* as loudly as I could.

Andrew left his table and offered me his handkerchief. "Are you all right?"

I took the cotton square daintily and dabbed my eyes.

"Tell me not all men are like him," I said with a voice so soft he had to lean closer to hear it.

Andrew sat next to me as I pressed my face into his handkerchief and pretended to cry. The heat of him warmed my side. While it was a tactic I'd used before, it was not the triumphant first impression I'd imagined giving. Why did I have to be weak in order to draw his interest?

"Is there anything I can do, miss?" he said, as if he were so much older than I was. Five months and seven days. Yet I was the miss and he was the hero.

I lowered the handkerchief and studied his face.

He pushed up his glasses. A nervous tick. I'd made him nervous.

Good.

"I could tell you a joke if you like," he said, glancing over at the books. "My friend Bill was just talking about a pirate who, uh . . . No, that wouldn't be appropriate."

I examined his embroidered handkerchief. "You're not helping your case."

"I promise I mean nothing untoward. I just can't abide seeing a pretty girl cry."

I fought to keep my face from shifting into a glare. *You mean you couldn't abide seeing a pretty girl not immediately trusting you. And were only pretty girls worthy of your compassion?*

Calm your storm, Elsie. Your anger won't turn him into Patch. "You don't have to—"

He cut me off with a smile. "—I know just what to do." And then he turned head over heels, hands to the ground, his suit-pant-covered legs sticking straight into the air. "You can trust a man standing on his head."

It was so preposterous. So unexpectedly unfashionable that I let out a laugh and he fell over, knocking into the bookshelf with a playful awkwardness I think Bea would have really enjoyed. We both panicked for a moment as the shelf wobbled, but then stood steady.

I put my hand over my lips to cover the laughter that erupted inside me. It would break the Matron's heart if he heard me snort. But the unexpected humor had cleared the cobwebs of the dream I'd been caught inside.

He grinned at me and brushed his hair off his forehead. "There. Now you're not crying, and you've made a friend. Day's looking up."

There was something so earnest about his face.

I'd vote for him.

"You look familiar," I said. "Have I seen you around?"

"At Hank's cafeteria," he said quickly, "and at the bakery yesterday."

My breath caught. Andrew turned away quickly, grabbing a book from the shelf, I think perhaps to hide behind.

Hope fluttered through me. "I'm surprised you remember me."

He looked away from his book. "You leave an impression."

I smiled smile number three, very bashful, and interested, before ripping my gaze away. "I still don't know if I should trust you. That boy who made me cry was that soda jerk at Hank's. You probably know him."

"Him? No? Not really." His voice was gentle.

I tucked my skirt under my knees and turned. "But you took his drinks."

He looked away. "That was . . . It was my friend's idea. I swear I didn't even drink," he whispered. His voice had dimmed so quiet not even the people on the bookshelf next to us could hear him. "I hate the stuff. Richards dared me to drink a whole bottle of his parent's gin on my fourteenth birthday, and I vomited the whole thing on his mother's pear tree. That tree has never recovered fully."

I gave a gentle laugh, which turned genuine as his cheeks flushed red.

"You can tell I'm really good at talking to girls." He leaned back, like he was planning on bolting.

I touched his elbow. "You're doing fine. Most boys don't bring up vomit until at least the second date."

He chuckled with me.

I held his handkerchief against my chest. "I find it refreshing. Honestly." He met my eye, and I gave him my very best smile. "I'm Elsie, by the way."

"Right." He rubbed the back of his neck. "I should probably tell you my name before I tell you my most embarrassing of stories. I'm Andrew."

"Andrew." I said his name carefully; like it was something I wanted to remember, like something important. "It suits you. You're not an Andy, or heaven forbid, a Drew. Are you?"

I asked the question, but I knew the answer. The dossier said he never liked nicknames, and I thought that might be something he felt odd about. Most boys have a childhood name, a Billy or a Sammy. I could just picture a five-year-old Andrew crinkling his nose when someone tried to call him Drew. I believed he might have been born an old man, and there was nothing like being the wrong age for his body to make him feel as though he were an outsider among his peers. My favorite trick was to find a man's insecurities, and let him know that was my favorite part about him.

Worked like a charm.

I moved closer so our knees touched. "*Andrew* feels like a strong name. Weighty. Important. Like you could see it on a dollar bill one day."

I dropped his secret ambitions like a lure. He inhaled quickly, staring at me like he was memorizing my face and this moment. Like I'd mentioned his most secret of dreams, the goals too big to even believe possible, and I believed in them.

Snap the lure tight and the boy was caught. "You're going to be a great man one day. I can already tell."

"I don't care about great," he said softly. "I just want to be a good one."

"Don't you think it's possible to be both?"

"I don't know." He tossed his hair and looked at the book he'd picked up. *The Ladies Guide to Plain Sewing.* He put it back on the shelf. "What do they say . . . Absolute power corrupts absolutely."

"Lord Acton," I said, naming the quote. "Though I like Shakespeare better. *I think the King is but a man, as I am. The violet smells to him as it does to me. The element shows to him as it does me. All his senses have but human conditions. His ceremonies laid by, in his nakedness he appears but a man.*" His cheeks flushed pink as I said the word *nakedness.* Which was why I included it. "I think power amplifies what is already there, and goodness can be amplified as well as vice depending on what you hold on to the tightest."

Then I blushed hard, because nakedness and holding on tight was perhaps too pointed a thing for an innocent girl to say.

"I hope you're right," he said. Not teasing me or following the baseness of what I was alluding to like Patch would have.

I smiled smile number two, the *go on* smile. "You're Rebecca's brother, right?"

He nodded. "Most people say that the other way around."

"That doesn't surprise me." I clamped my lips together and then shifted into a smile. "She certainly made quite the impression on me, sitting at my table unannounced."

"Well, you had art supplies." He huffed out a laugh. "My

sister thinks everything artistic belongs to her. She's colored in nearly every one of my textbooks."

I laughed softly and leaned into his shoulder. "I liked her very much."

"She really liked you too." The heat from his arm seeped into mine. "She'll be excited that I found out your name."

Rebecca had told me that Andrew was slow to catch on when a girl liked him, so I knew I had to be direct.

"Are you glad to know my name?" I pressed my shoulders together and glanced down, my cheeks pinking as I'd trained them to do. I licked my lips and looked up to him.

His knee began to wag, like he was an excited puppy. "Yeah," he said softly.

I smiled, and the rounds of Andrew's pupils widened.

"Would you like to help me find some books?" I asked. "What are you reading at the moment?"

"A great biography about President Hill. Did you know he was sick often as a child?"

"Really?"

He stood, and then offered me his hand to help me up. His palm was dry and steady, a little warm. I trusted him with my weight, and every trick I'd used had come from my training, but something was missing here.

I stood and adjusted my dress.

There weren't any sparks from our touch. When Patch grabbed my wrist, it was like my skin tingled.

But with Andrew, not a nerve lit up.

Which was fine, and completely to be expected, what with the pressure of this meeting, and with seeing Patch so recently. Feelings didn't go away that quickly, and they grew over time, so it wasn't anything worth panicking about.

It wasn't.

I followed Andrew as he spoke about what nonfiction title he was reading, very into biographies lately, and I should have picked up the conversation. I should have. This was my element.

But as we walked through the shelves, all I could think about was Patch lying in the round casing of a window as he read a book, and the way his hands brushed his brother's hair so gently as he lay against his chest.

"—historically, don't you think?" Andrew asked, and I realized I'd just zoned out completely as he described a book.

A book.

Was I *ever* in a heap of it?

I couldn't even think to lie. "Sorry. I'm . . ." *Use this, Elsie.* "I'm not feeling like myself."

He wasn't put off or insulted. Instead his eyes lit with concern. "That's okay. Heartbreak will do that."

I shrugged a little. "I didn't know him well enough for him to break my heart."

"What can I do?" His hands floundered, like he wanted to touch my shoulder but didn't dare.

I stepped closer. "Could you . . ." I pretended I lost my nerve.

He pushed his glasses up. "What is it?"

I glanced down and licked my lips, then looked up at him through my eyelashes. "Could you hug me? Please? It's just that I'm so far from home and . . ."

He stilled, his fingers fluttering, and his eyes searching like he was double-checking that I'd given him permission. And then he stepped closer with his arms held open. I leaned against his chest, and his arms wrapped me in close enough to him that I could hear his heart beating, his pulse quick where mine felt slow. He was shorter than Patch, softer too, and his arms were warm and comforting, but something was wrong. When I leaned back, his feet were pointing straight at me, while mine were pointing away.

I should feel sparks here, but he reminded me so much of my brother.

Loving Andrew was my path to mattering. My only chance to change his sister's future.

And I felt nothing.

No. I felt nothing yet.

He smelled like stories. Like old paper and clean dust. My absolute most favorite of smells. Surely that was the ground from which our love could build. I was nearly positive I found him attractive enough. Sparks weren't everything. And he needed help. He needed someone to help him feel confident, he needed kindness and guidance. I could change the world whispering into his ear. And he was a good man. They wouldn't have selected him if he wasn't. I wanted the life I could get with him. Honestly I did.

I could live my whole life behind him.

My hands broke into a cold sweat. And now my heartbeat sped up. Not with sparks, not with love, but with a surge of panic.

Andrew was everything I've hoped for, but it wasn't enough.

Priority one wasn't enough for me.

But if so, then what possibly was?

I pulled away and ran my fingers up my arm.

My gaze flitted down the line of the shelf to a piece of paper left on the floor discarded.

It was a hand-drawn picture of my face.

I let go of Andrew and crossed to pick it up.

It was Patch's drawing. But now the eyes had been crossed out with vicious black pen marks that sent a chill up my neck. I watched Patch stalk past the librarian's desk, his shoulders arched up to his ears, his steps furious. He grabbed his brother's wrist and yanked him out the front door without glancing back.

He must have dropped this here as he watched me hug the boy he's been asked to blackmail. The boy I said I didn't care about. The boy he would hate now.

"I should go," I said.

"Of course," Andrew answered. He watched the door. "Would you like me to walk you to your car?"

I turned.

He eyed the drawing. "I just want to make sure you're safe."

"Thank you," I said. "But I'll be fine. I can handle this."

"I'm sure you can."

"If you see him anywhere," I said quietly, "just stay away from him. Okay?"

"If he's a threat, I don't know if I should let you go."

Let me? I stared at the door and fought to keep a scowl from my face.

Andrew adjusted his vest. "Perhaps it'd be best to wait until he's gone?"

I flashed three fingers behind my back.

"Elsie, you ready to go?" Andrew stiffened, and I knew Mira was the one who answered my signal. "Oh, how are you, Andy? I didn't see you there."

Andy? The dossier said he didn't like that name.

"Mirabelle," Andrew said. She let out a playful scoff, and I gathered it was a shared joke.

"Elsie, you are taking forever," Greta said. Her hair combed out, but still a little grayer than its usual brassy blond. "How many books do you need?" I lowered my shoulders at Greta's kindness here; she was propping me up as a book reader, even when I hadn't played that strategy well enough at all. She made eyes at Andrew. "Oh hey there, good looking."

Andrew pressed up his glasses. "Greta. You all know each other?"

"We do," I said, taking a step away from him. "Thank you so much for cheering me up, Andrew. But we do really need to go. Mrs. Brown was expecting us home a half hour ago."

He looked at all of us. "Wait. You're staying with Mrs. Brown?"

"We are. Do you know her?"

"Not really, but I know her niece. Bea?" he asked.

Mira pulled Bea from behind the shelf where she'd waited. Bea shot Mira a look, and then she grinned wide and waved a little awkwardly. "Hi, Andrew." She hugged a recipe book to her chest.

"Oh. Wow. Hello." He glanced us all over, each girl he'd met and made a connection with now looking up at him like he wasn't in any trouble for flirting with her friends.

It couldn't be any worse than when he thought he was flirting with sisters or cousins. This wasn't his first time set up like this. Did he really think this was what everyone went through?

"Bea is one of my dearest friends," I answered finally. "She's the kindest person I've ever met. All of us girls from finishing school are staying with her for the summer."

"The whole summer?" His eyebrows lowered, and for a second his gaze flicked inward, like he was making plans, or mentally penciling my name into them.

Or our names.

I smiled my very best smile. "I've a feeling it's going to be a good one." Then I shifted into smile number three, slightly bashful, very interested. I stepped closer, taking up all his focus. "Thank you for your kindness, Andrew. And for the handkerchief. I'll find a way to return it to you." I could wash it and return it with a sprig of flowers and a note. Or . . .

"I'm sure we'll see each other around," he said. "It's not that big of a town."

I put on a smile and tried not to react that I'd left him the perfect opening to ask me out on a date, to declare me his favorite in front of all my friends, but he didn't take it.

My smile didn't alter. "Of course."

Mira took my arm in hers, and I locked elbows with Greta on the other side, and then the four of us walked in lockstep, our hips twisting our skirts, and when I reached the door, I glanced back. He watched us go. He lifted one hand in a wave. I bit my bottom lip and left quickly.

As we approached Mrs. Brown's car where Iris waited leaning against the driver's-side door, I passed Patch's drawing over to Greta.

She touched her lips. "I'm sorry. I had no idea he was violent. I thought—"

Iris took the drawing from Greta, and her eyes narrowed. She flashed a signal with four fingers, and Spinsters crossed from benches, or left empty baby strollers to join her. "Don't worry, Elsie. We'll double the watch on him."

"I don't think he's dangerous," I said. "I think he's just hurt."

"Worth watching anyway. And after what you've said about his bosses? A hurt boy can pull a trigger for something worse."

"That's not who he is. I know him—"

"—You've known him for one night," Mira said. "You don't know him."

But I did. At least I thought I did. I didn't know the boy who would cross out my eyes like this.

"You know how to handle good men," Iris said. "Trust me. I can handle the bad ones."

"I do trust you."

Iris shot a look at Greta. "Don't sneak past me again, this isn't just your future you're risking."

She left to speak with the pair of Spinsters, who scattered back into hiding behind women's invisible work.

"You did an excellent job," Bea said. "Andrew seemed very taken with you."

"I'm sorry," I said. And then I shook my head, because I'm not sure that I was. Was I supposed to be?

Mira unlocked her arm from mine. She still wouldn't look at me.

As I left, I replayed the entire conversation, the way Andrew's knee brushed against mine, the way he stared at me when I told him he was good enough for his most secret dreams, the way Patch looked in that windowsill with his little brother.

And how mad he must have been to cross out my eyes when I knew all he wanted was for me to see him.

By the time we'd filed into the car and Mrs. Brown and my friends were waiting for me to give my full report, I had lost my words again.

I'd lost them on a windowsill in a library.

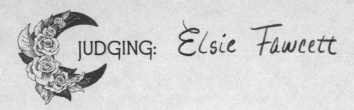

JUDGING: *Elsie Fawcett*

CATEGORY: First blush

Amount of Bloom:

Four florets, three soft, one lingering

Quality:

Firmness lacking, stoutness

Physical appearance at time of judging:

Appealing, well groomed. Slightly off balance but used to good effect.

Creative arrangement:

Well-matched, playful after a distracted and intense beginning. Impressive exit. Five-second reaction.

Faults:

Visible pest (watch for infestation)

TOTAL SCORE: 19 out of 20

Judge initials: MB

CHAPTER TWELVE

My friends were just outside my bedroom door, but I didn't want to leave. If I went out there, I'd have to cheer for them, I'd have to stuff down any feelings of jealousy or hurt, or guilt for the hurt that I caused. But in my room I could dream for myself. In my room alone, I could want this for myself, without worrying about taking it away from the girls who I loved.

In my room, perhaps I could finally figure out what it was that I wanted for me.

I found solace in the books on my shelves. Emily Dickinson knew that success had a song and a sting and a freedom too. Lowell, and Yeats, and Cummings created familiar rhythms that calmed my anxious heart. I held a copy of *The Dial* to my chest, and at once I was no longer alone. My poets understood themselves, and if I could spy glimpses of my own soul inside their words, then maybe they would have understood me too. Maybe they would look in my unpolished face and tell me I hadn't done this all wrong.

Once armed by my author friends, I read my mother's telegraph and penned one they'd send back, asking for the rest of my books to be sent up, and any clothes or powders she deemed helpful. I needed my mother's guidance if I was going to live my mother's life.

More noises came from downstairs, but no one ventured up and I still didn't feel ready to leave. Instead I turned the gramophone on to make noise of my own. If I was going to be a footnote in Andrew's story, then I would make them type as many sentences as I could get. I wanted every comma. I wanted every stanza, and I was grateful for this chance.

I was.

I nestled into a large chair with seven different books perched on the floor in front of me. I began my preparations by studying history. I pulled out the society's book and set to work while nibbling on the tea and toast Mrs. Brown had sent up when the woman took my note to be telegraphed.

I loved the history of our society. Those women were my heroes. Abigail Adams held her young son's hand and walked into battle, she made herself a spectator to death, to war, wise enough to let her child picnic above it. Her dear friend Mercy Otis Warren was a historian and a visionary, whose voice recorded a history that included the women and people often cut from it. Phyllis Wheatley came to

America chained on a boat and wrote poems about God and a life that was forced upon her and freedom members of Congress didn't think she should have. Phyllis's perspective and brilliance became the eyes of our body. Anna Smith Strong, a mother of seven, whose work as a spy for General George Washington influenced the tide of war, until those skills were thought forgotten and lost in child rearing, but instead she developed our codes. Other women brought fashion and beauty tricks. Some brought strength and compassion. Some brought anger, and how to keep going in the face of it. If these women hadn't met, if they hadn't joined together, I couldn't imagine the way the world would look.

As the society was forming, another woman, Penelope Barker, held a party and convinced the ladies of her acquaintance to boycott British tea. The media outcry was ugly. They called them harlots and cross-eyed and ugly. Men could rebel and be called patriots, but women rebelling was something to be belittled.

It was something to be feared.

After Penelope Barker's tea party, Abigail and her sisterhood knew that this society would need to be secret. Because as soon as you stand up, they knocked you back into your place. So we used our beauty as a shield and a cover. We hid behind the femininity and gentleness Abigail preached to others, but we stood up against injustice as she did too. We could be strong and fierce, soft and fragile. We could contain multitudes.

It was a miracle they ever agreed on anything. It was a miracle that distance and race and the ease of letting others fight for themselves didn't silence them. It was a miracle that they stood together at all. If they hadn't, I couldn't even imagine where we'd be. They were best when they listened to one another. Best when they worked side by side.

They wouldn't recognize what the society had become. I wondered if they would still be proud of us. I wondered what they would want for us in the future.

What would they think of the storm in my thoughts? What would they want for me?

I found Mira in the garage separate from Mrs. Brown's house, tucked behind a row of flowers. She sat on a stool, her short hair tucked behind her ears, a streak of grease darkening her cheek, as she searched for something inside a metal toolbox.

I leaned against the doorframe and smiled before I balled up a rag from the ground and threw it at her face.

She startled so high and let out such a scream that I couldn't help but laugh.

"Jeepers creepers. You scared me to bits." Mira pressed her hand to her chest.

I cocked my head to the side. "And here I thought you were fearless."

"No one's fearless." She sniffed. "Turns out I'm afraid of promise breakers."

She turned back to her engine, picking up some shining metal part and wiping it with the rag I'd tossed at her.

I didn't know what to say. I was in a good position to win Andrew, so now my only goal was to fix the things I'd broken between my friends. Knowing Mira, she wasn't waiting for an apology, and she wouldn't accept one if I gave one to her.

She reached for a socket set and offered me an icy shoulder.

She'd need a sacrifice. I ran my fingers up my arm. "You want to go break the law with me?"

She stilled, met my eye. Then her face broke into a grin. "Yeah, I'm in."

"We might need to steal a car."

"I said I was in. No need to sweeten the pot."

I let out a laugh.

Her eyes lit up. "Oh, and I know just the car."

"I thought you might. Let's grab our Bea and go off on one of those adventures we used to take. I need to clear my thoughts."

"And your conscience."

I looked her straight in the eye. "That too."

It was as close to an apology as Mira would accept from me. She shoved me and then ran forward with a laugh, like it was her way of saying I was forgiven. We raced, because anything with Mira ends up being a race, from the garage, up the front steps, and into the house.

"Watch where you're going," Mr. Brown said as we very nearly bumped into him on the steps.

"Sorry!" we called together. Mira stuck her behind out and cut me off up the steps, not that she needed to, and then we thundered into Bea and Mira's shared room, where Bea sat on the floor cutting fabric for May Kits with Iris's help, stitching the gauze while Greta plucked her eyebrows in a small hand mirror.

Iris stood quickly. "What's wrong?"

"Nothing," I said, my voice winded.

"Who wants to go on an adventure?" Mira said with her hands on both hips.

"Oh no," Bea said. "This will not be legal."

Iris grinned.

Greta squealed. "Can I come?"

Mira and I looked at each other.

"I've never admitted it," Greta said, "but I've always wanted to go with you when you go on these side trips."

"Of course you can," Bea said.

"Great. I'll go change my clothes."

She left the room, and I sighed.

"I'm sorry," Bea said quickly. "But we couldn't just leave her here."

"I think that we could," Mira said.

I laughed once. "Bea's right," I said.

"Thank you."

"And I'm sorry again that I smiled at Andrew during your turn, Bea."

"It's okay."

I stepped closer. "It's not."

Bea wouldn't let me apologize. "I mean it. I'm not bothered by it. I'd rather you flirt over me than treat me like the baby all the time."

"We don't—" Mira started.

"—You do! And don't get me started on your promise to help me win."

I opened my mouth and looked at Mira. "I didn't tell her."

Mira shook her head quickly.

We both turned to Iris, who we'd asked to keep it secret. She shrugged. "Bea's bribes taste better than yours do."

Bea looked down her nose at us and pursed her lips. "Throw whatever you want at me, ladies. I can still beat it."

My heart warmed. "Ah, look how smug she is," I cooed.

"We raised a monster. I'm so proud," Mira said.

"Stop it."

We grinned at one another, but then we stopped pushing her.

"I can't wait to show you all what I've found," Mira whispered. "She's a dream."

"Is this like when you found that airplane?" Bea asked.

Mira's face grew soft. "My sweet bird."

"Your stolen bird," Iris said.

"My neighbor's heirs never came to claim it. She's mine." Mira grinned. "At least until they do."

"I will not get in a plane again," Bea said. "I draw the line at possible death."

"But felonies are fine now?" I clarified, as Greta rushed

back into the room wearing the same skirt but a new simple white blouse with a scalloped collar. "Greta, get that in writing. Bea just agreed to commit a felony."

Bea's eyes bulged. "I did not."

"No take backs," Greta said with a grin she threw my way for including her in our joking.

"Is stealing a car a felony?" Mira asked.

"It's a *car*? We're stealing a car?" Iris laughed out loud, and all of us shushed her.

Mira's eyes twinkled. "It's Mr. Brown's car. Maybe we shouldn't shout." Then she disappeared out the bedroom door and we had to follow her into the hall.

Bea grumbled. "Maybe we should just ask him."

Greta wrapped her arm in the crook of Iris's. "Where's the fun in that?"

"I don't know," Bea answered. "I find not going to prison loads of fun."

"Maybe we should leave a note." I could feel my face heating. "And we must be mindful of the law; the last thing any of us need—"

Mira interrupted me. "What we need is to be young and free and alive."

She was right. There was a reason why all my stories ended with a happy ever after. No one reads the chapters after the I do. The story ended with the closing of the veil.

You clip a rose before it fully blooms.

We sneaked out of the house with too-loud steps and away from the garage I'd expected as our final destination.

Instead we crept behind the house and into the wooded countryside. As we ducked under the branches of the trees our steps grew as quiet as they'd been trained to be, but our giggles were unmuffled in the afternoon breeze. Mira led us deeper through the brush. The way was long, each step settling into a rhythm as I followed my chattering friends through the trees to an ivy-covered, dilapidated outbuilding that might have once been a barn or a large shed.

"Oh look, Bea," Greta said when we finally stopped. "It's your house."

"Be kind," I said.

"Jokes on you, Greta," Bea said. "This is actually much bigger than my house."

Iris laughed, and Bea stuck out her tongue.

Mira pulled a hairpin from behind her bangs and fiddled with a rusty lock on a painted door. She grumbled under her breath as she adjusted the pins inside. The lock snapped open, and we all clapped while Mira took a bow.

"And we are sure this is a good idea?" Bea asked with a wince

We crept inside. Mira smiled at her. "Just you wait for my next trick."

The inside of the outbuilding was cleaner than I expected, filled with five or six different vehicles, including the bread truck, Mrs. Brown's sensible town car, a Model T with a large trunk strapped on the back, and in the shadows at the edge of the building, under a protective blanket that Mira pulled off reverently, a glittering white convertible with polished chrome and curves that were meant for a woman.

"Hot cha," I said. "Swanky."

"The Duesenberg Model J, with Italian leather interior," Mira said with reverence.

"Oh my," Greta said, "this is just like the car Georgia Hale drove in to the premiere of *The Gold Rush*."

Bea glanced over her shoulder. "Why would they have this car here?"

"This is not a car, this is a Duesenberg Model J," Mira said, running her hands up the curved fenders. "She is my child." She grinned herself goofy. "My beautiful, shining child."

"Mr. Brown does not have this kind of money," Greta said. "This car has got to belong to the society."

"Okay, this is fun and all, but are you sure we should take her?" Bea asked, her panicking voice back. "This has got to be the most expensive vehicle the society owns. This is the priority one of cars, and there's a reason why they locked that door."

Mira did not pull away from the car. She sniffed the leather.

I pressed my hands together. Bea was right. "We could get in a lot of trouble here," I said. "If they catch us we could lose our chance at this mission."

"We'll be careful," Greta said.

No one moved forward. This was a rebellion above any

we'd taken. This wasn't like the time Mira started that air-plane but it didn't have enough fuel to make it down the run-way. This could get us kicked out. Not only if we got caught.

If Iris told.

And there was reason she would. I didn't want to risk her future, just for an adventure.

Daylight streamed across Iris's brow as she looked at each of us, probably calculating how anxious we all were and how much we needed a moment of freedom, versus the risk. She looked back at me and sighed. "We stay out of the city lim-its so no one will spot us."

"Really?"

Iris's grinned and tension in my jaw I didn't know I was carrying released.

Mira whooped and jumped into the front passenger seat without opening the door. She jangled a set of shining sil-ver keys and then turned to me. "Elsie's going to drive."

I sucked in a breath. "What? This is your baby. You—"

"—I believe in you too," Mira said firmly, no joke or spar-kle in her eyes. "You gotta know that."

I glanced at Bea.

"We're here for you, Elsie," Bea said. "And because of you."

"I'm sorry," I said for real. "I never want to hurt you girls."

"Don't be sorry," Greta said. "We all know how messy this can get."

"Are you sorry?" Mira asked Greta.

"Whatever for?" she said, and I honestly believed that she'd forgotten what she did by inviting Patch to the library.

I envied her. I couldn't seem to forget it.

Iris pulled open the barn doors, the squeaking hinges almost overtaking the sound of Mira and Greta squabbling over Greta's sabotage as they climbed in. I blocked it out. I couldn't think of Patch right now. I just couldn't.

I sat in the front seat, my bare hands running over the polished steering wheel. I twisted the keys, and the engine purred beneath me, strong and gentle as a wild animal.

Mira moaned, and I giggled in embarrassment.

I drove forward, revving a little for the fun of it.

Mira climbed over the seat and then sat on the chassis, with Iris and Bea clutching her calves so she wouldn't blow away. She raised her hands and whooped. Greta climbed into the front seat and wrapped her hair in a scarf and slipped on some sparkling shades.

I shifted into first gear and off we went, out of the building and down a pebbled road.

Second gear was heaven, but third and then fourth gear were power personified, and my toes pushed those pedals; it was my hands on the wheel. We galloped our way down that dirt road, laughing and shouting and squealing at the top of our lungs once we were out of hearing distance.

We might have got caught for screaming, but it was hard to hear over the wind rushing in our faces, and since we screamed right into the wind, it was likely the wind would swallow the sound anyway. I yelled like I wanted to be heard. I'd found my voice and it was made of thunder, and if I could generate enough noise I know I'd wake the cloudless sky and start a downpour.

But only sunlight answered our voices, sunlight that warmed my shoulders. The country road smelled like leaves and farm animals and freedom. Delicious like forbidden fruit. Like jazz music, or kissing a stranger.

Rebellion. My mother still didn't know how to drive, so she didn't know what this freedom felt like. She stayed home alone, waiting for my father to remember her enough to take her outside the house he'd abandoned, but my future would be different.

The wind washed away my dollface, and I knew that whatever future was coming would find me with my hands on the wheel.

No matter what choices were coming, I would make them for me.

And I would make them with my sisters by my side.

Sisters

Perhaps I'd been waiting
for a boy to hold my hand
when I simply needed to
hold my sister's hand a little tighter.

Maybe
kindness
and cake
and recipes
and forgiveness
and hands on shoulders
were stronger than a thousand kisses.
Stronger than a thousand wows.
Stronger than the smell of libraries.
Maybe sisters were enough.
Maybe sisters were more.

CHAPTER THIRTEEN

After, as we relaxed in Greta's room while we assembled fresh May Kits, we made a plan for the big party. It would be the next time we'd see Andrew, each of us done up to our best, each of us pushing to get that first kiss. The first kiss was like a Primary Election. It wouldn't be over, but once Andrew kissed a girl, things would be different. There'd be a front-runner, and if we couldn't find a way to create a kiss of our own, then the rest of us would work on support, and angle to snag one of Andrew's friends instead.

"So how do we play this?" I asked. "This is already complicated, so I think it's best we go in with a plan. There are several targets in play."

"Johnson is awful handsome," Mira said to Bea.

Bea nodded fiercely. "And a senator's wife is nothing to sneeze at."

"His family has loads of money," Greta said. "I'm sure your life would be all fancy cars and exciting vacations."

A scissor cut through flannel.

None of us would give up our chance at Andrew.

Mira watered one of her plants. "And Harper."

"Also handsome," I said. My mouth went dry. "Pass me some flannel won't you."

Bea held strips of flannel for Greta to pass down, but Greta just lay back on her bed with a hand mirror and a tweezer, plucking any wild eyebrow hairs. Bea sighed and then tossed the flannel stack, the strips separating as they fell to the floor.

I helped her gather a few and handed one to Mira. "Why aren't you helping us?" I asked Greta. "Your cycle starts next week."

She stared at herself in the mirror. "I prefer Kotex."

"At six cents a napkin?" Bea asked.

"And it's always so embarrassing when there's a male clerk." I focused on matching the fabric to its identical pattern. "I'd rather buy fabric and use the society's extra bandages."

"Besides, Kotex is far too large," Mira said

"I don't have that problem." I grinned, glad my large behind was good for something.

"I don't have that problem either," Iris answered from her seat, and Bea snorted. I smiled softly, carefully in case she'd spoken from a place of pain, but Iris didn't seem upset about it.

Mira lifted the May Kit in her hand and studied it. "You know, there's a business here," she said absentmindedly. "A sanitary napkin delivery service. If you think about it, there's . . . what did they say at the last meeting? Around thirty thousand women between thirteen and forty-five in the US? And if each woman has thirteen periods a year, uses eleven or so napkins a cycle, then each woman would use 4,576 during her menstrual life."

I grabbed a notebook to write down her figures. There were too many numbers for me to follow without taking notes.

"And even if you could only capture a third of that market, that's still the possibility of . . ." She paused as she did the math. "That's 45 million products needed. If you could find a way to decrease the costs while maintaining quality it would certainly be viable, and you could provide jobs to local women, perhaps paying delivery fees in free napkins."

"No. Women should always be paid for their work," Iris said.

"And not all women have periods," I insisted, "and not all people who have periods are women."

"Right. *Right.* You're both one hundred percent correct." Mira sat taller. "Our numbers would have to account for that. But if we kept the delivery area local, it could be a way of creating small incomes for local communities. Better hygiene, and freedom to leave the home, build community. It's—"

"Disgusting," Greta said. "Do you really want your name associated with menstrual blood?"

Bea tugged one of her braids. "I don't know how voters would feel about a president's wife owning a company of feminine napkins."

"Oh." Mira's posture fell.

I could see this for her. Just like I knew Rebecca would make a great architect. It was like Matchmaking. I think this idea could grow into her greatest love.

"How funny, I'd forgotten that might become my future," Mira said despondently.

I wouldn't give up my scheme to match her and this idea. "But there is definitely something there, Mira," I said in a soft voice. "You should talk to Mrs. Brown. Maybe even bring up the idea to the Matron Circle. Perhaps this is something the society could help make happen? I'm sure they could use more revenue beyond our dues. And we're always looking for ways to expand membership and loyalty bases."

"That's an idea," Mira said, some of her excitement missing from her voice.

It was clear she wanted to do this on her own. This was her puzzle to figure out, and maybe it was wrong of me to try to give it to the society.

My thoughts were blustery. "Do you really think we can't have a job?" I still hadn't reached out to that editor, though I kept that card on me at all times.

"A job is fine. Education is fine," Greta answered. "Starting a business, however?"

"Why not?" I asked.

The room turned silent. "Yeah, why not?" Iris lowered her scissors.

Bea bit her lip. "I guess it might be intimidating to male voters."

"And women themselves might not like it," Greta said.

"Why?" I asked again. "I guess they might be jealous or—"

Greta put down her mirror. "No, it's not jealousy. There is a status quo, Elsie. The men rule their businesses, and the women rule their houses. And as the future wives of powerful men we need to reflect that."

I closed my eyes. "Then why were we given our brains?" I muttered quietly.

I swore I didn't mean them to hear. I would never have dared say it out loud before I'd claimed my own name or found the thunder in my voice.

"It's challenging to run a household, to rear children," Bea answered. "It will take every aspect of your brilliance to do it well. And it's important work. Just because it's not a man's work doesn't mean it's not valuable."

Greta nodded hard. "You're devaluing thousands of years of influential women."

"I'm not." I dropped my shoulders. "I'm asking a question. Not one of our lessons has taught us this. No one said we couldn't have dreams, or seek for influence beyond our own families." They both sat back. "Why does asking this question strike such a nerve in us?"

"It feels dangerous," Bea said after a second. "There are threats everywhere, and the society keeps such a difficult balance already."

"I think we've been too cautious. I think it's right for us to ask for more. Why aren't we demanding that the society should be giving us what they give our husbands?"

That's what I wanted. I wanted the society to see me as a person worth helping. I wanted my dreams to matter as much as my brother's did, as much as my husband's will.

"Growing up, people always asked me what career I'd want," Iris said. "They'd talk to me about college, opportunities for training, and really listened to my goals. And then once I transitioned to the point of passing, it was like those questions just stopped. Less people asked my opinion, I was no longer looked to for answers. People looked at me because they thought I was pretty. Which I am, obviously. But I think they forget that we're more than just pretty things to look at."

Greta shook her head so sharply, it was like she'd shaken her brain to ensure my words didn't take root inside. "You're wrong. You both are devaluing our whole lives. A wife is a partner to her husband. A creator of children, a builder of communities."

She didn't see how our position within the society was intended to prop up men? "A helper."

"A partner," Greta insisted. "You're young. You're still

hurting because of what I did, inviting Patch to your meetup, and I'm sorry I did that. But as the oldest of us, I have to tell you what a holy privilege it is to be loved, to be cared for, to bring life and nurture those children. The ability to mold our children is a monumental task that will change our society for good or for ill for generations, and to denigrate that into nothing? It's irresponsible."

She spoke like the words she was saying were written by someone else.

"Greta's right," Bea said. "There's a balance. We've got to think of the abused wives and children we've relocated. The society needs to be kept secret in order to protect them. If we seek for more power, the men will stop us. They will destroy us."

"I'd like to see them try," Iris said with a confidence I didn't feel.

"I wouldn't." Was Bea right? Patch's bosses were already watching Andrew, and we were hiding in his ricochet area. All those angry men we've silenced and stolen from might find their anger if we showed off what we'd done.

I've read the articles about the suffragettes, seen the comics about women. I've seen men *and* women hate any woman who seemed to be seeking power, when that same ambition was celebrated in a man. I knew that, and my storm inside me didn't care. I wanted more. I wanted it to be fair. I wanted to be remembered.

But not for breaking this society.

"If your oaths aren't enough, Elsie," Greta said, "you

can always leave. Go to college, start that business, run for office. I'll be sure to clip the cartoon drawing of you and remember you back when your teeth fit inside your mouth."

They were right. Perhaps I was devaluing the work because it was a woman's. Perhaps I should have let it go.

But I couldn't. The thunder in my voice was too loud to silence. I had value that wasn't quantifiable by which man I stood next to. They were wrong. I knew it.

"Our dreams matter as much as the dreams of the men we'd marry," I said with fervor. "If Andrew wanted to start a business that would do half as much good as Mira's brilliant idea, you know the society would support him in it. You know we would. So why are you pressing Mira to forget her own idea?

"That's not what our founders demanded when they started this society. That's not what we do for women of different romantic notions, or races. If you were standing in that room back then would you tell them they needed to be silent and allow their husbands to speak for them? No! What is the point of representation if we can't dream? Mira, do you want to do this?"

Mira startled and then nodded. "It sounds like the greatest adventure ever."

"Then you do it. And we'll help. We'll convince the society to support you. They will understand. We have the power to make changes in our society, and our society has the power to make changes in the world. And if you're not willing to do that, Greta, then *you* are the one who is break-ing your oaths."

"Fine." Greta sniffed. "You go right ahead, Mira. What's one less in competition for Andrew?"

Mira picked up a hairbrush and started combing her hair. She'd turned away a little, so we couldn't see her eyes, like something was wrong.

"There's nothing saying she can't still have him," Bea insisted. "We can have dreams *and* love."

And that was why I loved her. "Exactly."

"Except . . ." Mira closed her eyes and lowered her hair-brush as we turned to her. "I don't want him."

I didn't reply.

Mira looked at me. "I don't know. I guess I've always liked the challenge of it, and I loved all you girls, and when it was Andrew, when I thought I wanted it, that I'd finally met someone who would meet my high standards. I've always loved reading romantic stories, and I want this big life, so I thought one day everything would click. I thought that attraction would just come one day. But I don't want him."

"How come?" Bea asked.

"I don't really want anyone like that. I care about peo-ple like siblings, but I don't feel romantic love. You girls always talk about how handsome the men all were, and I guess in a way I could see it aesthetically, but I've never really felt attraction." She gestured with her hands, and her voice grew in volume. "I don't feel attraction. I don't have a need to kiss *anybody*. I fall asleep thinking about engines, not ball gowns or bedrooms. I'm not physically attracted to men or women or anyone." She swallowed. "I love the society, I love what we do, but even my ambitions aren't big enough to keep trying to pretend to be someone I'm not. And we know Andrew wants a physical relationship. We know it, and I don't. I don't want to fake physical attraction. I don't want a false life."

"We won't make you choose one," Greta said.

Iris touched her arm. "What you're saying is more common than you think."

"It is?"

"Do you think you might be asexual?" I asked. "Or maybe aromantic?"

Mira shook her head. "I'm not a Spinster, though. I've always liked boys."

Iris's voice was gentle. "I'm a Spinster, and I like boys."

"That's different."

"And so maybe are you."

Mira's head kept shaking, she lifted her hand over her lips as she processed.

"There are a lot of people I'd love to introduce you to who feel the same way," Iris said. "They have amazing lives without romantic love. And some find a romantic connection without physical attraction. And some live happily in platonic relationships. And that's not even mentioning all my friends outside of the society. There's a big world out there, and so many more ways to live than we're told."

Mira barked out a laugh, or maybe it was a cry. "That knocks my socks off," she said with emotion. "Asexual. Huh. I need . . . Can you get me some more information?"

"I have some books you can read," I said.

Bea threw her arms around her. "We love you, Mira."

"You're not broken," Iris said. She held both of Mira's hands in hers and leveled down. Mira squeezed her eyes shut.

I put my arm around Mira's shoulders. "You know I love you, and this is a part of you, so I love this too."

Mira scrunched up her face, and then she lifted the hairbrush like it was a weapon. "If you girls make me cry I will hit you."

I laughed. We gave her space. She didn't always like to be touched.

"I always thought I was the only one," Mira said after a second.

Iris shook her head. "There are lots of people who feel this way."

"But I . . ." She wiped her nose. "I don't want to train with the Spinsters. I'm not really a fighter."

"Says the girl who just threatened to hit us with a hairbrush," Greta inserted.

"I'm a threaten-to-hit-you girl, not an actually-going-to-hit-you girl. There's a big difference, and you know it."

"Says the girl who put me in a headlock," Greta said in the same tone.

Mira lifted one finger, but I didn't wait for her to get lost in a tangent. My brain was positively humming. "You don't have to join the Spinsters. There are plenty of queer people in different designations. And besides you know the society could always use help as a mechanic, or a driver."

Bea nodded. "I'm sure they'd even be willing to send you to school for it."

"And you've got your business idea too." I grinned.

Her face lit up. "Engines every day and helping women? That sound like my own version of heaven." As she turned to us, her smile disappeared. "But let's keep this secret for now."

"What?" Bea asked.

"Why?" Iris and I asked at the same time.

"I don't want to leave you. I want to see you all settled and happy, and I'll do everything in my power to help get you there."

Greta bit the inside of her cheek. "But you're not going to claim Andrew or Johnson or even Harper?"

"No, I won't be taking your men." Mira made a face.

"When you tell anyone is up to you," I said.

"Of course it is," Bea agreed.

"I'd like to keep it to just us for right now," Mira said. "I want to know all the pieces of this before I let anyone else into this part of me."

"That makes perfect sense," Iris said. "It can sometimes take a little while to make sure the labels fit."

Mira nodded, and it was like a weight had been lifted from her shoulders, or a light added to her eyes. She knew who she was, and what she wanted. And the society I loved would support her.

So maybe I could find a way to get them to support me. Maybe my dreams could matter too.

Maybe it was time for me to open my eyes and figure out what it was that I actually wanted. And then go after it. Because I won't be going after it alone. "From now on," I said, "our lives matter as much as theirs do. And our dreams can happen if we support each other. It's our job to help each other. It's our job not to stand in each other's way. So the question I want us asking is not, What dress would Andrew like me best in, or How will this flirtation strategy work, but *What is it that I want to do with my one life?* What is it that I want for me?"

"Absolutely," Iris said emphatically as I sat back, tired as I always was after a good speech, and I looked at my friends. Mira's eyes were shining, and Bea's gaze was steady. And Iris nodded like she was ready to take up right where I left off.

"The society already supports our identities," Iris said. "Why not our ambitions?"

"Why does this world belong to the men anyhow?" Mira asked.

"And why are we giving everything to a society that supports men and not us?" Bea whispered.

Greta rolled her eyes again and looked into her hand mirror; then as we sat in silence, the mirror drooped and she met my eye. "Maybe there's more than one way we can matter. Maybe there is more than one way we can make our families proud."

For a second, a crest of panic ran up my neck. My words had just convinced my friends to risk something dangerous. If the society didn't change with us, where would they be? What was I asking them to give up?

The rules had always kept me safe. Small, yes, but safe. The thought of breaking free from them was terrifying.

But maybe it was time we started making our own rules.

I nodded to them all, then I said one more thing.

"And maybe it's time we stop saying maybe."

They told me

I would be a shadow
of the statue I would have to build.
But they never questioned if Andrew resented
being clay.
Or if the light that warms my shoulders as I build
Makes shadows disappear.

What if the artist could shine as brightly
as the statue?
Or what if we pulled all the statues down
And make every person build themselves.

CHAPTER FOURTEEN

They dressed us to go on a date when we were ready to go to war.

Pearls at my neck and dripping from my ears, my curls perfectly placed, my lips bowed. Each of us sitting on kitchen chairs in Mira and Bea's room as Beauty Makers made us their canvas.

Mrs. Brown was ready first, looking tall and fine in her silks and curls. She cleared her throat, and we looked over.

"Not to put any undue pressure on you for this outing—"

"Because priority one isn't enough?" Mira interrupted with a grin.

Mrs. Brown was not amused. "But whichever one of you claims the first kiss will become an official suitor. And that girl has just received an invitation from the Matron Circle to have tea next Saturday."

We erupted into excited chatter. Even the Beauty Makers put up their brushes.

Mrs. Brown sat carefully on Bea's bed. "The front-runner and I will be invited to speak with the Matron Circle, and if they approve of the match, one of you will begin your mentorship with the line of First Ladies."

A mentorship. A chance to speak with our future leadership, a chance to speak and have influence, and to make sure the decisions our society makes are based on what is good for the individual as well as the man.

And all we had to do was earn the first kiss.

It had to be me. It had to.

Still, after we'd decided that our lives didn't have to depend on a man to carry us, it made the pressure of this so much lighter. No one cried. No one stressed if the Beauty Makers chose something we didn't like to wear, and we didn't fight when we decided how we were going to balance a flirtation with Johnson and Harper as we each took our turns with Andrew. Tonight the rules were looser; each of us would get a chance to push our relationship as far as possible before someone broke in to steal our own turn. It should feel like a race, or a rumble, but I trusted that we would support one another.

We weren't fighting for a chance to matter. Not really. Because we all knew that we mattered without a boy to prove it.

We knew our future was ours to claim.

I slipped my grandmother's hair clips behind my ears

while we snacked on Bea's scones and listened to the music Mira played on the gramophone. Even Greta loaned out her fancy scientific perfume, and as we rubbed our wrists together and then behind our necks, Mira and I both baaed like sheep and then collapsed in a pile of giggles, not worrying about wrinkling our dresses.

Then we stood together in front of the mirror, each of us curled and polished and shining, and each of us looking into our own eyes in the mirror like we were looking at *someone* worth seeing, not *something* worth seeing.

When night came, the crescent moon lifted like a spotlight that shone on our bare shoulders. Mrs. Brown and her husband were driving their own car, but before they pulled away she offered the sparkling keys. Mira snagged them in her gloved hands

"I'm driving!"

"It's a . . ." Mrs. Brown startled. "Don't you need to know which car?"

Ha. "Um . . ." Mira looked at me with wide eyes before she turned and pretended we hadn't stolen the car already. "I'll figure it out, I'm sure." She walked straight to the Duesenberg. "Oh, my sweet beautiful child"—I smacked her arm and she looked over—"that I've just met now for the first time."

"How did it get dirt on the rims?" Mrs. Brown said. "I swear we had it washed."

I turned away so they wouldn't see me trying to hold back a snort laugh.

"What a beautiful car," Mr. Brown said. "Whose is it?"

Greta smiled. "It's mine of course." She glanced over as Mira glared. "But I'll let Mira drive. This once."

"Ah. Well. Good. Do you need directions?" Mr. Brown said, as if we hadn't made the plans ourselves.

"We'll follow you," Mira said. Mr. and Mrs. Brown walked to their own car with their hands clasped gently. They both looked so fine in their finest clothes. And despite the lies we kept from him, they seemed so well suited and happy with each other.

I glanced back at the large house. This life the society was trying to give me was a good one. I think I'd be happy if Andrew chose me. It wasn't just the life or the power I could get with him. Love stories were magical, and while I'd not seen a happy marriage in my own home, I couldn't help but think of all the weddings I'd attended, and the smiles of my friends. Andrew was a good man. He was smart and kind and genuinely caring. Winning his love wouldn't be a bad thing, I know it wouldn't. This might be my happily ever after. If only I knew if I could fall in love with him. One touch of a hand wasn't a good test to see if we had sparks. Maybe without the pressure of needing to win this, I could test whether I wanted it. Tonight I could really test us as a couple. If I could just get Andrew to kiss me, then everything would be clear. And then I'd earn that meeting with the Matron Circle.

Maybe belonging to that circle of powerful women was

my new dream. Maybe that and real love would be enough for me.

It was definitely a safer goal than the thought that kept whispering in my ear.

That maybe the name on that future ballot could be mine . . .

Mira turned to me. "How would you feel if we took the top down?"

"You'll—you'll mess up Bea's hair," Greta spluttered, finally realizing what tactic to take to influence Mira's opinions, though I'm sure the only hair she was concerned about was her own perfect corkscrew waves.

"We'll take it down on the way home," I said, mollifying Mira. "It'll be so nice after we've sweat off all this makeup."

"It might get chilly," Iris said as she slipped into the back seat, her dress sparkling and full of fringe and her eyes perfectly shaded. She looked stunning, and I couldn't help but notice that one of the Beauty Makers had spent a considerable amount of his attention on her. "I don't want anyone to get sick."

"At least one of us will be warm from a kiss," Bea said. Her painted red lips curled into a smile. We grew quiet. As much as we were united now, we also were pretty competitive, and it was like Bea's words had signaled the start of our favorite sport. While we knew we would survive not winning, I know each of us would still do our best to snag that kiss first.

"It might be me," Iris said. "That Harper fellow is quite handsome."

Mira started giving Iris tips on how to charm Harper, but while she talked, I glanced between Greta and Bea. Greta's arched eyebrows marked her scheming face, and Bea let out a little sigh as she glanced down at the shawl the Beauty Makers had insisted we both wear to cover our large arms.

"You look lovely," I said. And it was true; her dress was well cut and a gorgeous golden color, her long hair was curled into a loose ponytail that hung over one shoulder. I pulled the hair clips from my hair and slid them behind Bea's ears. She tried to protest but Mira started the engine and I turned away.

We followed Mrs. Brown's car like a carriage leading them to a ball, and not a charity dinner, driving far out of the town limits, down freeways and into the city proper. Massive geometric buildings cut towering figures looming over the road, but in the distance it looked like the stars had landed in bright clusters, the city alive and sparkling and ours.

The party was to be held in the ballroom of a glittering hotel. The Duesenberg drew eyes and gasps when it parked in front of the entrance. Greta and Mira got out; I watched them with awe that felt so separate from me. Greta's drop waist and glittering headpiece made an actress of her, and Mira too in plunging lace, dark lips, and a slit dress that made her long legs go on forever.

Bea made a small sad sound. "Do you ever miss something before it's gone?"

I took her hand in mine. And then Iris opened that back door. It was our turn to share the spotlight.

We followed as fast as we could without running, though my heart had begun to pound as the five of us entered the hotel lobby. Gold gilt framed the marble floors, brass lights flickered, leaving the feel of fantasy and magic, and the tall gilded doors opened for us. And the belles of the ball, the girls all eyes turned to as we entered the ballroom, were my dearest friends. We were like princesses. Bea's hair was bright and curled at her neck, her skin gently painted with life. She looked made of oil paints, like an artist's best muse stepping from out of the canvas. Iris walked confidently, gorgeously, the fringe on her dress swaying with each step. And I felt just as beautiful, just as powerfully made up, the volume of my beauty turned to blasting.

I was proud to walk beside them all as I eyed the reaction of the well-dressed crowd sitting at tables or circled into groups. We were a force, the five of us, each done up in our scarf dresses and curls, pearls tracing my hairline, my jeweled dress twinkling like a wind chime.

But Bea's words nestled into my bones. And I knew this was the last night of us. My friends. After Andrew chose the front-runner, everything would be different. We'd still be friends, but one of us would be settled on our way, and we would never have tonight again.

The rest of the room was filled with powerful men in

tuxes and tails and women in their best, who turned and watched us cross to the center of the room behind Mrs. Brown. I spied two Wives from our original group, and it was so good to see them all looking so well. Nora was large with child, sitting with her husband the future ambassador. Her silver dress glowed against her dark brown skin, and she was surrounded by several nosy women who kept asking about her due date, and what names she'd give her child. If the five of us were princesses, then Nora was a queen, happy and magnanimous as she glanced our way and waved her hand, big and welcoming. She scrunched her nose at me when our eyes met. I'd missed her. She had such a way with science and biology, and such dreams too, of moving to New York, to Harlem. I was glad she found her match and that they'd made their way to the city. And her husband, Mr. Livingston, looking so dapper in his tux, tall and Black and handsome. When he spied us he averted his eyes when they landed on me.

As much as I'd liked speaking about the beetles with him, I'd prayed for her to be the one he chose. They were the match. Anyone who saw them knew it. And now they'd have their baby, and live in that big old house in that big old city.

For a second, I felt an ache hit me down to my bones. I wanted that. I wanted a partner and a friend and I wanted a romance like Nora got. I was so lonely, even with my friends right here, even with a lively party and all the beauty I could possess. I had everything, but I didn't have love.

And I wanted it. Deep down I wanted a love that made me want to write poems.

I glanced down. I was never taught to pray for myself. But I closed my eyes and I made a wish for myself. I wanted this night to be one I would never forget. My silver dress swayed with fringe, the hemline higher than I'd worn before, my stockings silky and flesh colored. The band was playing, raucous and lively, and I could not stay inside my thoughts for long. The room was a haze of conversations, laughter, and cheers. It was a party, and I was out with my friends, so I shook my curls and pressed my bare shoulders back. The thin cotton scarf the Beauty Makers insisted I wear to cover my arms slunk to my elbows. The room was filled with powerful people of so much influence, coming together to meet and hobnob, under the guise of helping a charity.

No, that was impolite. Helping people in need was important too, and I should be glad for it. I was the one who saw the night by who I could meet, how I could use it. There were educators here, professors who let women into their colleges, let them become doctors or someone of note.

Jeepers but I wished I could become a someone.

I had a dream, but what I didn't have yet was a plan. Maybe I wasn't doing enough. Maybe I was already losing my chance. My hands shook and I clenched my fists and fought to keep my thoughts from circling.

The society could get them to help me.

There were a thousand paths at this party. At least one

of them could take me to the White House. So why did I keep thinking the quickest path would be from behind a white veil?

Andrew would be here somewhere. If I could get him to kiss me, then I'd be the front-runner, and that meant speaking with the Matron Circle. If I could just speak to someone with more power, I was certain I could get them to see me as Andrew's equal.

And if we had sparks then . . . well, that path didn't seem so impossible. Plenty of women I admired had taken that path.

But my most secret dream, that idea I had since I was little, had no path. No woman has done it before. So why not try to win Andrew?

"Anyone have eyes on him?" I said through smiling teeth. Perhaps he was late.

"Sunlight blossom?" Iris suggested, naming a scattering technique where we'd all take off in different directions.

Mrs. Brown nodded. "Then chat and host. If we don't spot him, leave it to the Gossips and Matrons. We will put him back where he needs to be."

We turned our backs to one another and started to socialize with those in front of us, scanning the tables while smiling, each of us warm and welcoming as if this crowded ballroom were a home we were hosting these powerful people inside. But even as we offered the *how do you do*s and *how are your children?* I'd been trained to give, we made an urgent hunt for our missing target.

It took me two minutes and five belly laughs at jokes I did not find that humorous before I reached the wall. I turned back. Mira and Iris stood across the ballroom from me, shaking their heads with confirmation. Greta and Bea had met up, both of them chatting across the room from me. Mrs. Brown crossed to a large woman with a glowing smile.

He wasn't in the ballroom. He must have been diverted somehow. My curiosity burned. Where could he be?

The woman speaking with Mrs. Brown had soft brown hair, pinked skin, and Andrew's eyes. I rubbed my forehead. I knew her face from the family picture in his dossier. Mrs. Brown had found Andrew's mother.

I stood taller, wanting to make a good impression if she glanced over. I wondered if his mother knew my own; perhaps they'd been in the same training group. Perhaps she raised Andrew with the same focus and force and forgiveness as my mother gave Nathaniel, proud that her mission as his mother had led to a priority one, as my mother was so proud of Nathaniel's priority three.

Andrew's sister Rebecca wasn't here. This wasn't a party for children.

Across the room, Greta stood alone now, her hands clasped tight as she stood near a wall and waited for the spotlight of everyone's attention to fall back on her. Her gaze darted about; her nerves clear even from here as she searched the room, her perfect polished look now forgotten as the servers laid plates of Oysters Rockefeller at the tables.

She smiled, but her smile was a small thing.

A not-wanting-to-be-patient-for-one-more-minute thing.

Where was Bea?

I wondered . . . Andrew wasn't in this entire massive room where he should be. She might have found him.

A server entered through a back door, pushing a shining platter on wheels. And I knew exactly where Bea would look first.

I slipped through the door, around servers and wait-staff, into a world of people whose names I didn't know. The halls were less lit here. The floor less shining, yet still clean.

Perhaps he needed a breath of air, space from all the pressure I knew we were putting on his shoulders. I searched through the hallways and offices. No Andrew.

I followed a server through the swinging door of the kitchen, and I found him with my youngest friend. Andrew looked grand in his suit and tails, and Bea was perfection, as they leaned next to each other, peeking at the dessert cart, looking as charming as it was possible to be.

The first to respond to the target was a strong play for a night like this where we'd all need to fight for a chance to talk to Andrew, especially since she was already in the lead. She was establishing dominance here, and I grinned, despite myself, because I was so proud of her.

Bea pressed her cheeks with her hands. "Round truffles covered with chocolate and gold filigree."

"I mean it's not my mom's lemon drizzle cake," he said, his smile cutting dimples into his cheeks.

"But what is?"

"Not a single thing. She adds just the right amount of raspberry filling and pairs it with a glass of ice-cold milk."

Bea smiled. "Sounds like heaven."

"Doesn't it?"

"We should skip the one-hundred-dollar plate of steak and potatoes and go steal a dinner made entirely of desserts."

"That sounds positively rebellious."

Bea arched an eyebrow. "Almost a scandal. Or a stomachache."

"But worth it."

Bea laughed, and it wasn't the trained giggle I'd heard her perfect. It was the kind of laugh she made when it was two in the morning and Mira was telling her naughtiest jokes.

She'd skipped past her training, and I realized that for her this wasn't a game. She was being real here.

And he was clearly charmed by her. Andrew leaned against a wall. He looked good in a coat and tails, his soft frame fitted behind good tailoring. Really good. His hair had the perfect amount of pomade, his glasses lighting his eyes, his smile genuine.

I knew we could find our sparks. What if he was the love story I was missing?

"You know, I thought once about becoming a dessert chef," he said.

"Really? I didn't know that," Bea lied. We all knew it. Lying didn't sit naturally on her face, and the edge of her lips turned down.

He smiled, though, not catching her. He didn't know her like I did. "Foolishness, I guess."

She lifted one shoulder. "There's nothing foolish about finding a way to make money doing something you love."

He met her eye and smiled warmly. "I like that."

He liked her.

Bea's skin flushed, and they both stared into each other's eyes, the sparks that I was just starting to feel for him, clearly settled between them. They both gazed at each other like there was no one else in the kitchen, no one else in the world. Bea stroked the seam of his tuxedo collar and then looked up at him through her eyelashes. Andrew bit his lip and leaned forward, closer to her, like he was attempting a kiss.

I had to do something quick, or else this girl Mira and I had sworn to help would win this whole thing on her own before any of us had our turns.

CHAPTER FIFTEEN

"**B**ea! There you are!" I said quickly. "I've been looking all over. Mrs. Brown needs you desperately."

It took her a second to look away from Andrew's gaze, and when she faced me, her eyes twinkled. "Really?" she said. "So soon?"

Soon? If I gave her another minute she'd be ironing her wedding clothes.

"I know," I said anyway, sticking to the prepared answers. "It's so early in the night, but she's snagged a heel and twisted an ankle, poor lamb. And since you've had so much experience tending to your father's leg injury, I thought she'd do best under your care."

I'd handed her a compliment as scripted, although I knew I shouldn't have interrupted. But Andrew wasn't hers yet. Greta still needed to take a turn after me, and then Bea would get another chance. We'd go round robin at least three more times. We were supposed to aim our kiss for the end of the night, not before the party even started.

I mean part of me wanted her to win, but I couldn't make it easy for her.

This was a priority one. Shouldn't Andrew have a chance with each of us before we set his whole life in motion?

And I wasn't ready to give up on my chance for love.

I faced him and gasped like I'd just realized he was there, and I let every ounce of surprise and joy show on my face. "Andrew! I didn't know you'd be here! What fun!"

He created space between him and Bea, and I knew that it wasn't too late. His eyes warmed when he saw me in this dress. I was his type too.

"Perhaps we should all go help her," he said, "is the injury serious?"

"Oh," I touched my chin. "That wouldn't be proper. Mrs. Brown is quite immodest in the ladies' restroom."

Andrew looked away in embarrassment, and Bea mouthed the words, *Two more minutes and it would all be over.*

We have all night, I mouthed back. She'd have several chances to kiss him again tonight. Andrew turned, and we both slipped our smiles back on. "Bea is quite capable of handling it."

I needed to stop complimenting her. It was so hard not to, though. I just loved her to bits, and my Matchmaking instinct wanted to smoosh their faces together and command them to kiss already.

But I needed to stop giving everyone else my dreams.

I lowered my shoulders. I'd been trained for a moment like this since I was twelve. He was dead set on one opinion, his desire to kiss my friend, and I needed to charm him into changing his mind and his vote, into kissing me.

This wasn't personal; this was the life I'd have if I chose him.

These were also the skills I'd use if I was the one seeking political office.

This was politics. And the skills they gave me would translate over, I knew it.

Bea's eyes softened as she turned to Andrew. "I should go, but I do hope you'll find me later."

"Of course I will," Andrew said. "Maybe I could ask you to dance?"

She titled her head to one side and clasped her hands together. "I'd love that."

"Great!" he said too eagerly. He glanced at me, and his voice mellowed. "Cool."

Bea met my eye and wiggled her eyebrows before she turned dutifully and with a confident sway of her hips toward the ballroom.

I stopped and traced a circle on my cheek. He looked at me then. And I knew I had to surprise him. "You never told me that joke about a pirate."

He flushed pink, and then laughed. "That wouldn't be proper, I—"

"You can trust me, Andrew," I said. "I would never judge you."

He still seemed a bit hesitant, so I said the first joke I could think of. "How do you make a pirate angry?"

He looked at me now, curious and somewhat charmed. "How?"

"You take away the *p*."

He blinked twice. "Irate," he said as he got the joke. He laughed once and then lowered his chin like a coconspirator. "Why wouldn't anyone play cards with the pirate?"

He was playing back. My smile turned genuine. "Why?"

"Because he was standing on the deck." That wasn't the naughty joke, but it had done its job. I gave an enraptured laugh and touched his arm. I'd caught his full attention. Now I called back to our first meeting. "Oh, that reminds me. I read that biography you mentioned in the library."

"President Hill wasn't a pirate," he chuckled. "At least not in that biography."

I leaned closer. "He sure lived an extraordinary life."

"That's partially to do with his wife," Andrew said.

I glanced at him.

"It was her connections that opened those doors, and you could see her thoughts in those personal letters, to see just how much of an influence she was in the policies President Hill championed."

"I'd never noticed that," I said, as though I hadn't studied Dorothy Whetly Hill's every word.

"It makes me wonder, really, how much of women's influence has been ignored by history. I believe we need to celebrate women, in all the different ways they're made."

In that second I saw why the society chose him. "I think I could fall for you," I said without thinking. But his eyes, or his ego, warmed to that, and I realized raising my love level was exactly the right play.

I glanced down, establishing a barrier to protect myself behind. "I don't want to be forgotten. I want a partner who will listen to my thoughts, see wisdom when I speak it."

"That's the kind of man I want to be."

"That kind of man could change the world."

"Change isn't enough," Andrew said with an eyebrow raised. "Bad men change the world too. I want to make things better."

I smiled at him approvingly, and his shoulders lifted. "Then you'll need a partner who will help you."

"Someone kind," he said, and in that second I knew he was thinking of Bea.

"Someone good," I corrected. "Sometimes the kind answer is to not make noise. A good person will defend those most in need, even if it means saying something necessary that might hurts feelings."

He looked at me in a new light.

"We should probably get back in there." I said in a soft voice. It was a test.

I didn't move. I could feel a chance at something developing here, and I didn't want to let go of it, before Greta took her next chance, or Bea won the whole game. I needed to figure out if we had sparks.

He didn't move either.

"I'm sure my mother is expecting me in there. I should . . ." Andrew stared at the doors that led to the ballroom. His eyes seemed stormy, and for a second I could imagine him like a brooding hero. A Mr. Darcy staring into a foggy forest. He sighed.

"What is it?" I asked too fast.

He scratched his neck. "It's nothing."

The hallways were empty. "You can tell me, Andrew."

His face seemed shadowed. "I hate these things." His voice was soft but firm. "Isn't that ridiculous? I'm too ambitious for my own good, and I know I need to make these connections, but it doesn't feel genuine. It feels—"

"Like a meat market," I supplied.

"Well, yes."

"I wonder what that's like," I said with an eyebrow raised.

"It's just that everyone is always so quick to introduce me to their friends. *Meet Mr. Greenough, Andrew.* He's the dean at Harvard. Or meet this other stuffy old man who will look at you like you are both his only hope for the future and somehow also a catastrophic failure waiting to happen. Or meet Mrs. Grant and her many daughters, or Mrs. Reed who will teach you how to dress better, or Mr. Landis who will help you find a better hairstyle to fit your face. It's like they are molding me into someone else. Someone better."

I touched his arm, and he sighed.

He pushed his glasses up. "I'm sorry, I shouldn't have said anything. I want to be seen, but I really don't want to be judged."

I drew a breath and squeezed his arm. "That's hard." I'd thought of his privilege, the pressures, or the opportunities we'd given him. But I'd never thought about how it must feel to be used.

But I couldn't feel sympathetic for long. He was squandering chances I would die for. He was annoyed to meet people who could change his life for the better. He had resources so many other people could never dream of, ways paved for him that were barred to others.

I didn't let these thoughts alter my expression.

He shrugged. "It's not hard. It's a blessing. I get it."

I swallowed my storm and tried to forgive him like I'd been trained. "I've had my face painted so many times, my image molded to become someone different. Better. I'm judged every time I walk down a street, or for what dress I choose, or what color I paint my lips. And it all makes me feel like what I think or what I want means nothing, like what they see is all I am. It's impossible to think of myself as big enough for my own dreams, when I don't think I deserve them, unless I paint my face in order to reach them. But if I have to pretend to be someone else in order to reach my goals, then is it actually me who's won them?"

His eyes were such a soft color, they seemed to burn with a candle spark of intensity as I met his gaze. "Exactly," he said. "I hate pretending."

"I think growth feels like pretending to most people. But honestly, I don't think that everyone in there is being false. I think there are a lot of people here who genuinely do care about the world, about making things better."

His presence was near enough and warm enough to realize how close we stood. Close enough I could see my reflection in his smudged glasses.

I pulled off his glasses and wiped the fingerprints and dust away with my cotton shawl. He stood very still as I slid those glasses back over the bridge of his nose.

"There," I said, my voice quiet. "Now at least you'll be able to see those people you're about to meet. Maybe if you look close enough, you'll see there are good people standing in front of you."

"I can see one," he said softly.

He meant me. He reached his hand forward and twisted his fingers around mine. A chill ran up my neck.

Try, my mother's voice echoed. I glanced down at our hands and rubbed my thumb up his finger. I glanced up at him through my eyelashes and inhaled heavily.

Someone should be here to interrupt this. I know that Greta knew where we were by now. She should be here.

"We should go in there," I said with a shaky voice. "There are people in there who are dying to meet you."

"We should."

Again we didn't move. We breathed together, but I didn't dare look at him. I didn't dare smile or push it forward. Greta still needed her turn, and then Bea again. But my ambitions would not let me step away. He smelled like stories. His jaw pulsed with our nearness. If my friends were here watching, I would have done what I was supposed to do. But Greta was late. Why was she late?

This was an opportunity.

I met his eyes. My training and my beauty left his gaze swimming with desire and hunger. I felt my lips sliding into a smile. "No more stalling, Andrew. Be brave. Open that door." I arched my chin and looked him right in the eye. A challenge and my consent in one look.

He leaned in closer, his eyes closing. But I kept mine open, aimed for his lips like I'd been trained to aim, and I kissed him, soft and short, for two seconds like I've been trained to kiss him in the peach kiss. I drew my chin down, giving him the victory, making myself the trophy. Leaving him wanting more, leaving him breathing in want where I felt nothing but lips on lips.

My training gave me the look that would draw him back. I knew the smile that would end the kiss but leave that line open for the next opportunity. I knew what to do to give my friends their chance, no matter how late Greta was.

But I knew his name and his future and I wanted to find our sparks. I wanted Nora's happy ending. I wanted him to choose me. I wanted the power and the path, and was it so wrong to let a good man love me? So I twisted his collar in my greedy grip and I drew him back to me and I kissed him like I was thirsty and would drink him dry. Like if I kissed him hard enough I could claim his life. Not my place beside him, but the place in the center of it. The place on the ballot. His place in history. I kissed him like I could blot out his name and pencil in my own.

He drew back, breaking the kiss like he was breaking the surface of a whirlpool I was dragging him down. We both gasped for air.

I touched my lips and didn't meet his eye. I couldn't. My shoulders tensed with shame, because even with all the passion that I possessed, there was nothing there between us. Not a single spark. I knew sparks. Patch had lit me up like a firework.

If Andrew chose me, I'd have to pretend every day of my life.

Bea wasn't pretending. Didn't Andrew deserve something real?

Didn't I?

"I'm sorry," I whispered. "I shouldn't have . . ." I met his wide eyes, and my words trailed off.

He swallowed and stepped closer to me, and only then did I realize how far he'd had to pull away from me. "That was . . ."

My lipstick had rubbed on his lips. I rubbed it off with my thumb, and his lips curved in a smile beneath my hand.

I knew my training had charmed him well past sense. I knew his loyalty would mean he'd close the door on his feelings for Bea and be mine until I let him go, or proved myself unworthy.

I was the front-runner now. I'd won the competition and the mentorship with those women who led our society. I'd won his heart.

But did I even want it?

CHAPTER SIXTEEN

Andrew's hand gripped mine as we walked through the server door. Tables full of elegant, powerful people turned their eyes to watch us, but I didn't feel like Cinderella at the top of the staircase, I felt like a wicked stepsister who had stepped into Cinderella's story.

Mrs. Brown watched me with her appraising eyes. Andrew brought my other hand to his mouth and kissed my fingers at the exact second that Bea glanced over.

My body went cold.

Greta danced with Johnson, both of them captured by each other, and I suddenly realized why she hadn't come to stop me from kissing Andrew.

She'd found her own path.

So now I was stuck on this one.

Andrew's mother made her way to us, like she was attached to a string someone else pulled forward. "Well, I guess it's time for us to meet my mother," Andrew said. He put a smile on like donning a mask. "Don't worry, I will protect you."

I rubbed my collarbone. Andrew and I could bond over our strained relationships with our mothers. Didn't that just spell love?

Smile number five. *The hostess.*

"Andrew, darling," Andrew's mother's voice carried, as though Andrew inherited her gravity-inducing voice. "Wherever had you gone off to?"

"Mother." He scratched the back of his neck.

"Don't slouch, darling," she said in a quiet but firm voice. "You'll wrinkle."

"Sorry." Andrew stood taller, but something in his expression seemed defeated.

I came to his rescue. I offered my hand demurely and met her eye with head held high. "It's good to meet you, Mrs. Shaw."

Andrew's mother smelled of rose petals and vanilla. She took my hand with vigor, her smile proud and satisfied. "And you too, Bea."

The smell soured.

"Mother, this is Elsie."

"Ah," she said as she tallied me up like the ingredients in a recipe, each part parceled, some clearly on her list for substitutions. "You're Rebecca's favorite."

"Of all your children," I answered quickly, "Rebecca is my favorite as well."

"Ouch," Andrew said playfully. "Let's hope you didn't kiss Rebecca like you did me."

I winced, both from that accusation I could not take as a joke and for the secret kiss he'd just shared so loudly. There was no taking it back now.

Across the room, Mira had joined Bea.

The answer, of course, to a moment like this one was to underplay any awkward feelings. "I love your dress, Mrs. Shaw. Is that a Lanvin?"

Her perfect posture did not change. "It is."

It wasn't a play. I loved the wide pannier skirt, and the soft blue silk with romantic embroidery. "I love her. Her work is so feminine and detailed, not so stark and crisp like Chanel."

Mrs. Shaw frowned. "Agreed. Chanel's style seems to design based off a uniform."

"But which uniform I wonder," I said with my eyebrow raised knowingly.

"I have my theories." She looked me over again as if reevaluating. "Her sympathies seem well established."

Rumors said Coco Chanel had an overfondness for a new party growing traction in Germany. "They seem all the rage in Europe." Even after the last war, fascism seemed to be infectious. It was growing at an alarming rate.

"Yes, it's concerning," Mrs. Shaw said.

"We'll have to watch for her fall show." I didn't mean the dresses.

"You women and your ribbons and bows," Andrew said. "I say if it fits and it's on sale, well then, it's good enough for me."

"And that, my dear boy, is why I do your shopping," Mrs. Shaw said with a smile I struggled to copy. We'd been talking about more than ribbons and bows, and to be dismissed so quickly was an unkindness I didn't think he was capable of bestowing.

He might like me for now, but how could he see me as an equal if every word of substance had to be kept secret?

Over Andrew's shoulder, I spied my friends across the busy ballroom. Far from me. Theirs were the only faces that reflected what I'd done. Greta glared openly, shaking her head in disgust, while Mira gave her words of solace to Bea, who mouthed the words *I'm fine, I'm fine* so clearly they scratched themselves into my bones. She did not smile.

My chest felt tight. "It was good to meet you, Mrs. Shaw," I said as warmly as I could manage. And I meant it. We'd established the start of something. We weren't rivals over Andrew's influence, we were allies. Our oaths made sure of that.

"Shall we make the rounds?" Andrew said, his mask of a smile in place.

I leaned into his side and spoke in quiet tones. "You're enough, Andrew. Don't make me clean your glasses again."

His false smile softened to genuine.

"There you are," I whispered.

His mother watched us go with surprised approval, and I knew I'd just aced an exam.

Only to jump right into the next one.

Butter knives were crossed at tables I was supposed to avoid, knives perpendicular at tables where people needed to meet Andrew. Flowers hid messages inside arrangements, with ivy set at tables filled with scholars and poets who held wisdom more than stature, oak wreaths at tables with military men. I guided him by the codes, my hand in his arm a rudder.

From table to table, Andrew introduced me. My name was briefly in the mouths of people who could change my life forever. They said my name, spoke to me about poetry and politics, and I smiled the smile I'd been trained to give, and included Andrew inside the conversation in a way that made him look better, in a way that made him shine.

All those connections. They knew my name, but they left caring about Andrew's future. All those powerful people only knew me as a possible asterisk in Andrew's life.

And we were both miserably bored. Perhaps the problem with being pawns in a hundred-year-old society was that it made you feel like you too were one hundred years old.

Across the room, Bea and Mira were laughing with one of Andrew's female friends, Greta slunk over Johnson, while Harper danced with Iris. They seemed young and free, and I was leashed by the hand held in my own.

A cork flew past my head, and I turned suddenly. Champagne. Andrew stiffened next to me. I glanced about. We'd met the mayor and several police officers in this very room, yet alcohol was flowing now without even a pretense of hiding.

The man holding the glass, whose name I'd just heard but somehow immediately forgotten, offered us a glass. He had a slick gray mustache and a stark black collar.

"No, thank you," Andrew said, answering for us.

"Don't be a wet blanket, man. It's a party." He gave us both a glass.

Andrew's shoulders curled, and I suddenly remembered him buying several glasses for his friends when we met. He'd fallen under male pressure before. But now he stood steady. "You know my parents are the head of the local temperance league, right?"

A flash went off, and I turned.

"Cheers to your parents." The man lifted his cup in a toast, and then he drank. "How about you, dollface?"

I knew in that second that Andrew needed support, but that he also needed the good opinion of this man whose name I still could not recall. I had to say no, but I had to say no in a way that made him feel like I had said yes.

Essentially, I needed to filibuster.

"I believe it was Mark Twain who said that 'it is the Prohibition that makes anything precious.' So while it's a delicious rebellion for you to say no to the temperance laws, it is our own delicious rebellion to say no to an offer you've made so kindly." I put the drink down on the table, and Andrew copied me. "I wish you a pleasant evening with your drink, and that we shall endeavor to have one without it. Our task, I dare say, is much harder. Shall we, Andrew."

Andrew and I walked away, and once our backs were turned we both started laughing.

"Was that a British accent?" Andrew asked.

"I can't say the word *endeavor* without sounding like an Anglophile."

"Shall we dance and make merriment?" Andrew asked with a poor excuse for a British accent.

"Indubitably." He took my hand and swung me around, and then he pulled me into a proper distance for dancing. There was a friendly level of comfort in Andrew's arms. I definitely felt a kinship with him, or perhaps a friendship? Perhaps that would grow into something more. Perhaps this wasn't hopeless.

"All this money," Andrew said after a minute. "It seems wasted, when there are people going without food."

"There are also people here who could change that. By law or charity or taxation."

His jaw tightened, but he kept his smile in place. "Don't let my father hear you say that. He's not a fan of our high taxes, despite all the good they do."

"Then maybe your father is one of those people whose opinions you could change. Your voice carries weight, Andrew. You can make the changes you'd like to see."

He looked down. "I hadn't thought of that."

Another flashbulb went off. I turned to find the camera, but it was too crowded.

"Tell me more about your family," Andrew said. "What's your father like?"

I missed a step. And for a second I heard my father's voice telling me that a good girl was silent.

And Andrew noticed. "Oh. I'm sorry. I'm truly sorry. I didn't—"

"—You didn't do anything wrong. My father is very much alive."

"Oh good."

"I just don't really know what to say. About my father. I'm protective of him, I guess. I don't know why. I hardly see him, and when I do it's always at some event or another where he's looking at anything except me." I smiled softly. "He's always surprised at how tall I am, how mature. Every time he sees me he says, 'Is this my little girl?' and for a second I am. I'm that little girl who hung on his knee, or who danced in his arms, or who played with the dolls he'd bring back from his trips."

Andrew stared into the crowd, his eyebrows pressed together in concern he didn't voice.

"It's strange, really," I said. "I'm never angry with my father even though he deserves it, but I'm nearly always mad at my mother."

"It's a protection," Andrew said in a voice so calm. "You know your mother's love can withstand your anger, but your father's . . ."

If my father saw the storm inside me, I doubt he would stick around. "People usually come to me to be understood like this," I said sincerely. "I don't often share these things about myself."

"Well, I'm honored."

"I think it's more than that. I think you understand me."

"You're easy to talk to," he said, again turning the conversation on me.

I touched his arm. "Perhaps our brains are similar."

"I . . ." He glanced over like he was weighing whether or not to trust me. "I'm mad at my father quite a bit." He let out a soft chuckle. "But I have no arguments with my mother. We're not particularly close, although she's extremely involved in my life. Some might say too involved. My friends specifically think my mother is far too involved in my choices. She's placed all her ambitions on me, but I don't think she sees me at all. She wants me to be important. Not happy."

"Are you happy?" I asked.

He scratched his neck. "I'm . . . happiest when I'm helping others." He glanced at me. "And I'm very happy to be dancing with you."

I put on a smile and then turned quiet as we swayed to the music. For a moment I'd forgotten to pretend. I liked spending time with him much more when I didn't have to pretend to be falling for him.

Because it was pretend.

But was a friendship so bad?

In the crowd someone held up a camera to his chest, a large silver flashbulb at the side. He was dressed as a waiter, or a reporter, looking like an outsider in clothes too old and worn compared to the tuxes and tails around him, his dark hair hanging over his eyes and his strong nose. Then he looked up through his hair and I froze.

Patch.

How was a human being so beautiful? All those sparks I couldn't feel for Andrew sent my stomach warm and my fingers tingly. How did he get in here? I know the Spinsters had raised their watch level on him. There were far too many influential people here for them to have lost track of him. How did he get past the Gossips and the Spinsters?

His eyes were storming.

A moment I should not have asked for lingered in the silence of our stares. He pressed the trigger on the camera, the flashbulb bright and blinding as a bullet.

He took that picture for himself. Perhaps to hang on his wall or press between pages of our favorite book.

But that was just me being romantic and foolish. He wasn't here for me. The flash earlier. He'd taken a picture of Andrew holding a glass of alcohol. He was here to black-mail the Shaws, and who knew how many others of these people.

I flashed a signal to Iris. She caught it with one glance, searched the ballroom, spotted Patch as he ducked past a server. I turned back to Andrew.

The Spinsters could handle him. They'd take the camera

away; they'd get him to leave. And then they'd do something to scare him away from the Shaws for good.

But a chill ran up my neck, and no matter how I tried to silence it, I saw Patch's little brother, that boy who depended on him for everything.

Had Patch done enough to deserve the Spinsters' punishment?

If the society could be wrong about Rebecca, how did I know they wouldn't be wrong with how they handled Patch?

I needed to help him.

And dancing with Andrew felt like when I was little and Nathaniel would dance with me on his feet. I didn't think I'd ever feel anything more than kinship with Andrew. I didn't want a relationship that started with a lie that would tear me away from my friends, and leave me alone in a life that would be made of pretending.

No goal was worth that.

"I'm so sorry," I said. I needed to go, but I needed to say something that would insure he wouldn't follow. "My stomach is cramping. I need to use the restroom."

He blinked, like it had never occurred to him that women use the restroom too.

"Of course."

I could have said a thousand things and kept Andrew on my hook. But I'd said that. And the comfort between us, the romance Andrew was forming for us both shattered like a broken glass.

I think I wanted to be free of him before I ran to Patch.

And I was the world's largest fool for doing so. I fled from his arms out the door toward where Iris had led Patch, but as I walked, for the briefest of seconds I looked back over my shoulder at the path I'd stolen, and now was rejecting.

Andrew's friends had claimed him, and Greta swallowed them all in her spotlight. I knew Patch wouldn't have let me leave like Andrew just did, but Andrew looked back at me with his eyebrows lifted and his gaze steady like he would let me come back after I'd done what I'd needed to do.

Like he hoped I would come back to him.

My shoes clicked against the marble floors. Mira matched my steps, and Bea joined us, and together we followed the closed doors and hairpins shaped into a letter *A* that Spinsters always left behind them. We always marked dangerous paths with the letter *A*.

We passed the laundry and the kitchen and office rooms until we made our way into the parking garage just next to the hotel. It was roofed with carved scrolls made of cement, the center arch painted with an exotic scene. The cars looked like flat, rounded squares as we crept down the cement steps. Parking garages weren't safe for girls like us. So we stood close.

"There." Mira pointed.

Iris had him with his arm pinned behind his back in the space between two cars. We raced forward.

"What are we doing?" Bea huffed.

I didn't know.

"Are we fighting him or are we charming him?" Mira asked with a heavy breath.

I didn't know.

"Stop," I shouted.

Iris turned.

I gathered my breaths like a shield around my shoulders. "Let me talk to him."

But heaven help me, I had no idea what I was going to say.

CHAPTER SEVENTEEN

Iris shoved Patch into the back seat of a Buick Marquette. He slid through and tried to unlock the door on the other side, but a Spinster whose name I didn't know stood directly in front of the window. The glass windows were square and tall so there wouldn't be much privacy from the women surrounding the car.

I climbed in.

Iris stopped me with one hand as she held Patch's camera in the other.

"Don't break that," Patch said in a soft fury. "It's not mine."

And he'd taken that picture of me. I glanced at the camera that was full of blackmail and I thought only of the shot he'd taken when I saw him.

Iris didn't blink. She studied me carefully, like she was looking for anxiety in my actions, and maybe I was panicking a little, but that wasn't why I'd run out here. I knew I needed to talk to him. If I could charm him calm again, then they wouldn't need to hurt him. "Be careful," she said to me.

"I will be." I could do this, I knew it. I sat down on the light leather-padded seat.

"And we're right out here," Iris said to Patch like a threat.

She closed the door. I pressed my dress down. Breathe. You can do this.

Patch was quiet for a second, his eyes more hurt than angry, though you couldn't tell by his voice once he spoke. "What the hell, Elsie."

I swallowed hard. "It's good to see you, Patch," I said, though that was a lie. Or at least it should have been. I'd missed him, missed the quirk of his smile and the way his dark hair hung over his eyes. I missed this feeling, that even with my friends right outside the car, we were all alone.

But I didn't miss his anger.

"You got some lady goon squad?"

I almost wanted to laugh, but there was no humor in his eyes. "I won't let anyone hurt you." I scooted over a little. "Are you okay?"

He rubbed his arm and looked out the window. "My arm still feels like it's bent up too high, like maybe she just pulled it out of the socket."

"I'm sorry." I didn't say anything else, just looked at him. His pale eyes beady in the shadowed light, his lips snarled, and his eyebrows creased so hard I knew it would one day be a wrinkle. I thought silence would calm him.

"And you." His neck and shoulders were tight as he turned to me. "I get wanting to kiss and run, like I've done that a few times myself, but you know I got to keep looking into the Shaws, so why are you dancing with that mug?" I turned away. I couldn't let him see my expression.

I didn't want to give him any hope.

But even looking away must have been too big a clue, because the anger in Patch's voice melted away, and now all that was left was pain. "I thought you were my girl. You were supposed to come to the library to meet me. When your friend asked me I thought . . . I don't know, I thought you'd arranged it. So I messed everything up with a drop-off, and I'm up *to here* in trouble with my bosses, and then I come to leave and you're snuggling up with that yahoo?"

"I'm sorry."

"I didn't like it."

"I'm sorry."

"What's that mug got that I ain't got, 'cause it sure as hell ain't passion. You two look like you're grandparents or something, like you can't even stand him."

I looked over, his words hitting their mark, and Patch softly traced his fingers over my neck, and a chill of pleasure nearly made me lose all sense. "He got this?"

Warmth puddled in my stomach, and I closed my eyes tight.

A Spinster banged on the glass, but I didn't pull away.

"You deserve passion, Elsie." His fingers trailed down my neck to my collarbone, and goose bumps raised those tiny hairs on my arms and neck. His eyes found mine, and it wasn't just passion he seemed to be offering; it had to be love.

"I owe you an explanation," I said. "And an apology."

Patch dropped his hands. "No. You don't. It's money."

My dress felt too tight at my waist. "It's not."

"You don't think I'm good enough for you."

I turned silent, like my father always told me to be, and then I looked at him. Really looked. Not at how beautiful he was, or the image in my head I'd painted of who I thought he could become. He was the boy who'd lost his parents. He was a boy who'd been broken. And I couldn't look him in the eye and tell him that he was right. I did want more than him.

But maybe I was too full of myself. Who'd I think I was anyway?

He shook his head with disgust. "All you want is to trick some idiot into paying for all your stuff and I'm not your guy, because I can't pay for your shiny dresses. I get it."

"You don't know me." And I didn't know him. Not really. Even when we spent that whole night together, we'd spent far more time kissing then we did talking. "I wasn't honest with you."

"I know. I don't care that you lied." He laughed then, once. "I don't even care that you're a stuck-up fancy girl who thinks you're too good for me, or that you've fooled that idiot Shaw into some con of a relationship. I'd still take you."

Oh my foolish heart.

I closed my eyes, because I knew if I looked at him for one second more I would have kissed him. I knew I would. So I could only see darkness behind my closed eyelids when his rough hand took my hand in his. I breathed in deep and caught the scent of alcohol so strong, it seemed almost like gasoline.

"Tell me we're over," he said in a voice that rumbled.

I opened my eyes and while his voice had sounded so steady, his expression was clouded with worry. I knew the society would let me go with him.

And I knew that I wouldn't go. It wasn't the money; it wasn't even all my ambitions that made me pull my hand from his. He gripped my hand tight.

It was that every time I tried to leave him, he tried to make me stay. It's that if I chose to be with him, it would have to be on his terms.

Patch rubbed his bottom lip with his thumb. "You think that idiot could survive without everybody always giving him opportunity after opportunity?"

"Just . . . forget about the Shaws," I said, because he was

right and I couldn't think too hard about that right now. "They're nothing. This has got nothing to do with them." I let out a breath. "I don't want to be with you."

His breath hitched. "That's a lie."

"No, it's not," I said, though it broke my heart.

He sat back and ran his hand over his forehead, brushing his hair out of his eyes.

"I'm sorry. It's not you," I said, even though that wasn't completely the truth. "I'm not ready to be the half of something," I said. "I want to be more. I want to be whole."

His leg started pulsing and his fists clenched, and now I remembered his anger. Remembered the vicious way he'd crossed out the drawing of my eyes.

I watched him and lifted my hands to protect myself.

But he didn't hurt me. He swung open the door, and Iris yanked him out by his shirt collar.

"The lady said no," Iris answered.

"Iris," I said, crawling out of the car after him. "Let him go."

"What? No." Iris said. "He shouldn't be here."

Patch's jaw pulsed, "Believe me I don't want to stay."

"Let him go, Iris," I said.

"You sure?" she asked.

I glanced at Patch and then I nodded.

She let him go, and Patch adjusted his collar roughly.

"Can I have my camera back?" he said, the rage in his voice barely contained. "I can't . . . I can't afford to replace it." His whole posture stooped with shame for admitting it.

The Spinster pulled out the sheet of film, exposing it to the light and ruining those pictures. Ruining Patch's chance to blackmail the Shaws.

Patch yanked the camera from the Spinster's grip. He gave a dirty look at each of the women around him. "This con of yours isn't going to work. Elsie's not pretty enough to trick her way into a family like that."

"Oh he did not just say that," Mira said. I grabbed her arm and then Patch turned and stalked away.

I winced. Not from the words, which I knew weren't true, but from the way he thought that they would destroy me.

Despite our sparks, he only ever thought of me as pretty.

And the kind of man I would love would see me as so much more than that.

Iris flashed a signal with her fingers, and a few Spinsters got into a car to trail after him.

"I don't trust him," Iris said.

"He's just hurting," I insisted.

"Hurt men are some of the most dangerous."

"He won't do anything too stupid," I said. "He's got a little brother. He can't risk getting sent to jail."

"I don't know."

"Trust me," I said.

Iris nodded. "I do, but I won't let him come near you again."

Tears made my vision blurry, because I knew she wouldn't. I even knew it was for the best.

But it was only then that I realized it was over.

"Oh, Elsie. I'm so sorry," Bea said as she pressed against my side.

"What a sap," Mira tucked her chin into my shoulder. "He's a fool, and a jackass, and most of all he's wrong."

"Right?" I said, with my throat tight.

"He's a hired thug," Bea said. "If I see him again I'm going to kick him in the kneecaps."

I laughed once, and then I covered my eyes with my hands and they held me tighter, each of them saying kind words I couldn't listen to, not over the thoughts in my head that told me how wrong I was, and how much I'd hurt him. I shouldn't have even smiled at him. I should have ended it when they'd told me to. Mrs. Brown was right. It wasn't fair to him. I'd been trained to make boys fall for me.

I had no idea how much it hurt to watch them walk away.

They held me like that for several minutes, until their touch started to feel too tight and their attention seemed a spotlight on all of my flaws. "Can I just go home?" I asked Iris.

"I'll drive you," Mira said.

"Yeah, I'll come with you," Iris said. "I'll set the watch here, and then I can go." She whistled once and women slid through the shadows of the parking garage and circled next to a shining Studebaker.

Mira and I walked toward our car and Bea fell in next to us. I turned and stopped her. "You should stay with

Andrew. Mr. and Mrs. Brown can take you home after the party is over."

Bea shook her head, and a chunk of her hair slipped over her round cheek. "I'm going with you."

"Please." My voice broke as I tucked the hair behind my grandmother's pins. "You can fix things up with Andrew. If you talk to him. Dance with him. I—"

"—You are my friend, and you need me. I'm going with you." Bea held my hand steady. "Besides, it's a long game. There will be time for me to fix us later."

I closed my eyes and stopped fighting. If we left now, there was no way for me to be anything but the front-runner here. Would I be stuck in a life with no love in it?

I felt heartbreak and I never felt love.

But I let her stay with me. My thoughts swarmed until they became a fog so thick I didn't have to hear them.

I didn't have to hear anything.

Minutes later, Mira pulled the car around. We picked up Iris and we drove home with the top down, the wind and the night breezes chilling me to frozen. The stars blurred as we drove toward a town that was covered in dark clouds. I clenched my eyes closed and slunk back against the seat, but I couldn't hide from this.

I couldn't feel heartbreak for a boy I could have loved. I couldn't feel celebration for winning Andrew. All I could feel was Bea's head on my shoulder as she muttered soft comforting words.

But the boy who needed comforting was long gone now. And the life I'd stolen from her seemed to move further and further away.

———✦———

About twenty minutes later, the car in front of us swerved, and Iris swore under her breath.

"What was that?" Mira asked from behind the wheel. I sat up as another car drove directly in front of us, and the Asian woman sitting in the back seat turned to face us directly. I recognized her as one of the Spinsters who'd trailed Patch. She held both hands up.

Ten fingers.

My blood went cold.

Iris flashed both hands twice, and then Mira followed the car off the highway.

"What should we do?" Bea asked. She looked at me, but I turned to Iris. Ten fingers meant emergency. Ten fingers meant war.

And Iris was our general.

"I don't know," she said. She met our panicked eyes. "Not yet."

I took three sharp breathes before I could speak. "It's not Patch," I said. "It couldn't be." The chill breeze smelled of smoke. As we followed the car in front of us, a hot wind blew toward us, and I saw that those thick gray clouds I'd thought were a storm were thick plumes of smoke.

Coming from the direction of Andrew's house. We drove forward in silence, down the quiet road past lilacs and pruned trees and freshly trimmed lawns until we passed the three-story house on the corner and saw the Shaw estate, tall behind its carved walls—sparkling, historic, and important.

And completely covered in towering flames.

CHAPTER EIGHTEEN

The air smelled of burning books.

Patch couldn't have done this. There wasn't time, not for the flames, the destruction, that covered the left side of the house to grow that massive. In the back, down a long stone drive, I spied movement in an open garage, not yet touched by flames. It was too quick to see who it was.

It might have been a spark from the new electrical system. Maybe a candle had lit too close to a curtain. It couldn't have been . . .

The car in front of us parked crooked in the middle of the road. Spinsters ran out, ran to help. Our car slammed to a stop.

"Stay here," Iris shouted as she opened her car door and ran toward the unlit outbuilding.

"No!" I whispered. I climbed out after her. It wasn't fair

that we let the Spinsters fight our wars for us, not while we stayed back here in safety. They needed all of us, this fire was too big to fight alone.

I staggered forward up the drive, fighting against the blistering heat.

A girl screamed. A little girl's voice turned even this blazing fire cold.

It was Rebecca. Rebecca hadn't gone to the party. And the sound was coming from the back of the burning house.

We ran up the drive and around the side of the house, passing under drifting ash as Mira kicked the gate open and we flooded into the large landscaped yard.

The house was rumbling, dark ash staining the polished stone. A window on the second story cracked open. Not wide. Just enough for Rebecca to stick her head out and gasp for air. Beneath her was a bed of soft grass.

"Jump!" I shouted to Rebecca. I was close enough that maybe we could catch her if she'd jumped. All we had to do was open our arms and I know we could save her if she'd leaped for me.

But she didn't hear me over the roaring flames.

In the time it took me to run under Rebecca's window, something had drawn her back inside.

"Elsie!" Mira shouted as she ran to the back door.

I raced forward. It was locked.

Mira screamed for help. I searched desperately for a way in. A small garden statue of an angel nestled next to soot-covered tulips. I grabbed it and swung at a window. The glass shattered, and I scraped the statue over the glass edge until there was a hole large enough I could climb in. The glass bit into my palms as I climbed up. Bea boosted me over and I made my way in. I didn't stop. Not to help them in, not for the pain or the blood dripping from my skin. We raced inside, ducking blistering beams. The Spinsters shouted for water in the front of the house, passing buckets. But I ignored them.

The smoke filled my lungs. I couldn't think. My feet slammed against the wooden steps and past art and beautiful things perfectly placed and scalded. It was so dark. So hot. Bea shouted warnings I didn't heed.

"Rebecca!" I screamed. Again and again. I couldn't hear her. I tested a doorknob. Blistering. I pounded on the door, and listened, past the screams and the roar of the fire. The floor cracked beneath me.

I tested another door, this one only warm to the touch. I swung the door open and a cloud of smoke blinded me.

It was her parent's room, filled with smoke rushing from the vent. Blankets covered a small lump at the center of the double bed, and when I pulled the blanket off of her face, Rebecca was still and perfect as a doll, her eyes glazed over with cities she would never build.

———◆———

Across town, Andrew and his parents were probably still dancing. Maybe Mrs. Shaw was complaining that her feet hurt. Maybe Andrew was talking with his friends about our kiss, or flirting with Greta. Maybe for the next hour or so they could live in a story they didn't know yet was a fiction.

Maybe for the next hour they would be happy and tired and have no idea that their night was just starting.

Just like ours was.

We followed the truck a Gossip had spied leaving the Shaws' estate. A truck I'd once been given a ride home inside. This time there were no barrels of whiskey in the back. He'd almost lost us a few times, but we weren't alone. Women painted the way to him from the front porches, as hand signals led us through the city.

We found Patch at the boardwalk standing in the pouring rain, juggling knives for no one, his empty hat on the ground waiting to be filled. It was too early for crowds, time of thieves and mothers, and a swirling storm making bruises out of the sky. The air was thick and smelled of fog and storms and cloying smoke.

I got out of the car and rain seeped into my hair and and blurred my eyes as ashy water ran into them. "Tell me it wasn't you. Tell me you didn't light that fire."

He didn't move. "What choice did I have?" he shouted through the rain.

I slumped back and Mira kept me standing. I couldn't hold myself up. This was my fault. This was my fault. My dress soaked against my back. The rain-soaked ground skid beneath my feet and mud seeped into my T-straps shoes.

Thunder rumbled above me, loud as a stomach without a meal.

Patch stood smug, with his chin jutted up. "You destroyed my pictures. I had to give my bosses something."

I covered my eyes and I sobbed, my throat raw and blistered.

Patch dropped his bravado and moved forward. His footstep echoed in my pounding ears. "It's just money. It's just stuff. And you know it ain't ethical for people to be that rich, not when people are going hungry. Now there's nothing he's got that I don't."

No one debated him, and he inhaled sharply. Lightning struck above him, lighting his storming eyes. "They weren't home," he said a second later. "The Shaws were across town. I know it."

"Not all of them," Bea said gently.

He shook his head, like if he denied it enough, it would take her words back. "No," he said. "They . . ." his voice trailed off and he turned suddenly still.

He swore once. Breathlessly. "I forgot about the girl."

He couldn't have hurt me more. I didn't think there was anything left inside me to break, but he found it. He found exactly the worst words.

He met my eye and I saw the moment the guilt tried to break him. He stared up and the storm streamed down his face and for a second I couldn't tell if it was tears or rain. And then his face changed as he covered his vulnerability with anger. With a sneer and jagged shoulders and a pulsing jaw. "You made me do this."

I roared because it was true. I ran at him, swinging my fists at his soaked chest. I hit him as hard as I could, and he didn't hit me back. He took it, like he deserved it. Like he'd been hit harder.

But it was true.

I hated him. With every breath in my chest I hated him.

But part of me still wanted to forgive him. I'd done this sure as if I'd lit the match.

I stilled my hands and looked at him, but he couldn't meet my eye. I knew he understood my anger. I knew he understood my fists. But every book he'd ever read had not prepared him to see a barefaced girl who would not take away his guilt.

But he wasn't the dragon. He wasn't the knight.

And I wasn't a princess.

We were both just people. Good and bad and broken. And responsible for our choices, and for their consequences.

I turned and left him like he was nothing. Each step heavy, each step full of wanting to look back, but not turning around. My bones ached for it but I wasn't weak. I didn't need saving. I wasn't the lies they told about me.

I was a woman and I was made of spine.

I heard the slap of footsteps as Patch ran away and no one chased him.

"What do we do with him," a Spinster asked Iris.

She matched my steps. "We hold him accountable. He's broken the law, now we let the law handle it."

I didn't know who would trail him, or who would call the cops, or who would leave the tip, or lead them to the evidence.

But throughout history, anonymous has been a woman.

My step faltered but I pushed forward. His brother would be fine. We'd watch for him. We could make sure he was placed in a good home, where he would sleep under a kind roof, and wouldn't go hungry again.

While Patrick Elliot Villipin, the boy I'd danced with, the boy whose hands I'd memorized, would sleep in prison. He didn't know it yet, but no one was coming to save him.

He didn't know it yet, but he wouldn't get away.

My mud-caked shoes followed my friends, with my head held high and my bones aching with a guilt I could not let myself feel.

He'd made this choice. Not me. His consequence was nothing compared to what he'd taken.

Somehow I found the car, and I opened the back door and climbed into the back seat.

Mrs. Brown would be proud of me. I didn't quit. I didn't break my vows.

Alone in the back seat, my legs tucked tight against my chest, my rain-soaked hair damaging the leather, I fought against the rumble in my throat, the downpour burning my eyes. I was stronger than this. I was a storm. I . . . Two hands touched my shoulder. One covered in jewels. One rough.

The engine turned.

And the storm inside me broke.

IN A LOSS FELT BY *the entire community, Rebecca Jane Shaw, aged 11 years, daughter of John J. and Rebecca Allen Shaw, died following a fire in her family home. Mr. Shaw is probably one of the most successful retail dry goods men in central Michigan, his family prominent in Mt. Pleasant for nearly forty years. He is a member of Wabon Lodge, Free and Accepted Masons, and also of the Bay City Masonic Consistory. Mr. and Mrs. Shaw are presiding members of the Mt. Pleasant Temperance League. So it is with shock that sixteen barrels of distilled whiskey were found in their family home, leading to the explosive nature of the fire that took their home and young daughter. Funeral services will be held Sunday afternoon at 2 o'clock at the home of Mr. and Mrs. Brown. Rev. John Roberts, pastor of the Presbyterian church, officiating.*

CHAPTER NINETEEN

I don't remember much of the next day. As front-runner, they wanted me to go over to help Andrew's family. To bring him something baked, and show him how well I could handle tragedies, but I couldn't get my head off my pillow.

Sometimes it hurt to open my eyes.

Iris lied for me and told them I had inhaled too much smoke, and maybe it wasn't a lie. Every time I coughed, I expelled shadows onto the handkerchief that Andrew had loaned me.

So Bea and Greta went instead. They were better in a crisis than I was.

Bea was better for him anyway.

All the nerves and twisting thoughts made my skin hurt. It felt like pieces of the fire still burned in my lungs and my skin was scalding hot and I couldn't do anything but lay in bed.

The words I loved were gone, except for the unkindest and most unforgiving. And none of my tools or tricks could get my nerves under control.

I was every bad name I'd ever called myself.

Mira and Iris lay on top of my bedcovers, all sharp angles and pressure against my skin.

I didn't like it. At first. I didn't love how soft and gentle they all were when my bones were made of rigid steel and bending hurt and I didn't need to cry at all. I didn't like how weak they made me feel, when I was trying so, *so* hard to be strong. I didn't like how sometimes one of their shoulders would block my view of Rebecca's drawing I'd pinned to my wall.

And then time passed. Maybe an hour or maybe a day. And nobody really spoke; they just sat with me until my body knew I wasn't alone in the dark anymore. Their softness finally melted into my own stiff muscles. But I didn't need to cry. I didn't need to say anything.

I just needed them.

They sent for my mother before the first day was done. I don't know if they expected her to guide me, or mend me, but they'd told her I'd fallen ill, and my mother came running.

I heard her when she came in, early Sunday morning. She went immediately to Mr. Brown and start asking him questions. He hadn't checked on me once, but she treated all men as the expert in all things.

Mira and Iris left, or maybe it was Greta and Bea by then, I wasn't sure when one had left and one had taken her place, but in any case, they'd left me in my room alone.

With each creak of her steps, my heart shrunk and my bones grew tired. I didn't fix my hair. I didn't wipe the makeup that had smeared under my eyes. I smelled dusty and of ash that no soak or scrubbing could wash clean. The nightgown I somehow wore was wrinkled, and I knew I would not pass my mother's inspection.

How could I when I would never pass my own?

The door opened.

My throat was tight. "I tried, Momma." I closed my eyes hard. "I really tried."

She came to me and tucked me into her arms. I lay stiff and didn't hug her back. How could I? I was her hopes. I was her reflection.

And I'd let her down. "I'm sorry. I'm sorry."

She held my head in her hands, but I couldn't raise my chin. I couldn't look her in the eye.

"It's all right," she said.

"It's not. A little girl died, and it was all my fault."

"It wasn't. You didn't light the match."

"But he did it for me."

"It's not your fault."

"Momma. It was." I closed my eyes, and my mother held me tight. "It was. And what we did to him was because of me too. Because of the choices that I'd made. I thought he was a hero from a story. I shouldn't have trusted him to be better. I thought because he was beautiful he had to be good, and I knew better. I knew better."

She shook my shoulders. "You are not that powerful."

I closed my eyes and tears crested my cheeks. "They trained me—"

"—you are not responsible for the choices he made."

"I smiled at him. I trusted him."

"That didn't do it. You can smile at anyone, that wouldn't make someone set a house on fire. He's the one who betrayed your trust, but you don't need to be able to predict the future. You didn't know. You didn't have to know."

"I kissed him."

"He did this." She brushed my hair from my cheeks. "You aren't a bad person for trusting someone who let you down. You don't have to know everything."

Those words were a gift. A magic balm that let me breathe. Let my bones bend, and let the panic dampen to a quiet roar.

She held me, and didn't say anything else. She didn't have to. Why was it so easy to blame her? To hate her? She showed up when I needed her, even though I wasn't my brother. How much of my anger was a shield because I was scared she'd hate me if she really saw me?

And I wondered what would happen if I forgave my

mother the way I've always forgiven my father. My father was not a good man, but he wasn't really a bad one either. He was just a man with a good name and a crooked smile who drank my mother's spirit dry.

I sat up and placed my head on her shoulder, held hands cold from lack of touch, and as we sat in silence, drip by drip I tried to fill her up with my love.

And the first step to loving my mother was to tell her my truth.

I stood from the bed I hadn't left, and I took Rebecca's drawing down from the wall. Carefully. It was the only art of hers that existed now; the rest had burned with her.

"This little girl's life mattered." I let her see the bare-faced me that I didn't think she'd like. "It mattered every bit as much as her brother's."

Then tears I should be too tired for, tears I thought were already well wrung from my eyes, crested over and blurred my vision. "And so does mine."

My mother gently took the drawing from my hands, and then she pulled one of Mrs. Brown's frames down from her wall, unbent the backing, and removed the stitched primer and slid the painting behind glass.

Like a monument. Like something scooped up and pro-tected.

She listened as I cried again. She held me. And after those last tears had finally stopped flowing she looked me in the eye. "It will all be okay," she said.

"I've messed everything up."

She patted my cheek, and I remembered the way my mother smelled of home. "I know, baby." I snuggled in, and my mother held me like I haven't let her in a while. "That just means you have the power to try to make it right."

"I don't know if I can."

She wiped my cheeks. "You can't erase what you've done, but you can try to make things better for those who were hurt by your choices. Trying counts, Elsie."

I sat back, trying to make myself small. There was so much I needed to fix. What I'd done to Bea. And I owed Andrew's family a debt I could never ever repay. But maybe if I could forgive my mother for wanting me to be less than I was, then maybe I could forgive myself for all the ways I've proved her right.

"You do what you can to make it better," my momma said, "and then you move forward. That's where your power lies. There will be other men. Your right match is still ahead of you."

I lowered my head. "No." I swallowed hard. "I'm not going to build my future around a man's life again."

Her mouth opened. "Elsie." She started to correct me, but I shook my head.

"I won't. The future I could have had with Andrew is impossible now. I can't face his family every day and know I'm the one who took their daughter from them. I can't. I'm not saying I won't fall for someone else someday. I'm not saying I might not want a family, but I'm not going to put my own goals, my own voice, aside in hopes that someone will take care of me. I can take care of myself."

"I'm sure you can, but, honey—"

"—And maybe that's okay." The muscles in my neck released, and I smiled a smile just for me, just because I felt lighter somehow. Even in the middle of all my guilt and all my failures, I felt released from my set path.

From her expression it was clear she didn't understand me.

I drank in fresh breath. "It's not that I don't want love. Love is something beautiful, except for every time it isn't. And I know good men, men like my brother, my grandfather, and the allies who've helped us. Maybe my future can still have marriage or children in it. But maybe it won't. Either way it's going to be my choice."

I didn't need her permission, but I searched her eyes like she could give it to me anyway.

"I . . ." My momma's voice trailed off, and we were so quiet I could hear the grandfather clock ticking. "I don't even know what that would look like."

She was right. "I don't know either. My whole life has been leading me to a white veil. Every fairy tale I've read, every nickel movie I've watched, the girl becomes a wife and the ending starts and we just have to assume it's happy. How can I imagine a life where my thoughts matter, if every story I'd ever thought for myself ended with a kiss and a vow to honor and obey someone else's life more than my own? It's like I've left my own story now."

She tapped my knee. "Or maybe your own story is just starting."

I let out a laugh or a sob, and my voice grew stronger. "Isn't that the loveliest thing you ever heard?"

I've always known what my life would look like, because my life was a gift someone else gave me. But maybe women would be stronger if we stopped accepting poison just because it was tied with a pretty bow. Maybe I would be stronger if I stood on my own feet. Maybe falling in love is the gift at the side of life, like icing on a lemon cake, not our only meal, or our only option if we didn't want to starve.

I'd been taught my whole life how to bake. Maybe now I could feed my own self.

"Well, I can't wait to read it," my mother said.

My mother spoke to me in a metaphor. She reached me in my own language. She showed up and she saw me and she didn't run away, even when I know she didn't understand me.

I clutched her hands in mine, and then I looked her in the eye. "No, Momma. I need you on every page."

Her lips pressed together, and her eyes started to glisten. She licked her lips and nodded, until tears crested her eyelashes and left a streak of bare skin on her made-up face. She squeezed my hands tight with fingers that were trembling before she cleared her throat and spoke.

"I thought you'd never ask."

I held my momma's hand tight, and together we started our next chapter.

The Matriarchy

My great-great-great-grandmother had dreams I'll
never know.
But I know her love by the softness of my momma's
lullabies.
My great-great-grandmother had thoughts about
politics that didn't change the world.
But I know her by the notes she left in the margins
of my great-grandfather's books.
My great-grandmother had a hunger that would
never be filled.
But I know her by the recipes we still follow.
My grandmother gave me my name and held me
when my fingers were so small I could twist them
around one of hers,
And I know her hopes when I look in the mirror and
meet my own eye.
Invisible mothers stand behind me.
And while their lives were ignored by history
I will not forget the women who made me.
I hold their hopes, their hungers, their thoughts, and
their dreams upon my shoulders.
And when I walk alone I walk with them.

CHAPTER TWENTY

On the afternoon they would bury an eleven-year-old girl, the air was hot and arid, and dry enough my throat burned as I tried to carry one of Mrs. Brown's folding chairs from the front shed to set in the overflow in the front parlor. Mr. Brown took it from my grip.

"Allow me," he said, protecting me from a weight I could have carried. He and the Johnson boys set up the chairs in simple rows across an empty dining room that overfilled into the front parlor, while Greta kept them all company. We were expecting quite the crowd.

But how many of them would be here to mourn?

Rebecca's obituary spoke more about her father than it did her.

There was nowhere for me to stand. My cotton dress clung to my back, and my thighs chafed in the heat as I left the front parlor and moved past the boys in the dining room into the kitchen. The kitchen was even hotter than the front parlor, and there wasn't room for me to stand in there either, not with Bea ordering everyone about like a grand chef. So I made my way back through the hall and through the entry and out to the flowering front porch where a soft breeze offered me some respite.

The Shaws would be here soon.

I breathed in deep. I felt so much loss it had nearly broken me, but this wasn't about me. This wasn't my grief.

Before I could breathe twice they turned up the walk.

Andrew's steps were shallow, his neck bent crooked as he held his mother's arm. His mother—oh heavens, his mother—walked with flushed cheeks, pale eyes, and a proud step. His father couldn't seem to fake even a wounded pride; he carried his grief like it weighed down every muscle. His skin was gray and pale, his posture stooped, but his tie was folded crisp and perfect.

Andrew's eyes were downcast, and his shoulders slumped as he helped his parents climb the stairs. His gaze slipped over me without catching as he helped them in.

I followed a few steps behind.

My mother joined me and took my hand in hers. "Give them room, Elsie."

I did. I'd give them anything I had.

All three of them stood in the entry before a portrait Mrs. Shaw's sister had painted a few years back of Rebecca Jane

Shaw, whose name mattered, and whose voice mattered, and who would slip away forgotten and invisible.

But not by them.

And never by me. She'd made an impact on my life that would change me forever, and ten years from now, or twenty, when her name was only ever uttered in passing by the three people standing here, I would be thinking about her and about the way her life mattered.

I would be fighting for her my whole life.

I studied the portrait, even though she looked so much younger than the memory inscribed into my thoughts. Her light hair hung low, curled up by her face, with pale skin and rosy cheeks, and a light blue dress that brought out the color of her bright eyes. The artist had caught some mischief hiding in her expression, in the curl of her lips and the arch of her brows.

The service was short and sad. The preacher didn't ramble on too long, and while there was grief in the untimely loss, in the children she would never have, in the life she would never live, he spoke as though he hadn't ever met her. Each word slamming on my back like a weight I could not carry without cracking.

Andrew was the only one who spoke of her drawings, of all those cities she'd drawn in the textbooks that had burned with her.

So many people came to watch. So many people came to judge. Whispers made their own requiem as the pastor spoke of forgiveness and mercy and grief and the crowd ministered through sharp looks and glowering mouths. Even as they made a memorial, Rebecca's life was overshadowed by the gossip of how she died. Even as they mourned her life, most had come to watch the family fall.

I could feel them forgetting her already.

After, while the society passed the casseroles to feed the spectators, and tried to give comfort to those who could not eat, I hid on the staircase as Bea brought a plate to Andrew. He sat in the front parlor in a chair by a window, his cheek lit by sunlight that didn't reflect in his eyes.

He didn't see me watching him from across the room. He didn't even see Bea standing there with flour on the hips of her flowered day dress, and rosy cheeks warmed by the too-bright sun.

A dining chair at his side was vacant. She slipped into it, and they sat together for a few seconds before he noticed she was there.

They sat together in silence.

She handed him the plate. "You've got to eat," she said softly.

He turned away. "Nothing tastes as it should."

She offered the plate again, this time with a careful smile. "I baked this, so at least you know it will be good."

He sighed and took it from her.

"I'm so sorry," she said. Her voice shook. "I'm so sorry for your loss."

His lips trembled and then pressed together. "She was my sister. That's not just a loss. It's like a wall of my house is gone." His voice slumped off. He rubbed his chest. "No, it's worse than that. I've lost that too. We've lost everything. And all I miss is her." His voice was choked with tears.

"Would you tell me about her?"

His throat constricted. "I can't."

"That's okay."

They sat in silence.

"Eat something, Andrew," I whispered so low I knew they didn't hear me.

Andrew looked at his plate and wouldn't lift the fork.

"She kept snakes in boxes," he said after another minute of silence. "Rebecca did. She loved to play outside in the creek behind our house, and would always come in with the bottom of her dresses soaked and covered in mud. She loved toads and insects and water snakes. She'd always bring them inside the house; try to keep them as pets, but she loved hiding them in my mother's hatboxes. My mother would scream every time, and we'd all laugh while Rebecca tried to save the creature before my mother threw it out the window." His lips curled in a smile that didn't hit his eyes, then crumpled into a pucker. He swallowed hard. "It's like Rebecca was a light inside my house and now we've all gone dim."

Andrew rubbed his temples.

"I'm sorry," Bea said again.

"Don't be." His jaw tightened. "My parents knew the enemies they were making. But standing for what was right still matters, even when it takes everything."

He was so good. They'd chosen the right candidate. She picked up his fork and handed it to him. "Eat something. It can only help."

She got him to take three bites before his hands dropped like they'd grown heavy. She took his plate and his fork back.

"I should see my mother," he said, but then he didn't move.

She touched his arm. He grabbed her hand and clung to it, his eyes closed. He held her hand like she was holding him steady, like for one brief second he could stop trying so hard to stand tall.

My heart hurt when he let her go. Bea watched him leave, with concern and her good heart, and absolute yearning, and I knew she wanted to take some of his pain from him. She stared into the open dining room, and then she picked up his plate and took it back into the kitchen.

After they left, I stared down at my bandaged hands. His words had become a motto, or a rule that I would have to follow from here on out.

Doing what was right mattered, even when it cost something. Even when it cost everything.

I knew I could ease one thing for him. I had one thing I could do to restore a tiny part of what my choices had taken from them.

I made my way up to my room and pulled Rebecca's painting down from the wall. I hugged the frame to my chest. It felt sacred now. But I didn't need it to remember her.

I didn't need a monument to Rebecca.

I would build her one of my own.

I crossed back down to the dining room where Andrew and his parents sat together. I handed the framed drawing of Rebecca's city to her mother.

Mrs. Shaw touched the glass softly. "You don't know how many of these I've thrown away." Her face crumpled.

"I'm sorry for your loss. For all of it."

"Thank you, Elsie," Mrs. Shaw said. She took my hand and turned my palm so she saw the bandages. "This . . ." She couldn't finish. She handed the frame over to Mr. Shaw, and it was like some window inside him opened and a spark of light came through. Then she stood and wrapped me in her arms. "Thank you for trying to save her," she whispered.

"I'm so sorry I failed." My voice didn't carry past our ears.

She shook her head and pulled back, staring at my eyes like she needed me to know she could look into them.

Andrew held my fingers, and when his eyes found mine, tears were cresting. I turned away.

"Wait." Andrew stood and then wrapped me in a hug. I fought my emotions as he hugged me, and as I drew away, his own eyes were shining and the skin beneath his nose was wet as well.

"Thank you," he said. He glanced at the art. "It means

the whole world"—he breathed in—"to have one of her drawings."

I nodded, and then I turned and walked away as quickly as I could, so they wouldn't know how much it hurt to lose it.

Because I knew it was nowhere near how much it must hurt them to lose her.

CHAPTER TWENTY-ONE

After . . .

Oh heavens, there was an after.

After the crowd had left behind stained, scraped plates and unfolded napkins and empty chairs, I watched Andrew and his parents take the two paintings they had left of their artist.

My mother held my hand as they packed the car they'd borrowed. My friends were helping clean up after everything, and I knew I should help them, but I couldn't turn away.

"Where will they go?" I asked. "Where are they staying?"

Bea joined my side.

"They're staying with Mrs. Shaw's sister. Her house is small for all four of them, but it should be temporary, once Mr. Shaw finds more work."

"Why does he need . . . I thought he had a fine job."

"Poor Mr. Shaw has been removed from his position," my mother said. "He was the face of the company, but now he's lost the trust of the public."

"But surely they have savings."

"Some," Mira answered. I turned. She picked up a couple of cloth napkins. "But not enough to rebuild. Enough to survive."

"But how . . . how will Andrew go to college? How will he meet his future?"

"He won't," Greta answered. She held a stack of stained plates. "They're going to remove his priority one." She smiled as she said it. "They've decided to give it to Johnson instead."

My anger rattled against my lungs. "Whom you just happened to have netted in."

"Good luck, I guess."

"Nothing is decided," Mira said. "The Matron Circle is still discussing plans. But Johnson's path forward was already moving neck and neck with Andrew's anyway. It does seem likely."

"And they'll just give Andrew's future to Johnson? Has he been vetted? Has—"

"—I don't know," Greta said as though it didn't matter. "Why don't you ask the circle themselves?"

I . . . "Why don't I?" I said with a burst of energy. I stood. "I've been invited to tea."

Greta leaned back, her expression wary of the energy that

had taken over me. "That was supposed to be yesterday, and they canceled it."

"Then we uncancel it."

I thundered into the kitchen with my friends following behind me. Mr. and Mrs. Brown sat at the kitchen table. Mrs. Brown had her shoes off, and Mr. Brown was rubbing her heels. She tucked her feet beneath her to quickly restore her modesty.

"Girls," she said. "Next time—"

"—The tea party with . . . those lovely ladies." I glanced at Mr. Brown to make sure he didn't pick up on any clues. He hadn't. "Is there a way we can reschedule?"

Mrs. Brown sighed. "I know the Shaws have already lost so much, but—"

I wouldn't let her say no. "Can we reschedule?"

She raised her chin. "I think so."

"Then I can fix this."

Every single woman in the room looked at me.

"I'll see to it," Mrs. Brown said.

"Good." I glanced at my mother and remembered my manners. "Thank you."

If I was going to convince the Matrons to give Andrew back his priority, then I'd need to gather evidence. I needed . . . An idea bloomed fully in my head.

"And I'll need to borrow the car, if I can."

I turned. There was so much I needed to do.

"Where are we going?" Mira said.

I grinned. "On an adventure."

"I'll grab Iris."

"I'm staying home," Greta said. "I like the priority right where it is."

Fine with me. "Bea?"

"I'll go with you on any adventure you'll take me on."

I grinned. "Momma?"

She startled; I believe she thought I'd leave her behind again. "Will these adventures be legal?" she asked.

"Not every time," Bea warned. Mr. Brown made a face and Mira laughed.

A spark of spirit lit my mother's eyes.

I stood tall. "I've got to go to work."

———————————❖———————————

I flipped my notebook to a blank page and began to write.

It wasn't poetry. Not this time. It was an article.

It was recompense. Andrew could fight this. No words would give him back his sister. No words could fix that.

But I knew I could find him a path back to the future I know he still wanted.

I could write his way out. I could restore his reputation. I listed ideas that I knew Andrew had opinions on that could influence his and his family's reputation. He could write about Prohibition, about economic stability, and about temperance, or about the dangerous effect of nationalism . . .

But I knew him better now. He'd want to talk about preparing financially for heartbreaking losses. He'd want to talk about how wealth was empty without people to care about. He'd want to write about doing what's right, even when it cost him everything.

I started writing notes, which turned into an outline for an editorial. My enthusiasm for the idea of fixing this made the article thicker and fuller, and perhaps I should have stopped. I wrote a full article in Andrew's voice. And there was a power behind writing from a man's voice, knowing that the world would turn to listen. It was exhilarating knowing these words would matter. We were built to forgive men like Andrew. The world was built to give them a second chance, and the charm I'd been taught to influence men could influence opinions as well.

There was a kind of power here, a whiff just strong enough to get drunk on it.

When I was finished, I held the article in one hand and it fluttered in the breeze from my open window. My brain had done this. This article presented a likable, smart leader.

But only if I signed it with a man's name.

The cold wind carried my thoughts with it.

If I'd been born a man, I knew my whole life would look different. If I was born a man, I could have had a man's future. My brother's future. Maybe even Andrew's.

But what a loss that would have been.

I wanted my life to make a bigger change than their

lives would. And that was an opportunity I'd only have as a woman. Because I could change things for all of us.

I took the card from the editor off my bookshelf.

Frank Groeing, Editor in Chief, *Park Village Gazette*

I could make things better. And then after, I could do what all my grandmothers had done. I could create life.

I could create my own.

⁑

Frank's desk was littered with papers, and a coffee cup had left a permanent ring on the oak. Tall oak bookshelves were stuffed full of law books and loose files. My mother tapped her toes and looked down at the ground as if the disorder was physically painful to her.

And maybe it was. I'd inherited my issue with my nerves from her.

"I'm sure he wouldn't mind a little help with organization," I said.

"Oh, thank goodness." My mother started sorting his papers.

His secretary looked over at us through the large windows as he made a phone call. Perhaps to the police, or at least the building's security. A crest of nerves made me shake my hands. An echo of the panic attack rushed over me, hot against the cuts on my palms. I don't know what triggered it, but it felt like an aftershock of nerves, coming from nowhere.

I lifted my chin and breathed through it. I didn't fail at everything. And I was trying. This was me trying. Trying counted.

Frank burst in. "Who are you, and how'd you get into my office?"

Get a hold of yourself, Elsie. I remembered my training and gave him a smile. *The hostess.*

And after a moment, the smile turned genuine. He was so grumpy and gruff, I just wanted to squish him up and put him in my pocket.

That was an odd thing to think. Focus. "Hello, Mr. Groeing."

"Ah, the girl from the restaurant," he said, his voice pattern staccato and sharp. He crossed into his office and took the stack of papers my mother was trying to organize. "You trying to set me up again?" He turned to my mother. "I'm sorry, dear, I'm sure you're lovely, but I'm not interested."

My mother was scandalized. "I am a married woman."

"And my mother. This isn't Matchmaking, Mr. Groeing," I said. Although, they would be very cute together. Mr. Groeing was a grump, but he had a heart of gold, and left quite the mess everywhere he went that I know my mother would enjoy sorting. My own father hadn't even noticed she wasn't home until my mother had called him. But it wasn't to be. My mother would never leave my father, just like I would never stop trying to make Rebecca proud.

My mother gave me her stubbornness alongside her anxiety.

Mr. Groeing hovered over his desk, his ruddy cheeks flushed. "Then what are you doing in here? And what are you doing with my files? I have a system."

I lifted my pages, now freshly typed, from my pocketbook. "It's a story."

He turned.

"A review?" he asked, genuinely interested.

"No. A scoop."

He took the pages and started reading.

I swallowed. I immediately wanted the pages back. Why did I think this was a good idea? Maybe it's not ready. Maybe I should have done just one more edit pass.

Stop saying maybe, Elsie. You can fix this.

Frank grumbled. "This is not your name."

I didn't answer. My name mattered.

That's why it made a good sacrifice.

"It's good," Frank said. He flipped the page.

Good? "Really?" I squealed. I cleared my throat. "I'll tell him you think so."

"Why didn't he bring this himself?"

I opened my mouth but didn't know what to say.

"His mother needed him at home," my mother said quickly. "We're bringing it as a favor from him."

"Oh right. It's a shame, that poor little girl."

His cheeks puffed out as he read. He scratched his chin, and then he crossed out a sentence. "Okay, fine, I'll run it.

But this is not how my business is done, do you understand me? You can't just come in here—"

"—I thought you liked strange?" I smiled adorably, and he grumbled under his breath.

My mother gave me an approving look. "Let's talk money," she said.

"I'll send the standard fare in the mail to the Shaws."

"Good," I said hesitantly. I believed women should always be paid for their work, but this felt like part of the sacrifice. My stomach was already full.

It was okay to want more, even if you already have plenty, just so long as you don't take it from someone who was starving.

My mother left the desk, its papers now arrayed into neat piles. She picked up his hat from his cluttered hat rack, sniffed it, and then made a face before she collected his coat and scarf. "I'll launder this and have it back to you before end of business."

"I see you come by strange naturally." As he flipped through my mother's stacks, his voice had mellowed.

Oh, he liked us. Before I lost my courage I lowered my shoulders and spoke up. "I'd like to submit some of my own writing as well."

"What do you have?"

"I didn't bring anything with me."

"I can't read nothing," he said, his voice clipped.

"I'm sorry. I will have excellent pages for you, I promise."

"Next time make an appointment."

I shook his hand quickly. "I'll be sure to. Thank you." But then a handshake wasn't enough, because he said I was good. Strange, sure, I knew that, but good? I could live off the glow of good for at least a month. I threw my arms around him in a hug, and he grumbled some more and scrunched his shoulders uncomfortably when I pulled away.

But the corner of his mouth had tipped up into a smile.

My mother and I left his office, and I walked straight to his secretary.

I gave him smile number five. "Hello. I'd like to set up an appointment for next week to talk about my writing."

He glanced at Frank, who waved his hand in permission.

"He's open Thursday at two?"

"That works for me." I had no idea if it did or not, but I would make this work. This was the first chapter of the story I was building of myself. Now what should I write about?

"What name is this under?" He looked up at me.

This time I smiled, and it wasn't to charm anyone. It was because somehow, even after everything, I still could.

"My own. Elsie Fawcett. Pleasure to meet you"

Then my mother and I walked out of the office to rejoin my sisters.

I gave Andrew my words one time.

But I'd never do it again.

From now on, I'd make sure that everyone who met me knew my name mattered too.

My thoughts mattered too. My dreams mattered too. I wasn't going to defer them for anyone. Not anymore.

I was going to fight for my own story.

CHAPTER
TWENTY-TWO

Mr. Brown must have crossed down the steps of that flowering porch to retrieve his paper before we woke the next morning, because it sat on the dining room table, next to his coffee and freshly poured breakfast as I entered the dining room.

I had to sit on my hands to stop myself from grabbing his paper.

Bea and Mira helped my mother bring in breakfast, both of them asking her questions I'd never asked about how she met my father, or what she put into these breakfast casseroles. I smiled and listened to her answers, interested in the woman my mother was beyond the title I'd always called her by.

Iris grabbed a slice of bacon from a platter as Greta came in, still dressed in her nightgown, and what a nightgown, long and ruffled sheer tulle; it seemed almost indecent with Mr. Brown here. Not that he noticed. He was so absorbed in the newspaper.

As was I. I scanned the front page, but my article, no, *Andrew's article*, wasn't on there. This irked a little. Frank had said it was good. Didn't good deserve the front page?

"I say we take a lazy day today," Greta said with an overly satisfied smile. "The tea tomorrow with the Matrons seems positively laborious." I glanced at Mr. Brown, but he was still so oblivious he might have missed Greta's loose lips. She turned those loose lips toward Bea. "Darling, would you be a peach and mix up a batch of cookies to bring over for my dear friend Bill Johnson. I do want to thank their whole family for all their help with the funeral."

Mira and I shared a look.

Bea cleared her throat. "No."

"I'm sorry, what did you just say?" Greta asked.

"You'll need to bake them yourself," Bea said. "I'm tired from cooking for all those people, and if you want to charm Bill Johnson, you'll have to use your own recipes to do it."

"Atta girl," Mira said. I grinned at her.

Bea nodded her head once, and then she scrunched down. "But I would be happy to check over your recipes if you need any suggestions."

I smiled. She really couldn't help herself, now could she?

"Oh, that's interesting," Mr. Brown said.

I perked up.

"What is, dear?" Mrs. Brown asked.

"A fellow invented an instant camera. Can you imagine? What is this world coming to?"

"Oh, that is fascinating," Mira said. "I wonder how that works."

"Anything of local interest?" I asked quickly.

Mr. Brown didn't respond. He'd gone back to reading.

"Well, I guess I could just buy something," Greta said. "When does that bakery open again?"

Mr. Brown touched his lips as he read, his eyes shining. Mira reached for my hand and held it.

"Wow," Mr. Brown said as he brought a napkin to his nose. "What a courageous young man."

"Who, dear?"

I squeezed Mira's hand.

"Andrew Shaw."

Greta stopped midword.

"He's written a touching and courageous article. Can you imagine? Right after his sister's funeral?"

Mrs. Brown read the article, and then she looked at me with so much pride.

I glanced at my mom, and then I sat tall in my seat. My nerves were still here, they were always here, but I knew now, that if my nerves could call me powerful and blame me for every bad thing that happened around me, then they had to notice that I could influence things for good too. Maybe I couldn't be responsible for everyone else's choices.

But I could make a difference.

It took the full day to know for sure, but by the time

we ate dinner, the Gossips reported that the people of this town had forgiven the Shaws' tarnished reputation. By the time I finished what I wanted to say and collected my own researching in my pocketbook for tomorrow's meeting with the Matron Circle, I knew people I will never meet were quoting my words, talking to one another about Andrew's strength to write them right after his sister's funeral.

I collected the Gossip reports hidden inside recipes I wouldn't follow, and I had my mother hold on to them.

I'd done it.

His family's good name could be remembered. And there were always scholarships, and opportunities for him would be quick to reappear. This could be made into his story of overcoming, the narrative we could sell as we propped him back onto the path for a priority one.

I had my argument ready.

And my own dream to make possible.

It was night when Andrew pulled up to the house and started the walk up the lane.

I was waiting for him on the front porch.

I stood, and he looked up from his hands. "Elsie."

I swallowed hard, but let him speak.

Andrew stopped at the picket fence. He glanced around, remembering the loss that had last sent him here.

I took a couple of steps toward him. "Good evening, Andrew."

"I didn't write that article," he said finally, his voice tired.

"Oh?" I said, trying to find a lie.

"And when I spoke to the editor, he said you turned it in for me."

"Oh." I picked at the embroidery on my skirt.

He leaned against the wood. "Why did you do that?"

"I wanted to help."

"By speaking for me?"

I winced though his tone was not unkind. "I'm sorry." I turned. "I thought I could help repair your family's good name, in order to try to make up for what I'd broken. It was my fault for bringing Patch into your life. I had to make restitution."

"That was never your fault. None of us blame you."

I did. I think I always would.

"What did you need from me?" I asked instead.

He glanced down, and I looked away.

"You're an excellent writer," he managed. "You made me sound more like myself than I do in my own words. It's like you know me better than I know myself."

The feeling of relief only lasted for a moment. "I don't. I know who you'll grow into though."

I grew up with him.

Andrew met my eyes, his grief-weighed eyes crinkling at the end. "I like who you see me to be."

I tapped the fence between us. "I like you too." He brushed a curl from the side of my jaw, I knew that he'd forgiven me for writing the article for him. The life the society had wanted for me was still right here. All I'd have to do was lean closer, build him up more. And for a second I thought about how big and full and easy my life would be if I could just let myself be loved by him. It wasn't a bad life.

But it wasn't mine. My dreams and comfort and the power I'd gain by being with him weren't enough for me to sacrifice a life with love in it. I couldn't say no to the possibility of a love in my future, even when I didn't know who it would be with. I wanted lemon cake with icing.

I wanted my goals, and I wanted my own chance at love.

"You remind me of my brother," I said.

"High compliment," he said, smiling, and all at once I knew that he knew about Nathaniel without me having told him his name.

"And that's the way I like you," I said softly. "Like a brother, or a friend, but . . ."

I twisted my hands.

The moonlight hit the curve of his cheek, and his eyes, still dimmed with grief, met mine.

"I'm sorry," I said again.

He leaned back on his ankles and let go of me. "It's all right. I'm sorry I must have confused . . ."

"I kissed you. You read every signal I gave you."

"Are you sure this is how you feel? Could your feelings

grow or change?" I closed my eyes, knowing everything I could gain if I just said yes.

"You don't love me, Andrew. You love the way you look in my eyes."

"I . . ."

He couldn't refute it.

"And I think there's someone else who you like better. You don't have to keep trying with me just because I kissed you like we were serious. You don't owe me your loyalty. I don't want it. That's not enough for me."

I smiled a smile for me. "I need something bigger for my life. I want to be a great person too."

Andrew blinked, and for the first time, I think he saw the real me. His mouth trembled, and he glanced upward. "I would never stop you from going after a dream. You should write more."

"I'm going to." I touched his arm, and he nodded, like I'd told him no and he respected that. "I can't love you like you deserve, Andrew. But I do look forward to seeing you in the papers."

Andrew studied me like I was a puzzle and the last piece just clicked in. His expression warmed to a smile. "I'll look forward to reading your words."

He offered me his right hand, his palm facing me but held still.

I shook it. Like an equal.

Like a girl.

Like a goodbye.

And then I walked away.

Bea waited inside the front entry of the house, her long hair down and curled, her face painted. She wore that pink dress we'd been trying to get her to wear, and she looked so lovely that I resolved to kick her if she ever decided to wear a different color.

"It's too soon," she said. "I should wait. I should let him grieve."

"Bea."

"We have plenty of time."

"You don't know that," Iris said. "The worst heartbreaks come from when you don't try."

Mira hit her arm. "Be brave. That boy is crazy about you."

Bea rubbed her arm. "I don't want to be second place. I don't want to be . . . leftovers."

"Okay," I said. "So that's what you don't want. But what *do* you want?"

She closed her eyes tight, like she was summoning courage, but when she opened them her expression was clear. "Him."

"Even if he doesn't have the priority one?" Greta asked.

"I don't care about the priority. I'd still take him without it," Bea said softly. "I could live in poverty every day of my life if I could have him." She was so sweet. And so naive. She pressed down her dress.

"Then go get him."

Bea grinned, and Mira whooped and swatted Bea's behind, and then we all moved to the front window to watch as Bea raced down that long path after him. I sat on the ground next to them, my chin on Iris's knee, Mira's elbow digging into my shoulder. I reached for Greta and pulled her toward the window where outside, Andrew turned, and the look of relief that crossed his face made Iris and me swoon, while Greta murmured about impracticalities and Mira wondered out loud that he'd better deserve her.

They talked there for a long time, long enough that Greta went upstairs to grab her chenille blanket, and we all made plates of leftovers from the funeral, and I started to panic a little about what I'd have to say to the Matron Circle in the morning. But then Bea took Andrew's hand and gave it a comforting squeeze and we all turned quiet. We watched as they kept moving closer.

And then Bea leaned forward on her tiptoes and kissed his cheek.

She dropped back down on his heels, and Andrew bent down and kissed her, short and sweet as a blackberry.

Iris awwed, but Mira and I were quiet.

I was happy for her, obviously, but also he had just told me he liked me, so perhaps it was a little soon to have recovered. I mean I was happy for them both; this was how it always should have been.

But also . . . it was *over* over now. Now I had no net, and tomorrow I was going to take the greatest leap of my life.

And when I glanced at Mira I knew that this kiss was the first step toward a goodbye.

When Bea opened the front door, I'd recovered, and

all of us catcalled her so loudly, I was certain Andrew had heard it. Bea blushed and then ran at us like she was going to tackle us, but instead it became a giant hug so hard and fast that the chair Iris was sitting on toppled over. We all broke out laughing, wiggling like a pack of puppies in a dogpile snuggling to find a spot of comfort as our laughter ended, like all laughter does. We didn't move from where we lay on the ground. Mira's head rested on my stomach, Bea's forehead on my shoulder, while the rest of her lay partially on Greta and Iris.

We stayed like that for a while, talking and gossiping about, I don't know, nothing and everything. I laughed until I snorted at Mira's stories, and later we climbed to the rooftops and searched the clear sky for stars, until Bea grew so sleepy she snuggled, wrapped in Greta's blanket, against Mira's shoulder and Iris declared it was too dangerous to be up so high, and then we slept in Mira and Bea's room, Greta and I staying up talking until morning while Mira snored, and Iris had left for her own room, and it was perfect.

It was the calm in the center of a storm.

It was everything.

For that one night I could pretend that this night could go on forever and we'd always be young and sisters and together.

But I knew better.

CHAPTER
TWENTY-THREE

Mira was grumbling about the late hour, and Bea was humming happily to herself and kept staring off into the distance and then smiling for no reason. I was too tired, too keyed up, but I was ready. Greta joined us at the curb as we waited for the Helpers to pick us up to go to tea. For a second a touch of guilt hit me for what restoring Andrew's priority would take from her.

But she looked at me and only smiled back.

She wasn't my enemy anymore. Maybe she never really was.

We climbed into the back of an unmarked car, and covered our own faces with embroidered pillowcases in order to protect the location of the Matron Circle. I have no idea how long we drove, although Bea, Mira, and I had run out of all the hymns we'd learned and had moved on to singing songs of a rowdier disposition, much to Mrs. Brown's consternation. Iris's low voice lent a deep alto to the drinking songs she'd taught us.

The car stopped. I fell over into Bea's soft shoulders, and she propped me up sturdily.

When the doors opened the light filtered through the cotton and floss thread, leaving sun-dappled blurs against the white fabric.

A soft hand took my own, and a woman's voice I didn't recognize told me where to step and to be careful as I scooted off the bumper.

I felt suddenly self-conscious as I walked, my bag of my reports and homework weighing heavy on my shoulder, and my shoes rolling on what I suspected was a loose gravel road. With the pillowcase over my head, I didn't know who was watching us, or where we were, though by the absence of street noise, and frequent birdsong, I knew it was outside a city somewhere. The air smelled crisp, like overly ripened apples and just cut grass, my dress warmed from a half-lowered sun. It was late for tea. From the grumble in my stomach I was well ready for supper.

They led us upstairs and inside a building, following a path I could not discern, my shoes clacking against a wood floor. Eventually we stopped and warm shoulders pressed against either side of me. My sisters. I reached for a hand, and I knew from her rough palms Bea stood at my left and from her cold skin Mira held my right. Once we heard the sound of a door closing, someone gently lifted the pillowcases off our faces.

The breeze felt so cold against my breath-warmed face, and I knew my curls had pulled straight because of the sweat that had turned even Greta's face a little ruddy.

The room we found ourselves in was as large as a ballroom and windowless, with walls papered in an ornate flower pattern, and dark millwork creating borders and chair rails. Round tables filled the room, covered in matching white lace cloths and surrounded by Queen Anne chairs. A large buffet table in the back of the room held tiered platters full of squared fudge and caramels, coconut cakes, and cherry chocolate creams. Crystal bowls filled with a sparkling pink punch and gilded plates stacked in a neat pile seemed welcoming.

The few other women in the room were dressed simply but neatly. A Black woman with a soft smile and a patterned frock gestured toward the treats. "Please," she said, "fill up a plate. The circle will join you shortly."

Another woman, this one white and old enough that her shoulders bent over, her small frame appearing shrunken in her soft purple dress, touched my hand with a soft, cold, wrinkled palm and squeezed as she gave me the warmest smile. "After you, my dear," she said, her voice rough but melodic.

I didn't know any of these women, but I felt so welcomed and so hungry that I turned to the buffet and loaded up. Bea was already questioning the women about the recipes, and Mira's cheeks were stuffed full of fudges.

"I'm Elsie," I said to the older woman.

"We know."

Right. I wanted to ask them more questions, to set them at ease, and get to know them, or who they were. Were they Helpers who were joining us, or were they members of the circle themselves? But how could I ask without poking into the secret that had sent me here with a pillowcase over my head?

So I kept my curiosity small, and spoke only about the food or their hair, the pattern on the wallpapers, and what books they'd been reading. They had us each sit at a different table, and more women filtered in, each of them hugging or gossiping as they grabbed a plate. The little older woman stayed by my side the whole time.

"I love your hair clips," she said. I reached up and touched the crescent moon clips.

"Thank you," I said softly. "They were my grandmother's."

She smiled, and I noticed the brooch on her dress was shaped like a crescent moon as well, with jade flowers like my grandmother's. I glanced about, and spied crescent jewelry hung on necks and ears and wrists.

"Was my grandmother a member of the circle?" I asked suddenly. Those hair clips I'd inherited.

"The council," she said.

I sat back in my chair.

"Not many legacies make it back to this room." She smiled softly. "I'm glad you managed it."

"What can I call you?" I asked, being careful not to ask for her real name.

"My name is Sarah," she said, "but I like you so much you can call me Grandma."

My eyes prickled, and a grief I hadn't thought of in years made my throat feel tight.

More women filled my table, each of them smiling at me as they sat, and then turning to the other women whose names they knew and whose families they didn't hesitate to ask about. Laughter erupted from Mira's table, and Bea sat with a pencil, jotting down what had to be a recipe. Greta sat timidly, her usual gregarious disposition smaller as the women around her knew her good name and still ignored her.

I met her eye and gave her a smile, and she nibbled on a cookie, lowered her shoulders, and leaped into the conversation.

My mother and Mrs. Brown seemed to know every woman at their table, and many women would leave their own tables to hover around my mother's, listening as she spoke of the fire, and I might be wrong, but I may have heard Mrs. Brown mention the words *Duesenberg* and *joyride* in the same sentence. The differences of each woman struck me, old and young, all shades of skin color and size, all manner of dress from expensive silks to simple cotton, each speaking as an equal.

The country wasn't like this. Just sitting together in this room was against the Jim Crow laws of segregation. We worked and we built together, but the evil our society was founded to fight still loomed large and unbreakable.

But this was the future we were pushing for. Behind the secrecy and weight of my oaths, this was where we were going.

And if I had my way, this was just the beginning.

I reached into my bag and pulled out my notebooks. The newspaper with my article was folded carefully, but still it had creased. I smoothed the paper.

Sarah reached over and squeezed my hand again. "Just breathe in and out, dear one. We're all ready to listen."

I looked at her and realized my nerves were blissfully silent. She smiled again, a trained smile that filled her whole face and left me feeling so well loved that I knew she'd been called Mother.

"Thank you, Grandma."

Her nose crinkled.

Miss Reynolds slammed her cane down on the floor, and a sudden memory of our training evaluations sent a chill up my neck. The room went silent.

Miss Reynolds sat at Mira's table, dressed in a garçonne suit she fit very well, a cane in one hand, a top hat balanced across her forehead, shadowing her sharp pale cheekbones and heavy lidded eyes.

Miss Reynolds was a legend, though, already so influential. Her mind was sharp, but her strategies and her training were sharper. Her position was what Iris was working toward. She glanced around the room and then lifted one eyebrow. "All the circle members are here, so let's start this meeting. I yield the floor to Maud Brown: Head Wife Matron of the northwest chapters."

Mrs. Brown stood.

I swallowed back my nerves, and my stomach would not settle.

Mrs. Brown looked over us all. "To our Matron Circle, and their council, I thank you so kindly for your invitation. I'd like to introduce you to our former front-runner, Miss Elsie Fawcett. She has a speech prepared, and as many of you have read from her files, I expect this will not be the last we hear from her."

I smiled at that unexpected compliment. Soft applause sounded, and I stood from my chair, picking up my notes and the newspaper, sliding around chairs until I reached the front of the room, and turning so those sitting faced me. Mrs. Allen and Mrs. Alvarez, our own chapter heads, sat together at a table near the back, and they both lifted their hands to wave as I spotted them.

I grinned, and the nerves I'd been fighting simmered down. At my nod, my sisters and my mother stood from their chairs and began passing out copies of the newspaper.

"As the women who selected Andrew Shaw," I began, speaking to the members of the Matron Circle who hid here in this council, "I'm sure you know well how good and how kind he really is, a fact that I can confirm with my own experience. Andrew is a good enough man that I would let one of my best friends date him, which is as high praise as I can give. And he's already lost so much. How can we take away his future? Look what one article could do. Look how this loss is already making him a kinder more compassionate person."

A woman spoke from the crowd. "It is a good story angle. Voters will eat that up."

My storming thoughts pushed me to close my eyes, because Rebecca was more than an election strategy.

Another woman spoke up. "I've always liked him and his mother."

"With the right wife to guide him . . ."

Good. Andrew's life was set.

Now time for my own. "I hope you will give Andrew his priority back. He's going to make a great leader."

Polite applause sounded and a few of the women turned back to their plates.

But I didn't leave the podium. I glanced at the women, and for a moment I remembered when I was a girl and I'd give speeches to the trees in my backyard. I remember looking at the line of presidential portraits at my school and imagining my own face among them.

I knew what I wanted.

And all of a sudden, I wasn't nervous at all. "I would make a great leader too."

The soft chatter that had started hushed. "I wrote that

article and changed minds with my words. You've read my test scores. Some of you have heard my speeches."

"A few times," Greta burst in.

I smiled at her. "And I would like you to help me run against him."

"What?" The crowd erupted in voices. Dissenting voices for the most part. But I couldn't hear them over the sound of my own voice announcing my own dream.

"But you won't win," Miss Reynolds said. The room silenced.

"I know. I probably won't. Even if I have your support, even if everything goes right, I know it might take a miracle to even get me into the primary. I know this. But still, it's possible. And I believe it is worth trying."

Another woman spoke from Bea's table. "You've seen how they treat suffragettes. You've studied history. Can you name a single woman throughout history who men would vote for?"

"Jeannette Rankin," I said quickly. "She proves it possible. She was just elected to the Senate."

"In Montana. The demographics are different in other states."

"Rebecca L. Felton," I continued. "Alice Robertson. Winnifred Huck."

"These women are outliers. Some were only voted in because of their husbands—"

"—Mae Nolan," I interrupted. "Florence Prag Kahn,

Mary Norton, and Edith Rogers. These women proved that this is possible. They were elected without the society's help. What could I do with it? I'm not here to ask your permission. I'm here to ask for your help."

Someone else spoke from my mother's table. "I'll tell you the same thing we told the suffragettes. The good we do must be done in silence, or men will stop us. If they knew how we've turned their heads, they would discard us. We've failed because we've taken too ambitious steps before. We have to look at our history. This would fail and we'd be—"

"—We'd be closer," I answered. "I'm not asking you to step out into the light. I'm not asking you for any risk that could bring harm to the women and children we've aided. We'd have decades to prepare for this, to find the right paths, the right arguments. With your resources if you help me train to run, I know we have a chance. And what's the risk? With Andrew Shaw at the helm you have an excellent candidate, and a story I've helped build that will be nearly unbreakable. One I probably will not win against. I know I'm asking you to let me try, and to let me fail. I know what names the papers will call me, I know the comics will try to make me ugly and mock me for my size, but I am not dumb, though they will call me that. I am not uncultured, though they will call me that, and I am not ugly, though I know they will use that too. I know I am asking for heartache.

"But I also know that even if I lose, and am abused by the press, I know that by standing up anyway, I will inspire some other girl to take up the challenge. And then if she loses, it will be by less. And then someone else will come along, and another, and then eventually, some little girl will see our fight and decide to join in and that little girl will win."

Tears blurred my vision, and the room was blissfully silent. My mother looked at me with so much worry, and also confusion. She couldn't understand why I was asking for a life of heartache.

But this life was what I wanted more than anything. This was my dream. This was the change I could make that was bigger than the change my brother would make, or Andrew would make. They could be heroes.

But I could be me.

My mother stood. "I say we give her a chance."

Bea and Mira stood and shouted—well, I have no idea what because they both spoke at the same time, but it was clearly in support. Then Iris and Mrs. Brown and even Greta stood and said something.

"I've had enough of Elsie's speeches turned on me," Greta said. "Let's inflict her on the boys for a change. Honestly I could use the break."

I narrowed my eyes, and she smiled at me.

Another woman stood, and then another. Each of them speaking in approval, some coming up with ideas I hadn't thought of, ideas I jotted down so quickly that I couldn't read my own handwriting. It was overwhelming, all those ideas, all those thoughts, shouted at once.

But I've handled storming thoughts before. And I could handle this.

And then Sarah, that little old lady who told me to call her Grandma, stood and said no, and part of my heart broke a little. Which was foolishness: I'd just met her, and I knew that if I was going to take this path, with or without the society's assistance, then I'd need to get used to people not agreeing with me. No, I had to get used to people hating me.

But maybe the point of life wasn't to be loved by everyone. Maybe the point of life was to make the right people angry. Then at least you knew you've stood for something.

More women were speaking, orderly now, because of the no. Speaking of plans, and challenges, and risks. Sometimes I responded, but most of the time women whose names I didn't know answered for me. My words, my mission had become their own.

But the path forward seemed clear. I would write my way to the top. If I could only write enough articles to get the country accustomed to the sound of my voice, I knew I could get them to listen. Then we'd use connections to build my political experience, and start with local politics and school boards, and then as my experience grew, so would the size of my elections.

But so would the size of my risk as well. And the level of criticism.

I'd be sticking my neck out, like a rose from a bush. The society wouldn't be able to hold back those gardener's blades, inching ever closer.

But I wasn't a flower, destined to bloom for a short season of beauty, then wilt and be cut away. I was a person and I deserved the right to dream. Women's dreams should be perennials.

Miss Reynolds slammed her cane against the ground again, and the room silenced. She stood with some difficulty. "It does seem a manageable risk to take. At least for our society. But, Elsie, are you certain you want to attempt this? It will get ugly for you."

I dragged in a breath, and then I nodded. "I've been pretty, and only pretty, for long enough."

Miss Reynolds nodded at me like she'd just approved of the way I punched. "Then let's vote." She gestured to the table, and I crossed back to my seat.

All the women lowered their heads to the tablecloths, all except for my friends and me, who took a moment to realize that we were supposed to put our heads down too. I ducked down and pressed my forehead against the linen, not looking up but not being able to close my eyes either, so I just stared at a small crumb of cake next to a stain of dripped punch on the tablecloth as I heard women sit up and the softest brushing sound of hands making signals.

My curiosity won out. To do this, I'd have to start breaking rules, doing things that good obedient girls didn't do.

So I peeked. There were eight women in the circle. About half were voting no. Even with all my arguments half of them weren't ready to support a woman.

Then another woman sat up and raised her hand to vote

yes. She met my eye after the vote was counted and put a dark finger up to her lips. The Head Gossip Matron was a Black woman. And her vote changed my whole future.

Miss Reynolds pounded her cane again, and the women around me all sat up in their chairs. I sat up, already knowing the answer but not believing it. It felt too new. Too fragile. It wasn't going to be real, I couldn't let myself believe it until it was called.

"The votes are in," Miss Reynolds said. She looked directly at me, no clue or joy hiding in the light of her dark eyes. She opened her mouth. "This is historic. This is foolishness. And this is about damn time. Elsie Fawcett, your motion has passed."

The applause thundered, sparks of smiles flashed, and my friends flooded to my side, and that was when it finally hit me.

My dreams might just come true.

They were going to let me try.

They were going to stand with me.

We were going to change our future.

Miss Reynolds put her hand on Iris's shoulder and she slipped a crescent moon–shaped broach from her lapel. She handed it to Iris, who gaped softly and shook her hand. Iris only shook twice before she threw her arms around Miss Reynolds's shoulders and jumped up and down.

I thought for sure I'd blown Iris's chances. I thought for sure that losing Rebecca and the Shaws' reputation had been the end of Iris's dream. But this is more than one good match. She'd just led us to a revolution.

She'd done it. We'd done it. This wasn't just my dream coming true now.

"Speech!" Iris shouted. "Speech!" Greta groaned and Mira whistled twice with her fingers between her teeth and the whole council turned to me, and I didn't have a speech prepared. I didn't think this was actually possible. Was this real? Did this happen?

I glanced at my mom and she looked back at me with tears sparkling in her eyes, applauding noisily. I stood. I didn't give them a speech. I gave them a poem.

"There is no path in front of us," I started, "except for the one created by our own steps. That's the only way to get somewhere new."

My friends looked at me with their hands clasped and their eyes glistening.

Was this really happening? "But more will follow us. And all those footsteps will create a path that others will push further. And one day we'll reach a new height. But for now, at least my face is mine. Our lives are ours."

My mother clapped twice, her expression so full of pride that my throat clenched. "It's a responsibility we have to take up and hold tight. So many people will try to take that responsibility from us. It's too easy to let them. It's work." I smiled. "Women's work. To hold on to our own choices."

A few women grumbled then and left the room. I watched them go. "And some women and some men hate us for doing that work."

I shrugged though it hurt and looked at the women who

stayed. "People hate storms. They board up windows to protect their children. They curse the winds and fear the lightning. Storms are terrible, beautiful, damaging monsters in the sky."

Now tears blurred my vision. "But without them, nothing grows."

I lowered my shoulders and stood tall. "So if you have a storm inside you, like I do, let it out. Throw open your shutters and the things that protect you. Don't wish you were a sunny day. Sunny days are beautiful, but too many in a row will drink you dry."

Some of the women couldn't look at me, so I softened my fervor to include them too. "There are those who must remain silent. There are women who are not safe to speak. Women whose storms are buried so deeply it will take a lifetime to find them. Women who don't realize they have the right to rain. Women whose storms don't look like anger. Women who rain compassion and kindness." I looked at Bea. "Women who will rock cradles with gentle breezes and watch out for neighbors. We need you too. We march with rain-soaked hands clenched tight, our fingers bound together, like our lives and our futures. If you are friends to more than just Abigail, join us. Be more than a happy ending to a story someone else wrote. Write your own story. Walk where there is no path. Pass this movement on to your storming sisters. Let the rains fall and the lightning strike. And let's shake those houses to their foundations."

After, as we sat in the back of the car and my friends planned and gossiped and made vague speculations of who the other members of the Matron Circle were, tears streamed down my cheeks, soaking the cotton pillowcase against my skin, and making the recycled air I breathed humid. But after I caught my breath, my lips curled into a smile and I looked up.

It was real.

They'd said yes.

For a long moment, I held my grandmother's hair clips in my hands so tightly that the sharp edges bit into my palm.

Crescent moons were the symbol of our society. I loved that the moon was always present in the dark, shining only through reflected light. That was us. After all, how many fairy tale characters were afraid of a full moon? How many women made themselves small to keep those wolves at bay?

But moons wax too; they don't always have to wane.

I couldn't help but wonder how much light would shine down when we were full.

I opened my eyes and pulled off the pillowcase.

I wasn't promised a happily ever after, but I knew I would be happily myself for forever after.

And that was a different kind of joy.

That was hope.

PARK VILLAGE GAZETTE

GREAT WOMEN ALIVE TODAY
— NELLE E. PETERS, ARCHITECT

BY ELSIE FAWCETT

NELLE E. PETERS is one of Kansas City, Missouri's most productive and leading architects. She specializes in designing apartment buildings and hotels and owns her own independent practice.

Reared on a farm on the prairie, Nelle fostered a love of drawing and mathematics early. "When I was a child I preferred to draw mechanical things—anything from a bolt with all its threads to a steam engine," Nelle Peters told me as I interviewed her on the top floor of her newest completed project, the Valentine Hotel on 3724 Broadway.

It's a long way from where she started. When she moved to Sioux City, Iowa, none of the architectural firms would hire her, but she didn't give up. She went back to those offices that turned her down "I talked and I talked and at last I talked myself into a job." Her persistence paid off in 1903 when

Dearest Nathaniel,

I've enclosed your sister's first two articles. She's sold a third, and is currently working on the fourth, each of them highlighting extraordinary women around the country. We've been traveling a great deal, and every night I fall asleep to the gentle sounds of her typewriter click-clacking into the night. I do worry that she isn't getting enough rest, but I've never seen her so happy and focused. That sister of yours is going to do great things.

Which reminds me, how is your wife?

ACKNOWLEDGMENTS

I'm writing this acknowledgment on 11/7/2020.

Today we elected our first female vice president. All day I've been inundated with images of little girls looking up at screens watching Kamala Harris speak, of women bursting out crying because they didn't realize how much this meant until it happened. I've heard of so many little girls who now know that they can do anything, because one woman did something impossible.

Today would not have happened without Victoria Woodhull, Lucretia Coffin Mott, Margaret Chase Smith, Charlene Mitchell, Shirley Chisholm, Tonie Nathan, Lenora Fulani, Joyce Dattner, Mamie Moore, Wynonia Burke, Sarah Palin, Jill Stein, Cynthia McKinny, and Hillary Clinton.

Winning matters. But losing can change the world too.

I owe this book to them.

There are other women who have inspired me and this book, and others who have aided in making this dream come true.

First my mom who taught me my whole life that I could be anyone I wanted to be, and then showed me how to serve, how to create peace, how to work hard, and how to love fiercely.

Next my agent, Jessica Sinsheimer, who told me I could do this, and who told me that I should. I'd given up on this book, and she pushed me to try it. Without her this book would not exist.

To April Clausen, without whom I would not exist. Thank you for every read and for every phone call and for every dropped off gift and every single act of true friendship. You are my sister.

Thank you to Holly West, my editor, who gave this book her shape. She pushed me to find the hope, even when things were hard, and the world was bleak. Her belief and her ideas made this book the story I wanted to tell. Thank you to Brooke Sokoloski for shipping Andrew and Bea before I did, and for all your brilliance.

I owe a personal debt of gratitude to Trisha Previte, who illustrated and designed this story, and who I think loves it as much as I do. Thank you for the designing the gorgeous cover and for every sketch and fixed paragraph. Thank you also to the cover artist Sofia Bonati for your stunning work.

Thank you to Cynthia Lliguichuzhca for your tireless work connecting this book to readers. Thank you as well to Ilana Worrell, Pat McHugh, Rosanne Lauer, Celeste Cass, and everyone else who has had a hand in publishing this book, especially those whose names I don't know. I'm grateful to my beta readers: Michella Domenici, Amanda Rawson Hill, Jamie Pacton, Sabrina West, Melanie Crouse, and to my friends in the PCC who reacted excitedly when I told them my idea.

Thank you to Kate Meadows, Alechia Dow, Leanne Schwartz, Cassandra Newbold, Megan Lally, Isabel Ibanez, Cindy Baldwin, and every person and organization who helped me be a better writer. I'm so grateful to my Pitch Wars family, especially class 2015, and to my Roaring Twenties Debut Group who survived publishing during a pandemic, and are still shouting and supporting each other. Thank you to all the authors who helped me feel welcomed in this industry, but especially to Tricia Levenseller, whose kindness I will never forget.

A special thank-you to Alechia Dow, Dr. Rosalyn Eves, and Jamie Pacton for taking the time to blurb this book.

Thank you to Cassidy, Misha, Chloe, Melody, Sarah, Elizabeth N., Elizabeth R., Izzy, Sever, Fritz, Clara, Amber, Arch, Grace, Payton, Rachel, Salayna, Raine, and Ella. Thank you to Chelsea, Kendra, Tina, Miriam, and Emily. Thank you to Julie, Sarah, and Amie for keeping me breathing.

Hey, Gina Francesconi . . . do you know what this is? Acknowledgment Party! Thank you for being my sister. Thank you also to Mama Geiger for giving me permission to be different.

And to my family, Mom, Dad, Jana, Tyana, and Ben. Thank you to my mother-in-law and extended family for your support, and for every mother who didn't give birth to me, but made me all the same. To my children, who I love more than I love books, or ice cream, or comfy blankets in front of the fire. You are my everything. To my Darren, my best friend. My love. My equal. My partner. I love you most of all.

Thank you to the doctors, scientists, medication, and therapists that help those like me with anxiety and mental disorders.

My grandma Norma Ball wrote poems. I wrote this book as a monument to her, because her name and her life mattered, even though you've never heard it before.

Thank you to all who do the invisible work.

And to every reader who read to this point. Your dream matters. But you still have to fight for it. We don't fight alone.

Tomorrow there will be more of us.